HER SHADOW SIDE

Jennifer West

PUBLICATIONS

Lycan Valley Press Publications
1002 N Meridian STE 100-153
Puyallup, Washington 98371
United States of America

First Edition

ISBN-13: 978-1-64562-038-9

For my people, dark and twisty.

This book was born in the in-between—between nap times, moon phases, and customers at the coffee shop.

It is my first novel, shaped in the quiet hours, in the margins of motherhood, and it carries the vulnerability and the chaos of a beginning.

To my Coven—thank you for keeping the fire lit when mine burned low. You are the witches who hold me, the ones who remind me who I am.

To my husband, Sam—thank you for your love, your patience, and your deep wells of understanding. You gave me time and space to chase something invisible, and trusted I'd return with something worth holding.

To my daughters—you are my greatest magic. This story came to life in the cracks and quiet corners of our days together. If you ever read it one day, I hope you don't take it too seriously.

I experienced two pregnancies and births during the writing of this book and since completing it, I've become a birth worker, honoured to walk alongside people through pregnancy, birth, and the postpartum period. With this knowledge, I would have written parts of this story differently. But I'm leaving it as it is: a snapshot of where I was then, a reflection of what I knew, felt, and feared most of all.   It is a reminder that we are always becoming. Always learning. Always deepening into our work.

And to anyone out there who picked up this book hoping for a little scare, this story is meant to be extreme. It's folklore and fear, identity and unraveling, the weight of motherhood, and the shadows we're told not to look at too closely. But beneath the fiction lies a very real truth—postpartum depression and psychosis are real—and they are not rare.

If you know someone who's recently had a baby, check in on her. She probably won't become murderous, but there's a good chance she's not totally okay. The postpartum period is deeply important to a woman's experience as she integrates becoming a mother. It should not be ignored. She should not be ignored. Check on her. Care for her.

HER SHADOW SIDE

PROLOGUE

ONCE THERE WAS a beautiful young woman called Niamh. Newly married to the town blacksmith, a man named Cathmor, and pregnant with their first child, she lived an incredibly simple and happy life in a small house atop a cliff overlooking the sea.

Early one morning in the dead of winter, their baby was born a girl. The entire town rejoiced at the news and lined up outside their door in the bitter cold for a chance to see the tiny babe, as it had been many years since a girl had been born in the town. Each person who came through the house left advice for the happy couple and a gift made of iron for the babe.

To help the new family adjust to their new life, Niamh's grandmother, Clodagh, travelled from deep inland to stay with them. Clodagh believed that, above all else, you must protect a new baby during their first year of life, when they are the most vulnerable. So, she placed the iron spoons, cups and figurines of wildlife all around the cot as the baby slept. She believed, as many people in the area did, that the fairies feared iron and wouldn't snatch the baby as she slept if she were surrounded by it.

Niamh thought her grandmother's superstitions, especially those about fairies, were ancient and laughable. As the months passed with no signs of the dreaded fairies, she replaced the iron bits with new spring wildflowers and pretty leaves she found on her daily walks in the forest near their home. Clodagh called her granddaughter a foolish child and warned her that, one day, she would regret being so blind.

One morning, after removing the iron items the night before and replacing them with flowers as she did every night, Niamh woke to find her baby girl changed. She no longer cooed like a dove, she no longer searched for the eyes of her mother, and no longer could her hunger be satisfied. Now, the baby cried for days on end and never stopped eating from Niamh's breast, draining her completely. Clodagh told her granddaughter she had made a frightful error and now, this was her punishment for not taking the stories seriously.

"You must listen to the old ways," she told Niamh.

But it was too late. Niamh's beautiful, happy baby was gone and in its place was a monster.

A changeling.

A cast away from the fairy world. A world that, until now, she had thought to be make-believe, a child's imaginings. Now, she knew how wrong she had been.

Each night, as Niamh lay in bed listening to her monster cry in the next room, she also heard a sinister giggle underlying the wail. It was as though she were being taunted, made fun of, for no one else could hear the laughter, and sometimes Naimh feared she was beginning to lose her mind.

A month after her baby was stolen, she couldn't take it anymore. She hadn't slept in weeks, her breasts were raw and bleeding, and she felt empty in every way possible. So, she walked with her monster, to the edge of the cliff, turned with her back to the sea, closed her eyes and, with hardly a thought, fell.

When Cathmor woke up in the morning he found his wife was gone, and their perfect baby girl cooing in her cot, returned to them.

CHAPTER ONE

He sat at a table in the far corner of O'Donnell's with a tattered paperback open in front of him and a steaming cup of coffee clutched in his hand. We opened the door, a bell announcing our arrival. Despite his obvious absorption into the book he was reading, he looked up. Our eyes met only briefly, but when they did, I looked away. An all too familiar heat turned my face, already red from the cold of the December day, an even deeper shade of crimson. No one, apart from my sister Mags, had ever really *seen* me, but in that moment, I was certain *he* did as well. The feeling it aroused was so foreign it caused my skin to burn. Not only that, there was also a distinct pulling feeling within me. It was as though a physical and tangible thread just materialized connecting me directly to him. It was ridiculous but I couldn't deny that I could feel it tugging me towards him.

The familiar smell of burnt coffee and old grease made both my nose crinkle and my mouth water. Riding the boundary of Shaughnessy, O'Donnell's was deemed the most popular place to hang out by the residents of the prestigious neighbourhood. There were other diners in the area that were no better or no worse, but, for whatever reason, someone originally decided it wasn't proper to be seen at *those* kinds of places. Though the décor of O'Donnell's hadn't been touched since it opened almost thirty years ago, and there was a certain level of dinginess covering the place, the people in my parent's circle considered it to be what they called 'vintage chic.' So, it was acceptable to gather in the cracked and faded blue vinyl booths and order burgers and milkshakes—but only at O'Donnell's.

When we were little girls, our father brought us for hot chocolates every weekend, and it was one of the few treats we looked forward to. As we got older, though, he brought us less and less. I pretended it didn't bother me, but I missed that time with him. I don't think it was because he didn't want to spend time with us, but because he assumed that, as teenagers, we didn't want to spend time with him. Parents don't realise we never stop wanting to be with them; there is just a period of time where we can't say it out loud.

We slid into our usual booth, which was too close

to the door this time of year, so every time someone opened it, we were hit with a blast of cold air, and I shivered inside my thick wool sweater. Mr. and Mrs. O'Donnell's oldest daughter, Shari, sidled up to our table to take our orders in a uniform that also hadn't been updated since the fifties. A faded blue pencil skirt topped with a matching button down that made her look older than she was. We always ordered the same thing, and I wasn't sure why we had to go through the motions every single time we went there. When Shari returned just a few minutes later with our drinks, I saw Mags's eyes flick to the left. She had noticed the boy in the corner, who was obviously looking in our direction, and the questions starting to form inside her head were growing greater with every moment, practically visible behind her green eyes.

Finally, unable to hold it in any longer she squealed, "Okay, who is that guy?" over the raucous sounds of the diner. She grinned at me, dark eyebrows raised behind her horn-rimmed glasses, waiting for an answer. "Come on," she teased. "He hasn't taken his eyes off you since we walked in."

"Shush! He might hear you," I hissed through clenched teeth as my cheeks once again burned with embarrassment. "How should I know who he is?" I tried not to smile, but I couldn't help it. My lips no longer belonged to me, and I couldn't keep them in place, no matter how hard I tried. Instead, they trembled with the effort, making my skin burn even hotter.

Careful not to look directly at him, I watched him out of the corner of my eye. I could tell he had light hair but impossibly dark eyes, and although he sat in the darkest corner, the area around him seemed alight somehow. Even if I couldn't look directly at him, he was all I could see. The thread tightened.

Mags was not as discreet as I was and openly gaped in his direction, smiling and bouncing in her seat. "His sweater looks like his grandma made it," she teased in a low voice, bringing my attention reluctantly back to her. I reached over the table and shoved her gently, with what I hoped was a serious look that said *stop it*. She picked up a dripping marshmallow from her cup with her fingers and popped it into her mouth, her smile never ceasing.

As she continued to giggle at her own joke, I wondered how she got to be so lighthearted and free. As identical twins, people always assumed we were the same. Carbon copies of each other. But, that's never really how it is, is it? I think, more often than not, twins are mirror images of each other, but the image reflected is like one from another dimension. Another version of yourself that somehow escaped time and is walking around right in front of you, showing you what you could have been or, perhaps, what you *are* somewhere else. In our case, I was her shadow side.

I shook my head and glared at her. "Come on,

let's get out of here," I said, looking over her head at the clock on the wall behind her. "She'll be expecting us home soon." I stood up and tugged Mags out of the booth.

Ordinarily, I would be in a rush to get home to avoid getting into trouble, but today I took my time putting on my gloves, scarf, and coat. When we were bundled up and ready for the short walk, I snuck one last glance towards the dark corner where the bright stranger sat, but found the seat was now empty, and a tiny pit of disappointment opened up in my stomach. I wasn't planning on doing or saying anything to him; I just wanted to see him one more time.

Feeling silly, I hurried towards the door. Then someone called out from behind us, followed by what sounded like a chair being toppled over. I didn't stop. In fact, I walked a bit faster, certain they couldn't be talking to me. No one ever did. I hoped Mags was right behind me, so I wouldn't have to look at all. I couldn't bear the embarrassment of turning, involuntarily hopeful, only to see someone, a boy—*the* boy—wave to someone behind me. As my right hand closed around the cold metal of the door handle, a warm hand slipped seamlessly into my left. It was a feeling so comfortable and so shocking to me, I wasn't sure whether I should run or never let go.

Slowly, I turned to find myself face to face with the boy from across the room. Mags stopped behind him, her eyes wide at the scene. She knew as well as I did how our mother would react when—not if—she heard. Vancouver was a big city, but the community of Shaughnessy was small, and everyone knew the Auclairs. They would all scramble for the very rare opportunity to have something on our family to gossip about.

"I'm sorry. I just couldn't let you go without saying something," he said, breathless from his dash across the restaurant. Which had, in fact, included knocking over a chair along the way. Mr. O'Donnell looked in our direction, annoyed but curious, as he picked the fallen chair up off the floor.

He really was beautiful up close. Maybe not in the classically handsome way, but in a way that made me incapable of looking away from his kind, mischievous smile. Behind large tortoiseshell glasses, his dark brown eyes were wrung with gold and his pale skin was such a striking contrast to them that I had the strongest urge to touch his cheek. To see if he was real. He had delicate features for a man, contributing to the beauty of him. Unruly hair curled on the top of his head and he badly needed a haircut, but he had that brightness about him I had noticed earlier, and I felt safe in it. I can't recall ever seeing someone like him, before or since.

Intent, he stared at me, waiting for some kind of response, but my mouth was suddenly dry, and I couldn't form a proper thought, much less words, so I just stared back at him in complete silence.

With a smirk that lifted just the left corner of his lips, he said, "Okay, you're right, I'll start. My name is Benjamin. Ben. What's yours?" He raised his eyebrows, indicating it was my turn to speak.

When I didn't, Mags came up beside me and pinched the back of my arm gently, making me jump as I crashed back to reality.

"Josephine," I managed in a whisper.

"Josephine," he repeated with absolution and familiarity, as though he'd always known. Always known me. Realizing his fingers were still intertwined with my own, I pulled my hand reluctantly from his, crossing my arms over my chest in an attempt to keep myself from reaching out towards him again.

"Unfortunately, *Ben*, we have to go," Mags said, in her flirty if not mocking voice, effortless as always. "Our mother is expecting us home any minute." She grabbed my hand and pulled me towards the door, but I stumbled over my feet as my body tried to remain turned towards him. I wasn't ready to leave.

"Can you meet me here tomorrow?" he called out after me.

Too loud. Everyone heard.

I could feel the eyes of the other customers searing into me and committing the scene to memory.

I knew I should say no because there was no way we would be allowed to come here two days in a row, but instead I whispered, "Yes," and though I thought the words to be almost completely inaudible, he responded with a slight nod.

"Same time?"

"Yes." Again.

"See you tomorrow, Jo," he said as he brushed past me and skipped out the door, beaming. The air, disturbed by his presence, surrounded me—warm and spicy before succumbing to the cold from outside.

The name stopped me in my tracks. Nobody ever called me 'Jo' except for Mags, and even then, it was only when we were alone. Our mother didn't approve of nicknames and always insisted we be called Josephine and Magalie. I thought, if I were to see him again, I would tell him not to call me Jo, but it sounded so natural and comforting coming from him and I knew that, in the end, I wouldn't ever correct him.

He ran across the street, leaving me stunned, my heart beating harder than it ever had. I took one more look around the diner before ducking through the door as well. No one was looking at us, but that didn't mean no one saw.

The walk home was bitterly cold. It had snowed the night before and the wind whirled around us, blowing the soft flakes into our faces. Walking backwards, bracing herself against the wind, Mags talked non-stop about what happened as if it was the most exciting thing she had ever seen in her life.

To be fair, it probably was. There was no doubt it was the most exciting thing that had ever happened to me which was sad, because really it was nothing.

"He *loves* you!" Mags shrieked, jumping up and down, her hands waving in the air, a huge smile across her face. "Can you believe it? Someone loves you!" She swooned, her hand dramatically draped over her forehead, old Hollywood style. "How does it feel? Are you forever changed? Are you going to kiss him?" she gushed, firing off questions faster than I could answer them. It was hard to concentrate on what she was saying, as my own thoughts flew through my mind just as fast as the words flew from her mouth.

"Don't be ridiculous, Mags!" I snapped, feeling suddenly very overwhelmed. "I don't even know him, and he doesn't know me." My sister's ecstatic face fell with disappointment at my words and instantly, I softened, as I always did with her. I held out my hand, smiled instead and calmly said, "Come on, we better hurry, we have to get ready for the party."

It was clear she hadn't quite recovered from my outburst; she was so much more sensitive than me, but she took my hand anyway and we ran the rest of the way home.

Chapter Two

Of all the rooms in the entire house, my mother's bedroom was, without a doubt, the most beautiful. Its walls were adorned with a thick forest green wallpaper inlaid with a delicate floral pattern, and heavy white curtains covered the large windows overlooking the gardens. Despite the things that happened there, it was one of my favourite places to hide. Often, she and our father went to parties, which meant they would be gone for most of the night. On those nights, I spent hours in there, pretending the room belonged to me. Pretending I belonged there. Long before she returned home, I was always careful to put everything back exactly the way she left it, never leaving any trace that I was there. I was a ghost.

On the rare nights when the party was at our

house, Mags and I were expected to make an appearance. Our mother always did our hair and makeup herself to be sure we were flawless. Constantly on display for our parents' friends, we were expected to look our best and act our best. As always. The Auclair girls.

As a child, I loved the attention and the excitement, but as I grew older, I developed an immense hatred for the parties. I hated the expensive clothes and the inappropriate make up, the pretence of propriety. Most of all, I detested the act we all had to feign so that no one would know the truth about who we really were behind the closed doors of this house.

Although only a childish fantasy, it was during those times alone with her I was able to feel, for just a moment, that maybe we were a normal mother and daughter. With her hands in my hair and her eyes on my face, I could pretend maybe she did love me. I sat before her vanity, lavishly stocked with every cream, powder and perfume I could dream of, and watched the reflection in the three mirrors, but it wasn't my reflection I focused on. I watched my mother's image closely and leaned back just enough to feel her behind me, but not enough for her to notice and pull away. My eyes followed her as she moved gracefully; each of her movements controlled and precise in only the way a practiced dancer's can be. It was also the way Mags moved.

Everyone always said Caoimhe Auclair was

beautiful, and if I didn't look too closely at her, I could see what they meant. She had a charming look, with delicate but somehow bold features, and, individually, each of her qualities were flawless. Her dark, wavy hair flowed halfway down her back and her green eyes sometimes shone the colour of emeralds. But what most people couldn't see was that her personality and cruelness made her ugly. Grotesque. The bright, colourful eyes everyone admired were filled with a deep darkness she hid well from others.

They also said that, although Mags and I were identical, I looked the most like our mother. Whenever given the chance, I examined her in the mirror, looking for the similarities they spoke of. Where her lips were full, mine were thin. Where her cheek bones were high, mine were lost in the roundness of my face. I gazed at my own green eyes in the mirror, comparing them to hers, and I hoped they didn't have the same darkness in them hers did. I hoped my character didn't make me a monster as well.

"You will not be meeting that boy, tomorrow," she said, interrupting my thoughts and meeting my gaze in the mirror, red lips pursed slightly, the darkness transforming her face like a mask she could pull on anytime.

That afternoon, when we'd gotten home from the diner, we entered the drawing room to find her sitting on the sofa with her legs tucked beneath her, a book open in her lap and the phone pressed to her ear. She was listening intently to a story being told on the other end, and from the look on her face, I could tell what she was hearing was not good news. It wasn't until later we found out someone had called to tell her one of her daughters was seen holding hands with a most "unsuitable boy". The rage simmered almost visibly under her pale skin as she hung up the phone, but the party planner was standing patiently in the doorway waiting to ask her thoughts on a few last-minute details. The woman was starting to look frazzled, as the bulk of the party was to happen in this room, and she didn't want to be the one to ask the intimidating woman who hired her to leave so the furniture could be removed.

I was grateful for her presence, though, because it meant my mother couldn't punish me right then. Not with an audience. She had to wait until we were alone, until it had simmered so long that it boiled.

Now was her chance.

"But I said I would," I replied, and although I tried to sound brave, my voice came out small, barely a whisper. I'd never had the guts to talk back to her before but that tugging in my gut was unrelenting and urged me forward.

Her eyes widened a little. I had managed to surprise her. In response, she wound her long, thin fingers into my carefully pinned hair and grabbed it, close to my scalp. With a tight grasp, she pulled my head towards her so hard my neck snapped back painfully, and despite my resolve to never give her anything, I cried out at the shock of it.

"I don't care what you said. You will not embarrass me again," she whispered in my ear through clenched teeth, her fingers tightening in my hair even further, pulling it until I could feel each individual hair start to pull away from my scalp.

The pain brought tears to my eyes and I tried to blink them away before she noticed, but instead they fell and slid down my cheeks in steady streams, ruining my makeup.

"Can you imagine what people will say? 'Josephine Auclair—the slut'." She pushed my head forward, releasing my hair from her grip. The relief from the pressure was so great I gasped for breath as her eyes met mine in the mirror. Steady. Piercing green.

"You don't even know him," I said, my voice strained, my throat tight. I willed my eyes not to fill with tears again.

"That's exactly my point," she continued, smiling with sinister delight. "If he were respectable, I would already know him and his family. I'm sure you'll meet a nice boy at the party tonight." She pinned my ruined hair back into place with practiced precision before coming to stand in front of me. With a soft tissue from a silver box, she dabbed the tears from my cheeks and wiped the smudged makeup from beneath my eyes. Her face was close to mine, inspecting me for any imperfections and I closed my eyes against the humiliation she stirred, but she grabbed my cheeks with one hand, her fingertips pressing into my skin. "Look at me," she hissed, pulling my face up towards her. She finished fixing my makeup with just a dusting of powder and a swipe of mascara. Like it never even happened.

I wasn't interested in meeting a "nice boy." I wasn't interested in meeting anyone at all, and I never had been until today. I was definitely not interested in any of the boys my parents introduced me to. They were horribly dull and as unromantic as this moment was for me. I could never see myself feeling for them the way I felt this afternoon when Ben's hand slipped into mine. Not only that, but the boys had never been interested in me anyways. There were going to be a hundred other girls at this party who wore the right clothes, knew how to have fun, and didn't act as though a storm cloud was watching their every move.

She stood me up in front of the mirror and inspected every aspect of my appearance. Starting at the top of my head and moving down to the hem of my dress that hit almost at my ankle. Picking, pulling and smoothing as she went. When she was certain my hair was perfect, my makeup was perfect, and my dress was perfect, she smiled at her work and said, "Now, on the bed."

Really, she didn't have to say it; I knew it was coming. And it was unspoken that worse would happen to me if I were to misbehave again. I turned from the mirror and walked towards my mother's four poster bed; the lightness of the wood almost glowed against the darkness of the evening. When the front of my thighs touched the white quilt Nan had made for my parents when they were married, I paused and took a deep breath as my fingers grazed the fabric longingly. Then, silent and obedient as always, I reached under the hem of my green dress, pulled my panties down to my knees and bent over the edge of the bed, resting my cheek against the soft blanket as I lifted my dress up.

I heard her open the top drawer of her bedside table, and I heard her take out the black leather belt she always kept there. I heard the silver buckle clink as it hit the side of the drawer, and I heard her quietly take the four steps it took to come to stand behind me.

I taught myself, over the years, to take myself away from here. I took a deep breath and I let it out slowly, relaxing my body into the mattress. I knew from experience that it hurt worse if I was tense, so I slowed my breathing all the way down and focused my attention on the rhythm. In and out. In and out. It had started snowing again and I watched each snowflake fall past the window. I named every single one of them. Jane. Mary. Jennifer. Alice. Kathy. Eve. Sharon. I rolled each name around in my mouth as I tried not to feel the leather bite my skin five times. Always five. I didn't cry out. I didn't make a sound.

I never would.

When she was done, she put the belt back in the drawer and stood, her hands clasped delicately in front of her, waiting patiently as I pulled my panties up over my raw, burning skin. I smoothed my dress down, turned towards her and told her exactly what she wanted to hear. And although tears burned hot behind my eyes, this time I was in control. I did not let them show.

"You're right, Mother. I'm sorry. I won't see him again," I said, lying to my mother for the very first time. I knew, even then, it wouldn't be the last. Everything shifted inside me in that moment. I saw a glimpse of what life could be, of what it should be, and there was no coming back from that. There was no way I could go back to living only as a silent shadow, always trying to remain invisible.

I suppose it wasn't true when I said the only person who had ever truly seen me before today was Mags. My mother saw me too, but it was in those moments when she saw me that I knew how much she detested me. It was when she saw me that I understood how it felt to want to disappear forever. But that day, in the diner I had been to so many times before, I got something just for me. Something to live for. Maybe even a way to escape.

Chapter Three

It was December twenty-third, the night of our annual Christmas party. Like every year on this day, our house, usually cold and dark, was transformed for one night into an enchanted place where I desperately wanted to be, instead of the prison it usually was. I really did hate all the parties, but there was something special about Christmas, and Mags and I looked forward to it every year.

Covered top to bottom in white fairy lights, the entire main floor of the house was lit up with the magic of December. A lavishly decorated Christmas tree grazed the ceiling of every room. Emptied of its usual furnishings, the drawing room was opened up and adorned extravagantly with even more lights, cedar boughs and Christmas balls, while a great fire crackled in the usually empty hearth, warming even the furthest corners of the room.

Guests poured in through the front door like the never-ending flow of champagne into the countless flutes which would be consumed that night, tightly wrapped against the cold in cloaks and jackets made of fur and cashmere. Long gowns of silk and chiffon of every colour floated down from the women on the arms of men, indistinguishable in black tuxedos.

Each one brought with them a gift and the small space under each of the trees started to fill with brightly coloured packages, all wrapped elegantly in bows. Every year, Mags and I dreamed of opening just one, but every year they were loaded into black garbage bags at the end of the night and delivered to the children's hospital nearby, or whichever children's charity our parents were supporting that month. Meanwhile, the only gifts we ever received were the ones our father brought us when he had to be away from home for work. He hid them under our pillows when he got home, sneaking into our rooms in the night so we would wake up to a surprise in the morning. They were always our little secret and always miniature, small enough to hide. A tiny clay bird figurine, glass marbles of different colours, a small girl carved of wood. They were sweet and we loved him for it, but we knew they wouldn't quite compare to the magnificence of the gifts that would go to waste once all the guests went home and the lights went out.

Popular Christmas songs flowed from the grand

piano staged in the middle of the room. The pianist was a young boy with dark hair, hardly older than I was. It was unbelievable someone so young could create something so beautiful. I watched his fingers fly gracefully over the keys. He didn't have to look at them to know where his fingers would land; he did it entirely from memory. His eyes were either closed as he *felt* the music, or they were open as he laughed and chatted with guests, enticing them to put dollar bills in the large glass bowl placed on the lid of the white piano. For a second, I thought he looked my way, but I had already started to close my eyes, and with them closed, I let the heartening sounds penetrate me. I consumed each note hungrily, tucking them away so that, later, when it got dark and I was alone, I could pull each one out to warm me.

Completely immersed in the song, I jumped when I heard the words, "Voilà ma fille," in my ear. My father swooped me up as though I weighed nothing at all and twirled me around before placing me back on the ground.

I looked up at him, laughing and said, "Hello, Daddy."

No matter how dark things felt sometimes, he was always a bright light that chased the darkness away. When he was home, even mother was happy, *her* darkness chased away as well. His charm was infectious and everyone he met loved him and sought after his time and company. With his blonde hair and blue eyes, he always looked slightly out of place against the darkness of the rest of his family. His "dark girls" he called us with pride. If only he knew how accurate his nickname truly was.

"Tu es très belle , Josephine, as always. Just like your mother," he said, his English only slightly accented by the French he'd learned to speak from his adopted family when he was very young. He smiled back at me so sincerely that the lines around his eyes made him look younger, not the almost fifty that he was.

My heart fell just slightly at his comment, but I knew he didn't truly understand what his words meant for me, because to him, it was the biggest compliment.

He wasn't completely oblivious. He understood his wife had her problems, although I'm absolutely sure he didn't know the extent of them. He couldn't have. He was away for work almost more than he was home. Under the glow of his brief returns, she was okay for a while, until he had to leave again. Regardless, he loved her completely and had since the first day they met.

"Merci, Daddy." I beamed back at him, because how could I not? He kissed me gently on the nose and told me to have fun before striding away, his eyes searching the crowd. I knew he was looking for her. He always was. When he disappeared from sight, I turned my attention back to the music, closing my eyes to absorb the notes once again.

As the song came to an end, a delicate brightness danced at the edges of the darkness behind my closed eyes, soft pink and lavender in colour, and I knew my sister was near. It was a game we played when we were little. I used to sit with my eyes closed tight so everything would be dark, and Mags would then sneak around the room on the very tips of her toes, as only she could, and I would follow her lace-like aura with a tilt of my head until, finally, she would burst out laughing because she couldn't hide from me, not ever. We tried multiple times to switch places. She would close her eyes and I would walk silently around her, but she could never see me the way I could see her. When I asked her what she saw, she always said "nothing". That I was the only one who could do it. That I was so much better at it than her. I knew she was lying because her blind gaze did follow me wherever I went, but not in the excited way mine followed *her*. It was different. Slower. Somber.

I opened my eyes and watched her bound balletically towards me, her eyes bright.

"Isn't it beautiful?" She glowed, as always, looking around at the transformed room.

She loved the Christmas party just as much as I did, though she wasn't as reluctant to admit it. She was able to enjoy it in a way I couldn't. Immersing herself right into the revelry, while I watched from the sidelines, observing, but never participating.

"I'll go get us some food," she said, not waiting

for my reply before bounding away towards the tables piled high with almost every type of food imaginable.

Even when she wasn't on stage, each step Mags took was as though it were set to music. She had been dancing since she could walk and always said she felt more comfortable in her ballet slippers than in shoes. Even her outfit that night made her look like the ballerina she was. She chose a soft white tea length dress with a ruched bodice, thin straps and a pink satin ribbon around her waist, tied into a bow at the small of her back. She wore her dark hair pulled back and twisted into her usual tight bun. As always, I envied her easy grace and soft beauty. Our mother loved that at least one of her daughters had inherited her talent and she had someone to parade in front of everyone she knew. I took the same classes as Mags and practiced almost the same amount she did, but I could never dance the way she could. She was the star, and I was forever in the background. Her shadow.

Across the dance floor, our parents laughed at the jokes of their many guests and then, seeing someone across the room that interested her, our mother kissed our father on the cheek and squeezed his arm before flitting away, the train of her red gown trailing behind her. She always wore red for the Christmas party; she was so predictable. This year her dress was made of a fine red lace. A high collar caressed her throat while cap sleeves showed off her delicate arms. The back of the gown was open, revealing an ivory oval of bare skin. The contrast between modesty and sexy was striking, just like her. Flaring out at her knees, the dress gave her the shape of a mermaid, complimenting her tiny waist and the soft curve of her hips.

Floating between her guests with ease, she made her rounds, fulfilling her duty as hostess and wife. Her eyes flicked towards me, and I saw her darkness flash behind her smile like a snake. It was the darkness she saved especially for me. I stared back at her, knowing that among the crowd I was protected. *For now*. She hesitated towards me slightly, before a faceless man in a tuxedo caught her attention and she moved towards him and away from me.

I turned my head back towards the buffet where Mags was talking to a boy I recognized from the neighbouring boys school. She held two plates of food and laughed easily at whatever he was saying to her. She felt me looking and nodded in my direction before laughing once more and leaving him behind. She was as uninterested in the boys here as I was but she had a much easier time pretending than I did. Mags returned with two heaping plates of food. Roast beef and mashed potatoes smothered in a rich wine gravy. Maple roasted carrots with peas so crisp and fresh, you wouldn't believe that it was December. Canapes topped with blue cheese, walnuts and a drizzle of honey were my favourite and Mags was sure to add extra to my plate. She was always thinking of me. We savoured each and every bite in satisfied silence. It was a rare occurrence to be permitted to eat this way and we didn't waste a bite.

When our plates were empty, she leaned in close to me, her warm breath tickling my ear and said, "Let's steal some wine."

Excited, I turned towards her. I couldn't believe what she was suggesting but still, my pulse drummed in my ears as I looked around the room for our parents. I saw them, together again, dancing in the middle of the crowd, looking at each other intently. If we were going to go through with this, now was the perfect time. "Quickly," I said, pulling Mags towards the bar without hesitation. We were so in tune with each other that we never really needed to speak. We knew what the other was thinking and we knew how the other would move in any given situation and we used that to our full advantage. Standing close behind me, I blocked her from the view of the other guests. When the bartender turned to help someone else, she grabbed a bottle of red wine and held it between us. Certain no one saw, we turned together seamlessly and walked from the room, leaving the sounds of Christmas and laughter behind. Free from the party, we dashed up the stairs to my room and collapsed on my bed in a fit of laughter.

"Oh, my god." Mags stared at the bottle in her hands, incredulously. "I can't believe we did it." Her eyes were wide, and her mouth hung open with shock. We'd never done anything like this before, and it had happened so fast, I could hardly believe that only minutes before we hadn't even thought of doing it at all.

"What do we do now?" I asked, staring at the bottle between us.

"I guess we should drink it," she giggled in response.

I took the bottle, which, lucky for us, had already been opened. In place of the cork was a silver stopper topped with a crystal snowflake. Removing it gently, I placed it on my nightstand and a drop of red liquid pooled beneath it. I wiped it away with my hand before it could stain the light wood.

"Do you want to go first?" I held the bottle out to Mags. "It was your idea."

She shook her head. "No, it's okay. You can go first," she responded, her voice a little higher than usual as she pushed the bottle back towards me.

I never tasted alcohol before and I wanted to look braver than I felt, so without another thought, I tilted the bottle at my lips and was shocked by the sweet tang of the wine in my mouth. It was bitter and scorching on my throat, but the unpleasant sensation was quickly replaced by a sweet warmth that started deep in my belly before spreading out through my entire body. Despite my efforts to hold it back, a stifled laugh burst from my mouth.

"Your turn," I said, handing her the bottle.

She took it in her hand, looking at me curiously before reluctantly sipping from the bottle. I could see it in her eyes, the precise moment the red liquid touched her tongue. They widened and then squeezed shut as she struggled to swallow. She stuck her tongue, stained red with the remnants of the wine, out in disgust.

"Gross! Why do people drink this on purpose?" she asked, but then the warmth flowed through her too, and her eyes softened in response. "Actually, it's not that bad." She laughed, handing the bottle back to me.

In between giggles, we continued taking turns drinking straight from the bottle. When it was empty, I hid it under my bed, next to the secret gifts from our father.

Sprawled back across my light blue coverlet, head to head, we lay in a heavy silence. The room was warmer than usual, and it swayed back and forth slightly, making my stomach turn and my head ache.

"Do you feel anything?" I asked.

"No," she lied.

"Me neither," I lied.

We both started laughing at the same time, which quickly turned into uncontrollable howling as tears streamed from our eyes. I wiped mine away with the back of my hand and took a deep breath. I didn't like the sensation of the room moving or the sick feeling in my stomach, but I loved being there with her, rolling around and laughing in a carefree way we usually couldn't afford.

As quickly and completely as the laughter seized us, sadness replaced it in me. The edge of my vision blurred, and the shadows closed in. Usually, I was able to control them, keep them in the shadows themselves, but it was almost impossible to do through the haze of the wine. My mind grew darker and darker, and the weight of everything sat heavy on my chest.

"Mags?" I asked, my voice thick in my throat.

"Yeah?" she answered, still shaking with silent laughter, not noticing I wasn't laughing anymore.

"Do you think we'll ever get out of here?"

"Of course! You are going to marry that Ben guy, and I am going to dance away." She fluttered her hands over us, like two pale dancers so dreamy and confident, like she knew, without a doubt, what our future was. I wished I could be so sure.

"I'm not going to marry him," I said. "I just met him today."

"But you will. Just promise that wherever you go, you'll take me with you." She turned onto her side, her head resting on her arm, and looked straight at me, her laughter gone as well. "Promise you won't leave me here without you."

"I honest promise," I said, because you can't lie on an honest promise. I didn't have to "honest promise" though. She still didn't understand I could never leave her, that she was so interwoven within me, I would be completely lost without her. She always pushed me to be a better version of myself. When she was around, the shadows were easier to control. She helped keep me level, she helped keep me sane. She always put in the extra effort for me because the truth was that she didn't have it as hard as I did and she knew it.

When we were born, our parents didn't know they were having twins. The day our mother went into labor, they only expected one baby and when she, Magalie, was born, they thought they were done. A complete family. When the doctor told my mother that another baby was coming, she wasn't prepared for it, and she didn't like to be surprised. The delivery of Mags had gone smoothly, but when it was my turn to come into the world, the birth took a different turn. My mother started to hemorrhage, and there was a time when they thought they were going to lose us both. We were rushed into surgery and an emergency c-section forced me from her body, leaving her cut up, broken and confused.

Being a mother didn't come naturally for her, but she could muster the instincts for the daughter she'd planned for, just not for the one she hadn't, the one who almost killed her. Me. Though she was never especially loving towards Mags, she was never cruel to her the way she was to me, which I was both grateful for and jealous of. I never wanted Mags to have to endure what I did, but I felt that sting of rejection over and over. Instead of cruel, our mother was mostly indifferent to her. Mags was invisible unless she was dancing. She had only one thing to offer as a daughter, and at times, she said it was like balancing on her pointe shoes all the time, afraid to fall, afraid to make a mistake. I tried to protect her from everything that happened to me, but I knew she saw it anyway. She always did.

Footsteps clicked up the stairs that led to our rooms, interrupting my thoughts. I hoped it to be only a lost party guest looking for the bathroom, or more likely, snooping around *pretending* to look for the bathroom, but it wasn't worth the risk. I took one look at Mags's hooded eyes and knew we couldn't conceal we'd been drinking.

"Hide," I hissed, just as the footsteps hit the landing.

Fortunately, we were usually in my bedroom, because Mags's was too messy to do anything in or spend any amount of time in. Her room was the one closest to the stairs, and the footsteps stopped there first before making their way further down the hall towards my room.

The only place to hide was underneath the bed. We scrambled off it, dropped to the floor and slid under, pulling the bed skirt down to conceal us just in time for the door to creak open. Thin heels clicked slowly across the wood floor, echoing through the quiet room. The woman paused momentarily next to the bed and a hem of red lace brushed against the floor. She stood still and silent for a moment, before turning and striding from the room, closing the door behind her. I put my finger to Mags's lips to silence her. We needed to stay quiet until we could be sure our mother wasn't going to come back.

We hid in cramped silence for what felt like hours, our limbs numb and our lungs tight with dust. Finally, when she didn't return and the only sounds we could hear rose faintly from the party below, we pulled ourselves out from under the bed. Mags looked a bit frayed; her dress was rumpled and dusty and her hair, starting to fall out of her tightly spun bun, stuck out awkwardly on one side. I imagined I looked quite the same, and when her worried eyes met mine, I burst out laughing. I'm not sure where it came from or how I even managed it despite the shadows, but the moment suddenly felt hilarious. At first, her worried look deepened, but after a beat it softened, and her laughter joined mine as the lightness from the alcohol returned and the seriousness of the previous moments were forgotten.

Chapter Four

An explosion of light struck my eyes as they flickered open. I expected to see the sun shining through the windows but was surprised to find it was only the dim light of my bedside lamp left on from the night before. My head throbbed, the pain coming in loud pulsing waves, and my tongue was like foul cotton in my mouth. Closing my eyes tight against the brightness, I rolled over, groaning to find the other side of the bed rumpled, but empty. Mags was gone.

I sat up in slow motion, massaging my tender temples as the shadows of early morning lurked around me. I was still wearing my party dress; the thick green velvet was badly creased and there was a small, but obvious, wine stain on the bodice. As I checked the clock, which said it was almost quarter after six, I noticed another small red stain that, despite my attempts to avoid, had soaked into the light wood of my bedside table.

As thick as it was, the fog in my mind cleared instantly when I realised the silver wine stopper was gone. Scrambling off the bed, I looked under it, hoping to find it had just fallen to the floor, but all I found was the empty wine bottle and the secret trinkets hidden there. It was gone, and my memory reached back into the night before, through the haze, and landed on my mother, standing silently next to the bed for a few breaths before leaving the room.

She knew.

How did I let it happen? How did I let Mags talk me into taking the wine? We hadn't done anything like that before, but the excitement of meeting Ben must have clouded my judgement, making me feel invincible. I buried my face in my hands as dread throbbed deep inside my body and tears filled my eyes. I contemplated the enormity of what I was going to have to face when I went downstairs, where my mother surely waited. Most importantly, I knew with certainty I was never going to see Ben again. He was going to be expecting me that afternoon, but there was no way I would be leaving the house.

The clock ticked closer and closer to seven o'clock, and I knew I couldn't get away with hiding in my room for much longer. I pulled some clothes from my closet, and I rushed on tiptoes down the hall to the bathroom across from Mags's bedroom. I paused at her door but heard nothing, and when I opened it to peek in, her room was empty. We had ballet lessons every Saturday morning and Mags never missed a single class no matter what; no matter how bad she felt or how sick she was. She said she had to learn to dance through whatever was bothering her. She had to dance no matter what, and I envied her that she could be so focused and serious about something. Now not only would I be in trouble for drinking but I would also get it for missing class. The fact that no one woke me up and forced me to go was a bad omen in itself.

Safe in the bathroom, I undressed quickly, and hurried into the shower. The water was so hot it burned my skin, but I let it. I liked it that way. I liked to feel it burning everything away. Burning me away. This morning though, the heat and the steam made the small space spin around me, and I braced my hands against the cool white tiles to steady myself.

I didn't have to reach very far into my imagination to grasp the brutal punishments that were waiting for me downstairs. She could whip me with the belt again, maybe this time with the buckle end. She could lock me in the basement, or, worse, outside in the cold. Really, the possibilities of what she was capable of were endless.

The scalding water started to cool, so I washed quickly and when I stepped out, the cold air of the bathroom was a shock against my raw, red skin. Wiping the condensation from the mirror with my hand, I looked closely at myself. My eyes were bloodshot and rimmed with dark circles and my skin was dry and creased. It looked as though I hadn't slept at all. It felt like I hadn't either.

Once I was dressed in a knee length brown suede skirt and white blouse I hated, but my mother loved, I brushed my long hair, parted it down the middle and tied it back in a low ponytail like always and made my way down the stairs. On the second-floor landing, I hesitated for a moment to gaze down on the hollow foyer below. All remnants of the party had disappeared, as if it never happened. No Christmas trees, no presents, no lights. It was all gone. Everything was clean, and all the furniture put back exactly as it had been. Exactly as it always was. It happened this way every year, but, always, without fail, it was both shocking and disappointing to have that little bit of magic snatched away so completely each time. It made me wonder if I wasn't going crazy. Like maybe it really hadn't happened. Maybe I hadn't stolen the wine at all. It wasn't often that I actually hoped that I was losing my grasp on reality. I knew I couldn't be that lucky.

When I finally made it to the dining room, I leaned my back against the wall next to the entrance and took a few deep breaths, trying to work up the nerve to walk in and get it over with. Before I could, my mother's voice called out, "Josephine, I know you're there. It's not proper to lurk around corners."

The sound of her voice made me jump. With one final breath, I steeled myself and entered the dining room. She sat at the head of the long table, reading the newspaper, picking at a single piece of dry toast and sipping her black coffee. It was her usual post party breakfast, to stave off the effects of the "single" glass of champagne that never seemed to empty. Her head moved towards me slightly, acknowledging my presence, but she didn't look up at me and she said nothing else. Despite the simple breakfast, she looked perfect, as she always did.

My usual seat, to her right, was formally set and waiting for me. I sat down in silence and only moments later, a gold rimmed plate was set down before me. At the sight and smell of the egg white and broccoli omelette—no cheese—my stomach rolled, and I knew I wouldn't be able to eat a single bite. I could hardly manage it on a good day.

Luckily, my father walked into the dining room right at that moment and saved me from having to eat anything. At the sight of him, my mother's eyes lit up and he bent down and kissed her gently on the lips. They stayed close, smiling at each other as if I weren't even there for longer than was ever comfortable, before he straightened up and took the pages of the newspaper my mother was done with. He rolled them up and put them under his arm before turning to me.

Finally acknowledging my presence, he said,

"And good morning to you, too. What? No ballet this morning?"

"No," I answered, my voice quiet. "They are just practicing for the Christmas show tonight and I'm not in it this year." I didn't miss my mother glowering at my words, though my father didn't seem to notice.

"Well, nothing wrong with relaxing for once. I'm sure you will be chosen next year, darling," he said before kissing the top of my head. "I've got meetings today, so I better head to the office."

I wanted to protest that it was Christmas Eve, and he shouldn't be working. I needed him to stay home with me. To save me. But I couldn't say any of that, and after one more uncomfortably long kiss with my mother, he left for work, leaving us alone again.

The acid inside me boiled with more ferocity than usual and I was unsure whether it was from the alcohol or from the silence coming from the space beside me, but the stillness of the room was killing me. She wasn't saying anything. She wasn't acting any different than she usually did. Maybe she didn't know. Maybe, she didn't see the wine stopper. Maybe, I still had a chance.

When we were children, I was afraid of absolutely everything, while Mags was afraid of absolutely nothing. She would forever charge fearlessly forward, and I would hang back, permanently hesitating. Eventually, I knew I had to find a way to adapt, or I would inevitably be left behind. One especially hot summer day we were on our annual summer vacation to Vancouver Island with our nan and grandad. They had a house in Ucluelet and we spent weeks there every summer without our parents. It was the only time where I could be just me. But that particular day when we were ten or eleven, I was standing on the edge of the small cliff above the calm waters of a hidden cove tucked into the Pacific coast and Mags begged me to jump with her. She'd been doing it for years, as had all the other kids who lived there year round, but I had never made the leap. Mags never laughed at me, but the other kids did, and I saw my sister start to edge closer to them and farther away from me. Afraid I would lose her to them entirely, I did the only thing I could think of. I whispered to myself the words *too late*, ran towards the edge, and jumped off without thinking. The gasps from the kids at the edge followed behind me; Mags's most of all. I barely had time to feel the fear I was so afraid of before piercing the surface. There, I quickly found myself not afraid at all, but comforted by the weight of the dark water surrounding me. When my lungs began to ache, I kicked my way to the surface and drifted on my back in the sun and let the deep sense of excitement roll inside me.

From that day on, whenever I was faced with a moment I couldn't escape from, I would whisper those two words and dive headfirst into whatever I was afraid of. *Too late.* Too late to think. Too late to talk myself out of it. Too late to be afraid.

"Mother?" I said. *Too late.*

She put down the paper abruptly, annoyed at the interruption, and shifted uncomfortably in her chair. After a deep breath, she responded, "Yes?" Eyebrows raised. Lips pursed.

"Can Magalie and I spend the afternoon at the library?" I tried to keep my voice steady, but the lie felt foreign as it rolled around in my mouth. "We have a paper due as soon as we are back from break, and we need to work on it." That was true at least.

"Did you have a good time at the party last night?" she asked instead of answering my question, a small smile danced across her lips. "I looked for you and your sister, but I couldn't find you anywhere." She crossed her arms over her chest and sat back in her chair, waiting for my answer.

"Did you?" I said, feigning innocence. "I spent most of the evening talking to Robbie McDonald, like you suggested." I lied easily and quickly, hoping the mere thought of me spending quality time with a boy she approved of would distract her from my apparent absence from the party. Amazingly, it worked, and a small smile curved her lips.

"Ah, the McDonalds are fine people," she responded. "Unlike some of the other trash who come to our parties."

"Trash, Mother?" What was she talking about? Was this it? Disgust tainted her voice, not the anger

I was expecting, and for once, it didn't seem to be directed at me. I sat silent, waiting for her to elaborate as my blood pounded in my ears.

"Yes, when I was looking for you and Magalie during the party, I found evidence that some of the guests had somehow made it upstairs to your room."

"My room? What do you mean?" Was she playing with me, or could this be real?

"You would think that if they had the gall to drink and do God knows what else in my daughter's room, they could at least clean up after themselves. Disgusting. Never mind, we will install locks so this doesn't happen again." She ate the final bite of her toast and took a sip of her coffee before continuing. "Just be home in time for dinner, and remember that we have midnight mass tonight after Magalie's's recital. Perhaps we can sit with the McDonalds." She picked up the paper again, effectively ending the conversation.

The McDonalds were slightly higher up in society than we were. Sitting with them would mean we got to sit closer to the front of the church, and that meant, in my mother's eyes, closer to God. I should have been more nervous about the fact that, not only had I not talked to Robbie the night before, I had never talked to him at all. Stunned, I stared down at my untouched breakfast, unsure how to handle the situation, but one thing I did know. I was going to see Ben again.

"We'll be home in time for dinner. Thank you," I said and then I ate every last bite of my breakfast so she wouldn't have any other reason to suspect me of doing anything wrong. When I was done, I excused myself from the table, went back upstairs to our bathroom and threw it all up.

When Mags got home a few hours later, she found me in my room. Although she had been able to get up and go to class, she didn't look any better than I felt. She too had dark circles around her eyes and a grey tinge to her skin, and she collapsed onto the bed beside me, groaning. We laid still together for a long time, understanding that moving was not an option. The room no longer spun when we moved as it had the night before, but the insides of our bodies moved in waves that threatened to break at any moment.

When I felt okay enough to move again, I rolled from the bed and looked out my door. The hall was empty and quiet. Most of the house staff had already gone home for the day to celebrate Christmas with their families. It was safe. I kneeled on the floor beside the bed where Mags lay and she turned to me, grey and questioning. I filled her in on everything that happened at breakfast and almost instantly the pink returned to her cheeks.

She sat up, kneeling on the bed, suddenly feeling much better. "Don't worry about Robbie," she said with a laugh. "He's always so drunk at parties, he won't be able to remember whether he talked to you or not. He'll go along with anything we say to avoid his parents finding out. Plus, he wants me, so I can use that to our advantage if I need to."

CHAPTER FIVE

FRESH SNOW BLANKETED the neighbourhood, muting the already quiet Saturday afternoon even further. Snowflakes the size of cotton balls fell steadily around us, as the sun began to make its early descent behind the trees already heavy with yesterday's snow. The streets, typically full of people, were quiet with everyone already home, celebrating the holidays with their families and avoiding the unusual amount of snow we were getting. The odd person drove by on their way home from the supermarket or walked by on the sidewalk with their dog, but otherwise no one was choosing to be outside today. The windows of all the houses were warmly lit from within. That is, all the houses but ours, which stood dark in between the Monroe and the Richardson homes brightly lit with coloured

Christmas lights. To anyone going by our house, it looked like there was just no one home. Like no one was ever home.

We walked in restrained silence until we turned the corner and were out of sight from the house. Free from its ominous glare, we relaxed against each other and moved faster to keep warm during the short trip, muffled giggles and excitement vibrating between us.

At the end of the street, we were presented with a choice—we could either go right, which would lead us to the library or left, which would lead us to the diner. Ignoring that turn towards the library and therefore disobeying our mother sent my pulse racing. Again, I had never done anything like it before, and the thought of getting caught was both terrifying and exhilarating, especially after what we had gotten away with the night before. We turned left.

As the tattered exterior of O'Donnell's came into view, the world around me slowed to an almost complete stop, though my heart beat faster than I thought possible. I wanted to stand still, to wait in the shadows until I was ready, but Mags pulled me across the street and, without allowing any further hesitation, opened the door and pushed me inside.

Though the streets were quiet, the diner was busy and crowded as always. The air inside was moist, warm, and smelled of French fries, stale coffee and too many people. I swiftly scanned the crowd, looking for anyone I recognised and, to my surprise, saw no one.

Through a slight part in the crowd, I spotted Ben sitting at the same table as yesterday, intently reading a well-worn paperback with a still steaming mug in his hand. He bit his bottom lip slightly, obviously concentrating hard on whatever story was unfolding before him. He was so cute and tousled I couldn't help but pause and watch him for a few moments, before finally, as if feeling my eyes on him, he looked up and saw me. His eyes widened slightly when they met mine, and he smiled in a sincere way I wasn't used to seeing from anyone but my father.

Mags huffed impatiently and pulled me through the narrow aisle between chairs towards Ben's table, where he was now standing and waiting for us.

"You actually came," he said, obviously surprised.

The entire time, I had been afraid *he* wouldn't be here when I arrived. I wasn't expecting him to feel the same way, and I wondered if his heart was also beating as hard as mine was.

"Of course," I said, as if it were no big deal that I was there. I smiled and took the seat directly across from him, with my back to the rest of the diner, hoping to make it less likely we would be noticed.

Though we hadn't passed anyone I recognised, I knew that didn't mean nobody recognised *us*. We were one of only a few pairs of identical twins in our community, the other two being boys a little older than us and then a pair of girls barely out of diapers.

Once we were both seated, Ben sat down in his chair and leaned forward on his elbows, his book now closed and discarded next to him. His eyes studied me closely and I watched them flick back and forth between Mags and me, as I had seen people do so many times before. He was trying to pick out the differences between us, though he was being much less obvious about it than others usually were.

"That's a great book," I said, gesturing towards it. Although the cover was so worn that the title was completely obscured, I recognised it immediately as *The Great Gatsby*—my own similarly worn copy was on my bookshelf at home.

"It's one of my favourites," he said, smiling at me.

Mags cleared her throat beside me, reminding me she was there and I hadn't introduced her.

"This is my sister, Magalie," I said. My words felt sharp and clumsy as they always did, but Ben didn't seem to notice, and he was completely at ease as he put his hand out to shake hers.

"It's Mags," she said and her tone warned him not to forget it.

"Nice to meet you, Mags," he said to her with a warm smile. "Do you two want something to drink?" Ben wagged his finger between us as he stood up from his chair.

"We'll get two hot chocolates with extra marshmallows," Mags said automatically, before I could think of a better answer, and in response I kicked her a little too hard under the table.

To be fair, it was what we always ordered, but today, in front of Ben, it sounded juvenile and embarrassing next to his cup of black coffee.

"Two hot chocolates it is!" He strolled towards the counter that stretched along the back wall and sat on a stool talking animatedly with Shari while she made our drinks. She laughed loud at something he said and the sight of them, comfortable together, plucked an unfamiliar feeling in me. One I didn't like.

"Don't embarrass me," I hissed at Mags under my breath.

"Don't embarrass so easily; it's fine!" she teased, totally oblivious to the fact that I was being completely serious. She smiled wide as Ben sat back down and placed a large white mug brimming with marshmallows in front of each of us. Turns out that Shari is a lot more generous with the toppings when a cute guy is ordering from her, even if it was obvious that they were meant for us.

"Thank you," I said, and took a sip of the scalding liquid , stalling, not knowing what to say now that the time had come for actual talking. Everyone else in the restaurant was deep in conversations around us and the air was vibrating with holiday fervour. Against them, I felt exposed and apart. My heart slammed against my ribs, and I took another sip from the mug.

"So." He broke the silence. "Who are you?" He asked the question as abrupt as I felt, catching me completely off guard.

Struggling not to choke on my drink, I managed to say, through a nervous laugh, "What do you mean?" The question was so heavy and personal, and the immense weight of it pressed hard into my chest. No one knew me—no one except Mags, that is, and even then, did she really? There was so much I kept hidden, so much I dared not say, even to her. How could I even begin to explain myself to another person?

"Who are you?" He asked the strange question again, and when I still didn't say anything, he continued, "What kind of things do you like? What do you do?" He leaned slightly towards me with his arms folded on the table in front of him and a smirk that only lifted the left side of his lips.

Who am I?

I'm a deep dark pit. I'm cold and empty. I'm not very many things. I'm not the person he imagines me to be.

Mags, apparently unable to withstand my silence any longer, jumped in and spoke for me. "Jo's the best. She's a dancer. Ballet. She's also one of the smartest girls in our class," she added, her voice full of pride and I felt ashamed of my anger towards her moments before.

Ben smiled and although he seemed genuinely interested in what she was saying, his focus never strayed away from me for long. When Mags was done speaking, he nodded towards me, eyebrows raised, urging me to answer his question myself.

"There isn't much to tell," I said, concentrating all my attention on the now half empty mug of hot chocolate in front of me, unable to look him in the eye.

"I don't believe you."

His unwavering confidence in everything he said, and the intent way he sustained eye contact with me made me want to squirm uneasily in my seat, as I searched for something benign to tell him.

"Our mother is from Ireland. She moved to New York when she was twenty with her parents and she met our father shortly after. He was there for business. They got married right away, moved here to Vancouver and then, we were born." I spat out the boring details of my family history, hoping it was enough to satisfy his ardent curiosity.

"Well, that doesn't have a whole lot to do with who *you* are, but it's a start." He watched me with the same concentration he gave the book he was reading earlier, completely absorbed. When I didn't say anything else, he pushed further. "Why would they leave New York?" He sat back in his chair, his arms crossed in front of him, still not looking away from me.

"Our mother never liked New York and our father lived here so it seemed like the best choice, I guess." Our mother also hated Vancouver, but Shaughnessy was far enough from the core of the city that she was able to ignore it was there.

"What do you do when you're with your friends?" he asked as soon as I finished speaking.

"Do you always ask this many questions?" I fired back at him just as fast. Mags remained silent beside me, which I was grateful for, though it was unlike her to be quiet for so long.

"No, not usually." He settled in, across from me, waiting.

Deciding he may as well know the truth, I confessed, "I don't really have any friends."

"How's that possible?" he asked with genuine concern and surprise.

"No one likes me," I whispered.

"I can't believe that," he responded, shaking his head slowly.

Mags's hand found mine under the table and I knew she understood what it took for me to admit that to anyone, especially him. She also understood that, for whatever reason, it was true. We went to the same all-girls school since kindergarten, and all the girls enrolled there came from rich families like ours, but they were all a part of a prestigious club I was never invited to. It was a club started before any of us were even born. The mothers of the other girls had gathered first for prenatal classes and then again, laying their newborn babies on a soft blanket on the floor, drinking coffee and stacking them up against each other. Baby showers. Birthday parties. Piano lessons.

The morning of our first day at school, I was eager to make some friends and to play with someone other than my sister, but right from that first day, I knew it would never happen. They enveloped Mags into their world with ease, but I didn't fit into their box as neatly as she did. They said I was weird and creepy. At first, they said it only when they thought I wasn't listening, but as we got older, they made sure that I was. Children are intuitive. They knew right away that there was something wrong with me, that something was different, though they couldn't figure out exactly what it was. Though they couldn't see anything obviously wrong with me, they knew.

"Who are *you*?" I asked him. Changing the subject, and staring back at him with a steady gaze of my own only made him chuckle with obvious amusement.

He laughed loud and easy. "Point taken," he answered.

"Where are you from? I've never seen you around Shaughnessy," Mags asked, finally speaking.

"I've never been to Shaughnessy before. I don't think I'd really fit in," he answered, looking down at his worn clothes. "Actually, I'm only in Vancouver for a few months to help my aunt run her cafe while she recovers from an accident."

Shari appeared at the table then with a glass carafe, interrupting the conversation to refill Ben's empty coffee cup. She lingered for a few moments too long after Ben thanked her before finally walking away from the table slowly, but Ben didn't seem to notice.

"I'm actually from further up the coast," he said. "I live in a small fishing town called Halliswell. Have you heard of it?" We both shook our heads that we hadn't, and he continued to describe the area with its dense green forest, endless blue water and the small town where everyone knew everyone else.

"It sounds incredible." And it did. I had never been outside of the lower mainland aside from our summer vacations to the island. Really, I'd hardly been out of our neighbourhood, which was nice, but orderly in a way that could feel oppressive at times. Everything was perfect right down to the way the streets lined up with each other, the flawless displays in the few store windows and the houses that weren't at all alike but looked the same anyways. Not a thing was ever out of place, and the thought of deep dark water lapping at the wildness of unexplored woods excited me immeasurably.

I sat back and let his deep voice lull me. He spoke so easily, as though he didn't even have to think about it while I had to plan every word I said in advance. I spent the next few hours just listening to him talk more about his town and his best friend,

Ami.

We talked about books, movies, and music, but he knew much more about it all than I did. Our mother didn't approve of us "participating in popular culture", but that didn't stop me from keeping a copy of *Interview with a Vampire* hidden under my mattress, and sometimes we were able to sneak away to see a movie at the theater if our parents were going to be out late, so I wasn't completely oblivious.

Mags asked him about his parents. He hesitated at first, but then told us they died in a car accident a few years before.

"I'm sorry. I shouldn't have asked," she said quickly.

"No. It's okay." He assured her and took a shaky breath before continuing. "They were driving home late one night from a Christmas party when their car went off the road. They weren't found until the next day, and by then it was too late." His voice broke as he told the story and tears shone in his eyes for a moment, but he recovered from the sadness quickly and I was surprised by his public vulnerability. "After the accident," he said, "I kept living in their house. I grew up there and I have lived there alone ever since."

I wanted to reach out and take his hand, to comfort him but I couldn't force myself to take that step and my hands remained folded under the table.

The bell above the door dinged for the first time

since I finished my drink and reminded me where we were. Shortly after we'd arrived, the diner had quickly emptied, becoming unusually quiet, and it was a wonder they were open at all. All that remained were the few men and women who had no families to spend the holidays with and instead sat at the counter drinking coffee until it was a reasonable time to move over to the one pub that would stay open tonight. When I looked around the restaurant at all the empty tables, I realised it was dark outside.

"What time is it?" I asked, panicked.

Ben looked at his watch. "It's almost four o'clock."

"Oh no," Mags said as she pushed her chair back out from the table at the same time that I jumped up and slid my arms into my jacket. "We're going to be late; we have to go."

Mags followed my lead and put her jacket on as well. "Thank you, for the hot chocolates," she said to Ben, taking the moment to stop and smile at him with those green eyes of hers.

Although he looked a bit disconcerted with our sudden upheaval, he also took the moment to say, "You're welcome," to my sister before turning to me.

Our eyes met and, despite our rush, it felt infinitely hard to leave him behind. "Can I call you later?"

"No!" I said a little too aggressively in my panic.

Hurt flashed across his face and I forced myself to calm before clarifying. "No. I'll call you."

"Okay, okay, we really have to go," Mags urged, breaking my gaze from him and bringing me back to reality.

He wrote down his phone number on a blank page ripped from the back of his book and slipped it into my jacket pocket.

"I'll talk to you later," he said, grinning. As we turned from him, he brushed his hand quickly into mine and gave it a little squeeze, making my heart and my stomach turn completely upside down.

The entire way home, Mags talked ceaselessly, but this time I didn't mind. I couldn't stop smiling. I was scared my lips were never going to relax, and our mother would see it all over my face as soon as we walked through the door.

As we turned onto our street, our house loomed above us, a large three-story Tudor with an obscenely large balcony jutting off the second floor, guarding the front door. During parties, cars pulled up under it and valets helped guests out before driving the cars elsewhere to be parked. Without the party and the cars and the valets, it looked absurd and out of place, as though it were put there by accident. Father told me once houses were sometimes built that way for protection, but protection from what? I imagined dropping things or pouring boiling water over the edge of the balcony onto intruders below. Seemed unlikely in

Canada.

Two dormer windows overlooked the balcony, each one belonging to one of our bedrooms. Mags's window emitted a warm glow from a lamp left on next to her bed. Mine was completely dark, but when I looked closer, there was a darkness even darker than just the absence of light. The darkness had substance and shape and stood staring out at us. Every hair on my body stood up pulling at my skin painfully. I squinted through the darkness, thinking I must be seeing things, but the figure remained framed in the window—motionless, staring.

I reached my hand out towards my sister and when her fingers intertwined with mine, I spoke quietly without moving my lips or even my head towards her, "Mags, do you see it?"

"See what?" Mags pulled her hand from mine and skipped ahead, leaving me alone on the dark street. "Come on! We're late."

When I looked back up at the window, the figure was gone, the darkness empty, and I thought maybe I had imagined it. Behind me, a streetlight blinked out. Afraid of the truculent darkness that surrounded me, I rushed to catch up with Mags.

Once inside the house, we hung up our jackets in the entryway closet just as our mother descended the curved staircase, dressed for dinner in an elegant hunter green wrap dress that fell just below her knees.

"Did you finish your papers?" she asked when

she reached the bottom.

"Yes, Mother," we said in unison, hands obediently clasped behind our backs, the way she liked. I held my breath and waited for her to comment on how long we were gone. She was about to speak again when our father came through the door behind us.

"Hey! Everyone's here. Sorry I'm late!" He kissed both Mags and I before turning to our mother. "Everyone wanted to get as much work done before Christmas as possible. It was madness."

"You two, go wash up and get changed for dinner, we're going to be late," she said to us without another thought, as she turned away and walked towards the dining room on our father's arm.

Safe in Mags's room, we laid side by side on her bed, marvelling at how we had gotten away with it, but still, the dark figure from my window haunted me. I saw it when I closed my eyes, lurking in the corners of my consciousness. Waiting. But for what?

"Mags?" I said, desperately wanting to talk about what I saw that night and what I had seen so many times before.

"Hmm?" She relaxed on the bed with her eyes closed, smiling gently.

She was happy and I didn't want to take that away from her, so in the end, I didn't mention the shadow I saw or the darkness I felt. Instead, I pushed it out of my mind and lay, head to head with my sister and thought about the perfect day I'd had.

CHAPTER SIX

AFTER THAT DAY in the diner, Ben and I met whenever we could. He was the perfect distraction from my daily life, and I quickly found myself forgetting about any possible consequences our relationship might cause. My mind played tricks on me—fooling me into thinking sneaking around was a good idea, that nothing bad could possibly happen as long as we were careful, and that any consequence would be worth it.

As far as our mother knew, we spent a lot of time at the library studying. I even told her that I picked up another dance class, and for the first time, I felt lucky she wasn't interested in my dancing, because she didn't question it, nor did she offer to come watch me as she did Mags sometimes. As long as I stayed quiet and obedient at home, I was able to slip in and out undetected.

Mags always went with me wherever I went, and it was no different when I went to see Ben. She came, not only as an excuse for me to be out of the house, but because we all genuinely liked being together. It was the middle of winter in Vancouver, and though the winters were usually mild, this year had been unseasonably cold, and seemed to be lasting forever. Because the air was frozen and constantly wet, there weren't a lot of places we could go or things we could do where people wouldn't notice us.

We couldn't risk someone telling our mother where we really were or what we were doing, so we spent a lot of our time in the darkness of the movie theater. The Hollywood Theater in Kitsilano was close enough to pile into Ben's rusted red Ford pickup , but also far away enough that there was a good chance no one would see us once we got there. We watched *A Star is Born* so many times we could recite the entire movie, and Mags would dream of being like Barbra Streisand's character, Esther Hoffman, except with dancing instead of singing.

"You know, the story isn't actually romantic right?" Ben reminded her. "Their relationship sucks and then he dies."

"Yeah, but look where she ends up," Mags responded as she twirled dreamily. "See? I could be famous," she smirked, as she whipped into a fouetté —one leg bent beneath her as she spun and lifted up on her toes again and again before ending with a flourish.

Ben rolled his eyes at her, but he couldn't help but chuckle.

When we weren't sneaking into the movies, we spent the rest of our time at the café off West Broadway where Ben worked during the day, and in the small one-bedroom apartment above, where he lived temporarily.

A few weeks before we met, his aunt Meredith had fallen down the stairs that connected her apartment with her café. After the fall, she'd required multiple surgeries to repair the breaks in her legs, and she was faced with a significant amount of rehab. Because her apartment was at the end of a long and narrow set of stairs, there was no way she could return home until she was able to climb them herself. The small café was all she had, and when his beloved mother's sister called Ben for help, he dropped everything and came right away.

We knew that, when she was finally able to come home, Ben would be expected to return to Halliswell, to his real life, and I might never see him again. It was inevitable and he never said it out loud, but I knew he couldn't stay here for me. So, we played games and we watched movies. He made us dinner most nights, and when we got home, we would have to choke down a second one so that no one would be suspicious.

Mags always came with me, and I was both

annoyed by and grateful for her presence. I needed her there because I knew that, without her, I would do something I would surely regret. In a way, I'd lost control of myself completely, and she was the only thing keeping me within the lines of the person I was supposed to be. But, with each visit to Ben, I came closer to the person I actually was, and not just the teenage cut out I had been cast as. My secret darkness receded while my public obedience was tested, and what was coming out of that was everything to me.

But Mags, she came with me every time until one night, I asked her not to.

"Are you really going to do this?" she gushed, sitting on the edge of our parent's massive bed with her knees pulled up to her chest.

Our parents were out at a party, and from experience, I knew they would be gone most of the night. As I usually did, I took the opportunity to sneak into their room and sit at our mother's vanity. Because it was a special night, we poured ourselves small glasses of brown liquid from the crystal decanter they kept on elaborate silver trays in practically every room. We giggled after each tiny sip of the burning liquid, and it wasn't long until our sips and our smiles got bigger.

I styled my hair the way our mother hated it the most—curled and loose around my shoulders. She always told me loose girls wore their hair loosely and that she would not have that kind of girl in her house. I then applied an amount of makeup that would probably have me slapped if I were caught, red lipstick to top it off. Next, I tried on a few of her dresses. Surprisingly, we were almost the same size, and in the end, I chose a dark blue knee length dress with cap sleeves and white buttons up the front. Standing before the mirror, for just a second, I saw not myself, but my mother staring back at me. Her roguish smile, turning up one corner of her lips. Her eyebrow raised.

I had done a good job of avoiding being completely alone with Ben until then. We had stolen moments when Mags went to use the bathroom, and I always thought she took a little bit longer than she normally would. We took advantage of that time to kiss. We touched and explored, rushed and excited, but were always forced apart when the bathroom door opened, and she emerged.

Now that our time together was coming to an end, I knew those stolen moments weren't enough. So, I went to his apartment that night knowing exactly what was going to happen. I went there with the intention of giving myself to him completely.

Too late.

When it was over, I went to the bathroom, looked in the mirror, and was surprised to see someone I didn't completely recognise looking back at me. My hair was tangled around my shoulders and my makeup was smudged, but I was happy.

The shadows stayed away when I was with him,

and in that moment, I really felt as though maybe they were gone for good.

CHAPTER SEVEN

Standing at the edge of a cliff, the wind blew my hair up around me, like hundreds of little whips lashing against my skin. The clouds changed quickly, from tiny wisps of white to undulating mountains of black. Lightning flashed, illuminating the opaque water below as thunder boomed overhead, and the storm was quickly upon me. A thick mist dampened my hair and clothes, plastering them to my body. When the rain started to fall, I turned to go back to the cottage, where my Nan waved from the open door, calling out for me to come home. As I tried to move towards her, little winged creatures appeared and started to pull me in every direction. Their miniature hands grasped at my clothes, my skin, and my hair. I wasn't afraid of them at first; they were playful, and I giggled as their wings tickled my bare skin. But then, they became more insistent and sinister, and when I looked closer at the fairies' tiny faces, the mouths I first thought smiling were actually full of sharp, dirty teeth.

Nan's voice called out to me again, calling my name, but I couldn't see her anymore through the impenetrable rain. I heard her again, but this time from behind me. I turned, but only the angry sea rolled below me. I couldn't find her. The creatures continued to pull at me, slicing my skin and tearing the fabric of my dress. Warmth poured from the cuts, ran down my chilled body to pool in my shoes. I turned around and around, crying out for Nan to save me, but she never came. My hands reached up to protect my face, instinctually stepping back from their claws, but my foot landed on nothing but air. And then, I was falling. Drops of my blood splattered the water, turning the sea red and filling the air with a salty copper smell before I plunged beneath the surface.

I sat up, safe in my own bed, gasping for breath. I could still feel the sting of my wounds, and tears clouded my eyes from the fear that still hammered inside me. Knowing it was only a dream didn't help; I was still in it, I was still falling.

My blanket pooled around my hips and my nightgown clung to my body. I shivered violently as my warm, damp skin was exposed to the cold air of my room. My breath continued to come in short bursts, but soon enough my eyes adjusted to the moonless dark and the familiarity of my space calmed my racing heart.

Nan had told me fairy stories brought over from Ireland ever since I was a little girl. She told me she saved these stories especially for me, but I knew she shared them with Mags as well, though I pretended not to know. No matter what, they were *our* stories, and over the years they became completely ingrained in my thoughts and dreams, a part of me. She died over a year ago and still, I missed the feeling of her sitting on the edge of my bed as she had almost every night since coming to live with us when we were still babies. Although the fairies always visited me in my dreams, it wasn't until she died that they gained a macabre quality, as if her life had protected me from their darkness.

A small fairy figurine stood watch over me from my bedside table. She gave it to me for my thirteenth birthday—a date which was, according to her, a magical age for children, because it was during that time, that in between place when they transitioned from child to adult, when everything begins to change. I thought it had more to do with the number thirteen itself, unlucky and yet coveted, but she didn't want to risk scaring me with her superstitions so she told me that if I kept the figurine beside my bed, it would keep me safe.

I closed my eyes and sank back into my mattress, letting the memory of her lull me back to sleep.

Then, the floor creaked, and I froze, suddenly aware that someone was standing directly behind me, watching. My heart slammed against my ribcage so hard I thought it would break through the bones.

"Mags?" I whispered into the immense darkness. My voice shook with desperation and hope that the sound I heard was just my sister coming to climb into my bed as she sometimes did when she had bad dreams, but no one responded. There was only silence and the thick night surrounding me.

The logical side of my brain, the side that ruled me most of all, assured me it was nothing, just the house settling in for the night, just the dampness from the winter rain expanding the old wood, but then it came again. The floor creaked excruciatingly close to where I lay, and this time, I heard someone breathing. Shallow. Quiet.

Don't turn around. Don't turn around. Don't turn around.

The words started an unceasing loop inside my head.

Don't turn around. Don't turn around. Don't turn around.

Despite the words I told myself, my body turned unwillingly, inch by inch towards the darkness behind me. My eyes remained closed; I was too afraid to open them. But then, something cold and dry touched the bare skin of my shoulder. A retching feeling pierced deep into my gut, and I recoiled from the touch. My eyes flew open to a dark shadow looming above me, so close I could feel the heat of it penetrating the frigid air of my room. A scream ripped from my lungs as I flew backwards out of bed, tripping on the bedsheets wrapped around my legs before pinning myself against the cold glass of the window. My skin crawled. The dark shadow remained completely motionless, as did I. I was sure not even my heart was beating anymore. Time stopped. The only thing moving in my world was the rain pounding steady against the windows.

The shadow, still unmoving, said, "You dirty whore," in a low, gravelly voice; a voice I recognised immediately, and that recognition only stoked the growing heat of fear in my belly.

"Mother?" The word was rotten in my mouth.

She didn't respond at first, though her voice continued spilling forth unintelligible muttering that I struggled to understand, but it was as though she were speaking a different language.

"You thought you could hide it from me." Her words, though still resembling something akin to a deep growl, returned to something I could understand. "You thought I wouldn't know you went out and got yourself pregnant?" she howled, and it was as though her voice reached out and slapped me across the face, shocking me back into the present and restarting the cogs of time.

"What?" The question came out more as a rush of air from my open mouth than an actual word. My chest heaved under the weight of the accusation, my lungs fighting to take in enough air.

She clicked the lamp on, filling the room with light, but although it dispelled the shadows, the darkness remained. My hands flew to my mouth to stifle another scream. The thing lurking before me was not my mother. Its face was blank, its eyes lifeless. The long dark hair my mother took such pride in hung limp and stringy around its shoulders; its makeup smudged into dark circles around its eyes, mascara running in two vertical lines down its cheeks; red lipstick smudged into a grotesque sneer. My mother was someone who always took great care with her appearance, and this was what worried me the most. My mother, a monster on the inside, was now a monster on the outside too, and I was shocked to realise this outward monster was also familiar to me. I knew it. I'd seen it before.

A deeply buried and long-forgotten memory clawed its way to the surface. We must have been only four or five years old. Not yet old enough to know how to use a calendar or to tell time, relying entirely on the adults around us to guide us through life. It was a typical morning, and we were sitting at the breakfast table as always. Mags and our father, who laughed and joked with each other across from me, didn't seem to notice anything was different, but I did. Our mother, always painfully punctual, wasn't ruling from her usual chair at the head of the table. Maybe I wouldn't have noticed the empty chair either if it wasn't for the immense relief I felt from being free from her eye for just a little bit longer, but as the seconds ticked by and she still didn't appear, the relief turned into something sour. It wasn't right. I knew something was wrong. It wasn't until our plates were cleared away that she appeared in the arched entrance to the breakfast room. It was a bit of a shock to see her that day. She was always put together, always in control. But there she stood, disheveled. She hadn't dressed yet and still wore her pink, silk nightgown with her white, silk robe thrown hastily over top. She just stood there in the doorway still, silent. It was obvious, even to me as a child, that we had done something wrong, but when I looked to my father for an explanation, I could see he didn't understand what it was that upset her any more than I did.

"Tout va bien?" He asked her. I*s everything alright?*

None of us moved or said anything else while we waited for her response. With a look I can only describe as absolute disbelief, she turned and rushed from the house. A car door slammed, an engine started, and tires squealed as she drove off in one of our father's cars, still in her nightgown and robe. Our father, finally able to move, jumped from his chair to chase after her, but he was too late. She was gone.

Mags and I waited all day for her to come home, playing quietly in my room, but she didn't come back. It wasn't until we had already gone to bed that the doorbell rang loud through the entire house. I was still awake, but Mags notoriously slept like the dead, and if she did wake up that night, she didn't emerge. I crept from my room and tiptoed down the stairs until I could see the foyer clearly from my hiding spot. A large man dressed in an RCMP uniform laid my mother on the chaise in the entryway. Her nightgown was dirty, ripped and smeared with red. My father took some bills out of his wallet and handed them to the officer before shaking his hand and thanking him for bringing her home. Then, he picked up his wife and held her in his arms like a child. She looked so small. Smaller than I have ever seen her, even to this day.

Concealed in the shadows of the stairwell that led to the third floor, I watched him climb the stairs one at a time, his head down. When he reached the second floor, I saw my mother's face clearly as he turned towards their bedroom. Her head hung limply all the way back and one of the straps of her nightgown swung broken against her face. Her eyes were wide open, and I thought for sure she had seen me, but her eyes were blank, like she wasn't there at all.

The next day, Father told us she was just a little bit sad because we all forgot Mother's Day. Usually, we brought her breakfast in bed and surprised her with gifts, but for whatever reason, that year, we didn't even think of it, and she'd waited patiently in bed for us to come upstairs.

After that day, things were different. They

weren't great before, but it was like the fine thread that was just holding her together had finally snapped.

A stinging slap across my cheek ripped me from the memory. The right side of my face burned, and my neck ached from the impact. When she hit me again, this time with her fist, it was so hard I lost my balance. My body slammed into the wall before crumpling to the floor. The blood from the first blow flowed freely and my fingers grazed my cheek, dancing across the warmth trickling from my broken skin.

She loomed above me, blocking the light and casting me in darkness, neither of us much more than a shadow.

"How dare you do this to me!" she screamed.

"I didn't… I… I didn't do anything," I said, pushing back away from her, sliding across the smooth wooden floor. No matter where I went, she was right on top of me. I couldn't escape.

"It was that boy, wasn't it? The one I warned you about. Or maybe it was every boy in this town, you little bitch!" she screamed with such fury as I had never before experienced.

"No, Mama, no, I didn't do it." On my knees before her, hands up as if in prayer, I cried. Each one of my tears hit the floor, creating a puddle beneath my knees.

"You filthy, fucking liar! You will pay for this." She pointed her finger at me and came so close that her sour spit sprayed across my face with each word.

My stomach retched again, and I thought for sure that, this time, I might throw up. But then, her head turned towards the door, as if someone I couldn't hear had called out to her. She straightened up, turned from me, and strode from the room, her white silk robe billowing behind her as she slammed the door. The sound of the key in the lock was deafening in the sudden silence of my room.

Aching, I pulled myself up from the floor and leaned against the cold wall. A shiver rocked through me when the bare skin of my back touched it. I didn't pull away though; the pain of it brought me out of the initial shock and, for a split second, took my mind off the throbbing in my head.

Yes, I knew I was pregnant, of course I did. I had known for a while; since last month when my period never came. It was confirmed when, even now, it was still absent.

But how had she discovered my secret before I'd even had the chance to decide what I was going to do about it? Before I could tell Ben he was to be a father, and ask him to take me with him back to Halliswell? I was hoping to be long gone before anyone even had the chance to find out.

Yes, I knew this could happen, and I didn't stop it, I didn't even try.

CHAPTER EIGHT

A SMALL VOICE, as familiar as my own, called my name through the dark. I scrambled out of bed to press myself against the locked door, longing for the comfort of my sister. Although only mere inches from her, I felt so far away.

I hadn't told her, either. At first, when I realised I was pregnant, I was too scared and ashamed. Then, the longer I kept silent, the harder it was to say anything at all. Keeping such a secret from the one person who was supposed to know me better than anyone in the whole world was enough to eat me alive, but sitting there with the door between us, I realised the truth was that I was actually disappointed in *her*; disappointed she hadn't seen it herself. Always able to see me so clearly, even with her eyes closed, somehow, she couldn't see this whole other person living inside of me.

"Mags?" My voice reached out to her and, despite my disappointment, I longed to tell her, if only to have someone share the weight of the night.

"What happened?" she asked, pushing her fingers under the door as far as she could.

I touched the tips of them with my own. This wasn't the first time one of us was locked in our room, though usually it *was* me. Although Mags was louder and more mischievous than me, I was almost always the one to be punished when we were caught. She would come to my room and sit outside it the way she did now, with her fingers under the door, enduring the punishment with me even though she didn't have to. We were always in it together.

The feel of her fingers against mine only intensified my guilt. I wanted to say it, I wanted to tell her, but the words wouldn't come. I couldn't be the one to let her down, and I knew that no matter how much it hurt, this weight was mine to bear alone. Instead of speaking, a sob tore from my chest, and I pressed myself even harder against the door, trying to make my way through it, closer to her.

She was quiet for so long that, if I couldn't feel her skin solidly against my own, I would have thought she had gone. Finally, she spoke. "Josephine..." She paused for a moment and then continued. "Is it true?"

She didn't have to say it out loud. I could tell from her voice and from her use of my full name that she knew. I could hear how it hurt her.

"Yes," was all I could say, my throat choked with guilt and shame.

At first, she didn't respond, and her quiet unnerved me, but then she said, "How could you do this to me?"

Her fingers pulled away from mine, the sound of her footsteps receded down the hall, and I knew I deserved it. I deserved worse, because the truth was, there was another reason I hadn't told her. I knew this pregnancy could be my chance to get away, and I didn't tell her about it because I wasn't sure my plan included her. I couldn't reconcile that idea with the one we had always agreed on. The one where we both got out. The one where we never left the other behind.

I felt certain that, if I were to leave, our mother wouldn't come looking for me. If anything, she would be relieved to be rid of me. Our father would look, of course, but realistically, by the time he knew I was gone, it would be too late. She would never let Magalie go, though. She was too valuable a trophy to let slip away, and I couldn't risk being dragged back with her.

Back in bed, my mind ran wild, but my eyes burned with exhaustion. I willed myself to fall asleep again, if only to take me away temporarily. I squeezed my eyes shut against the guilt raging through me, but I couldn't fall asleep knowing Mags wasn't speaking to me, so I reached up and knocked three times against the wall above my bed. We were once obsessed with the song 'Knock Three Times,' and we used it as a way to communicate during our fights. If I knocked three times, and she responded with three knocks as well, that meant we were okay. But, if she sent back just two knocks, that meant we were still in a fight. I was relieved when just seconds later, three knocks came back from the other side, and I knew that eventually we would be okay. She would forgive me. She always did.

I settled back into bed. Just as sleep began to take me away, and an intricate web of dreams wove around me, a loud forlorn wail pierced through the cocoon. It was a voice I didn't recognise, and I must have been closer to sleep than awake, because my dream reached out and snagged me before the wail could pull me away.

When I opened my eyes again, my room was engulfed in a dull early morning glow. Whatever I had dreamt in the night was gone, but the echo of the scream still resonated in my memory despite the fogginess of the morning. In the end, I attributed it to the abrupt feeling of falling that sometimes occurs right before sleep comes; something which happened to me often enough. I put it out of my mind when I glanced at the clock and saw it was already ten o'clock. I never slept later than six. Mother never allowed it, not even when I was sick, not even when she locked me in my room in the past. She thought it was frivolous and wasteful of a day granted from God, and she marched in every morning to make sure I was awake and ready to go.

I threw back the covers, went to the bedroom door, and turned the knob only to find it still locked. I wanted to pound on the hard wood. I wanted to scream and kick it open, but I knew it was pointless. No one would come. Mother's rules weren't broken by anyone in the house. Besides, I was on the third floor, and at this time of day, everyone would be downstairs, so no one would hear me if I tried.

I took comfort in the fact the servants would notice if I wasn't there for lunch as well as breakfast. My absence would give them something to gossip about, and that was something our mother would do anything to avoid. She *always* let me out, before anyone had the chance to ask questions. Worst case scenario, our father would open the door when he got home from work, but I couldn't see her letting it get that far. She always pushed things right to the edge where people might see them, but she couldn't risk her beloved husband knowing how far she really went in his absence.

The rain from the night before turned to a thick and heavy snow. The wind blew the large flakes so hard and fast I could hardly see anything outside my window. It always snowed a few times a year on the coast, but something about this snow was different. Unrelenting.

Cars were covered in all the neighbours' driveways, but no one was outside. The image from my bedroom window was missing the usual people shovelling their driveways or brushing off their cars. The silent scene was eerie, and I looked away, uncomfortable. Where was everybody?

With my clothes changed and my hair brushed, I sat at my desk to work on my French homework and wait for the door to open. I knew enough French from Daddy that the mandatory school curriculum was too easy and I finished quickly before moving onto math. I ran my tongue over my teeth, longing most of all for my toothbrush. I tried to concentrate on the work before me, but my eyes kept drifting to the clock. I watched the time tick by second by second. I watched as I missed lunch, and still no one came for me.

Hours later, my door handle shook, and for a moment, I thought I was finally being let out, but it was only Mags's voice who whispered my name. Tears flooded my eyes with a relief so acute that it hurt. She wouldn't be the one to let me out, I knew that; but I needed her, nonetheless. I ran to the door and stuck my fingers beneath it, waiting for the comfort of her touch, and was stunned when it didn't come. She couldn't possibly still be mad. She never stayed angry with me for long, no matter what we fought about.

"Mags? What's wrong?"

She didn't respond, but I could feel her there. I

could hear her heart beating, her pulse pounding alongside my own. She whispered my name again and this time I heard something in her voice that I hadn't before, desperation.

"Where's Daddy? Why hasn't he let me out yet?" I cried.

"He went away for work," she said, and with those words, dread filled me to the brim.

If he was gone, there really was no one to save me beyond the staff. No, he wasn't coming this time and besides being hungry, thirsty and scared, I needed to use the bathroom desperately.

"What? But I thought he wasn't supposed to leave until tomorrow. What about the storm? When did he leave? He shouldn't be driving in this!" The questions poured out of me dripping with fear, not only for myself, but for him as well.

The silence on the other side of the door remained thick. Finally, Mags spoke. "He left last night. He wanted to try to beat the storm."

"Hasn't anyone noticed that I'm gone?" The snow piled halfway up the window, blocking even more of the midday light. "What about Mrs. Bachelder?" I continued. She was the housekeeper and had been with our family since we were born. She moved from New York with us, and with no other family of her own, she was like a mother to us both.

"Mother told all of the staff that you went to visit a sick aunt in New York and she didn't know when or if you'd be back. She said that with you and Daddy both gone indefinitely, they wouldn't be needed anymore." She paused then, and I both feared and knew what she was going to say next. "Jo, she fired everyone."

I had always been able to hide behind the other people in the house. Mother couldn't hurt me too bad, not really, with Daddy around, and the staff. But now that they were gone, she could do anything, and no one would know. It was becoming hard to breathe and my room started to get smaller and smaller; the walls closing in on me.

"You have to get me out of here!" I screamed.

"Shhhh, Jo, it's going to be okay." Relenting, her fingers brushed mine beneath the door and as usual, her touch calmed me almost immediately.

My breathing slowed, my pulse returned to normal, and the walls of my room moved away from me.

She waited for me to calm down completely before continuing. "She said that if I interfered or if I told anyone the truth about where you are, she would lock me in my room too. What should I do? I can't just leave you in here."

Now she was the one starting to panic, and so it was my turn to calm her. It's how we did things. We couldn't fall apart at the same time because we each needed the other to put us back together again. If we were both apart, there would be no one to save us at all.

I couldn't ask her to help me. There was nothing she could do, and it wasn't fair to punish her as well. It was me who made the mistake, and it was me who should have to pay for it. Also, I knew that if Mags was locked up too, I would have no link to the outside, and I didn't know how important that link would be.

"Don't say anything. Don't do anything. I don't want you to get into trouble too."

A crash outside shook the house and the wind howled through the bare branches of the trees, but I could see nothing past the snow piling at my window.

"Mags, what's going on out there?"

"They're saying it's going to be one of the worst storms we've ever had." Her voice was quiet on the other side of the door. "They're telling everyone to stay indoors and ride it out."

Everything went dark and silent in an instant. "Mags?!"

"I'm still here; the power must have gone out. I'll be right back."

It was unusually dark in my room for this time of the day, and I quickly became nervous. The darkness pressed down on me like a heavy wet blanket, the scratchy kind made of wool that made my skin crawl. It surprised me how much noise electricity makes. Everything was empty and still without the constant hum running through the walls, and the silence was so loud I could hardly stand it. The wailing snow threw fluttering shadows over my walls, and I imagined them to be my fairies dancing, keeping me company. I was never alone. Not really.

Mags returned shortly and slid a candle and some matches under the door. "It looks like the power is out everywhere; I can't see anything outside."

"Can you stay here with me? I'm scared."

Before Mags could answer, our mother's voice called for her from the bottom of the stairs.

"I have to go. I'm sorry." She reached under the door, and we grasped at each other one more time, mirror images on each side of the wood, before she was gone again.

The time ticked by on the clock as the storm continued to rage outside. Snow continued to build up on the small patch of roof directly outside my window and it wasn't long before the wind had blown the snow to cover the glass completely, blocking all light. Everything was closing in on me and I was forced to finally light the candle. The sliver of light it produced was enough to pull the dark, heavy blanket back just enough so I could breathe.

By then, my bladder was so full I couldn't hold it any longer. I tipped the crumpled bits of paper and pencil shavings out of the small garbage can beside my desk. Bile rose from my empty stomach up into my throat at the thought of what I was about to do, but I had no choice. The humiliation of using a bucket for a toilet made my eyes burn and my throat tight, but the relief was so great and so necessary. It wasn't long before the acrid scent of urine filled my room, and it would only get worse the longer I was kept there.

My mouth was painfully dry and my stomach just as empty.

I called at the door, "Please, let me out!" When no one came, and no one answered my pleas, not even Mags, desperation overtook me completely. I slammed my fists against the wood until they were bruised and bloody, the skin split in multiple places. "Let me out of here!" I screamed and screamed until my voice was hoarse, my throat raw and sore. Hopeless, I rested my forehead against the door and began to cry, really cry.

With no one looking for me, it occurred to me that my mother could be capable of leaving me in here forever, and panic filled me. It poured into me like a glass filling up with water, only the water was black and smelled of tar and blood. My mind turned around and around like a carousel, each turn producing a more sinister possibility as the calliope's song grew more and more fevered, each turn scaring me more and more.

What if they never came back? What if she threw away the key and closed up the third floor forever? What if I wasted away to nothing and everyone forgot that I ever existed? I took a deep breath and tried to calm my thoughts. Shaking, I crawled back into bed and continued watching the seconds tick by, waiting for this day, the longest one I ever had, to finally end.

CHAPTER NINE

ANOTHER DAY PASSED by painfully slow, with no sign of either Mags or my mother. I knocked on my wall over and over but was met with only silence. I was all alone. The power was still out, and I spent all my time in bed trying to stay warm by wearing multiple layers of clothing and every blanket I owned piled on top of me, but the cold slipped through to my skin anyways and I couldn't stop my teeth from chattering.

The snow, piled high outside my window, taunted me. I tried to push it open to get at it, but either the window was frozen shut, or the snow stacked against it was too heavy for my weakened arms to move it. I watched the frozen water glistening behind the glass and imagined shoving handfuls of it into my mouth, my sandpaper tongue absorbing the moisture. I had long given up yelling for help. No one ever came, and I was too tired and too cold to get out of bed anymore except to use the bucket, but without food or water, even that became unnecessary.

The next morning, I awoke to a familiar weight on the edge of my bed. When I opened my eyes, there was Nan, sitting where she'd always sat, a small smile playing across her lips, though her eyes were filled with concern. She looked as she always did when she was alive, with her white hair pulled into a long braid that hung over her shoulder. An old-fashioned skirt fanned out around where she sat.

"Nanny," I said. "You came for me."

"Of course I did, dear." She smiled. "You called me, and here I am."

"I did?" I asked.

"Yes, darling, in your dreams. Don't you remember?" She gave a little chuckle and looked me over with love in her eyes. It was a love I missed so dearly, and, until that moment, I hadn't realised the absence of it was so dark.

The room brightened slowly and thoroughly, as though the sun was rising just over the horizon, pushing the shadows away. The light radiating from her was so warm it thawed my cold body. It felt good, it warmed me all the way through, and my thirst was taken away.

"You're safe, baby. Come with me and you won't hurt anymore."

She held her hand out towards me, and I wanted

so bad to take it, but just as I put my own hand out, a key turned in the lock and the door opened.

All at once, my nan was gone, the light was gone, the heat was gone, and my thirst had returned, as had the deep chill in my bones. I was back in my ice-cold room with my mother standing in the doorway, holding a candle in one hand and a glass of water in the other. She looked as she always did. Gone was the monster who locked me in here but still a monster remained. The sight of the water made my heart quicken. I wanted to run towards it. I wanted to grab it from her and drink the whole thing. But I couldn't make my muscles move. She bent down, put the glass on the floor, and then left the room, locking the door behind her once again.

Summoning all my strength, I pushed the blankets off me and got out of bed, my legs shaking with the effort. Without the meager protection of the blankets, my already cold skin screamed in shock as the freezing air picked its way through my clothes. Moving as fast as I could, I scrambled towards the water and collapsed to the ground in front of it. My shaking hand lifted the cup to my lips. Water spilled out the side and down my chin as I drank. I heard each lost drop hit the ground, like I could feel each drop within my mouth. It just wasn't enough.

Later that day, the power finally whirred back to life, filling my dark room with light from above. I flicked the switches of the lamps atop each bedside table, eager to illuminate every inch of the darkness I had been submerged in for days. The sound of the electricity was deafening, as though my room was full of bees, and it was vibrating with the weight of them. I covered my head with my pillow to keep the bees from seeping into my head, but another familiar sound forced me out from under it. Air flowed from the vents in my floor, and I scrambled out of bed to huddle over one of them; my blue floral quilt billowed out around it like a tent. I cried in relief as my limbs began to thaw, and I was sure I had never felt something so luxurious. It was better than every bath I had been drawn; better than any silk or velvet dress I owned. It was even better than sinking into bed with Ben nestled next to me. Settling in against the wall, I stayed there for hours.

"Jo?"

My sister called to me through the door, and the sound of her voice made my heart leap. I missed her. I missed her so much that I ached with it. We had been together every single day, from the very first moment when the cells inside our mother split and it was decided we would be two instead of one.

"Mags! Where have you been?" I hurried, as fast as my weak legs could carry me, to the door.

"Jo." Her voice was low, shaky, and hardly audible.

The single syllable of my name was more like a deep wail than a word and it stopped me dead. This voice was foreign to me, not the optimistic one I knew so well, and my body stiffened with dread. Something else had happened.

"What?" was all I managed to say, the word itself hardly choked out.

It was bad, I could tell. It was worse than anything we knew. It was worse than being locked in this room day after day. Her fingers groped under the door until they found mine and she held me as hard as she could, held me until it hurt.

The silence between us dragged on for what felt like an eternity, but I was grateful for the time. I didn't want to hear what she was going to say.

Finally, through strangled sobs, she whispered, "It's Daddy."

My throat felt like it was closing, and I couldn't breathe. I remembered the scream I heard that first night, the one I thought was a dream. The memory of it slammed into my mind, colliding with the stories Nan had told me about the banshee.

Mags didn't have to say the words. I knew my father was dead. I should have known.

"No. No!"

I heard each one of our tears hit the floor.

"They found him in his car on the highway. Thousands of cars were trapped on the road during the storm and everyone else was rescued, but they didn't find him right away. They think he had a heart attack and was gone before they got there."

We sat, a thin piece of wood between us, and cried, our fingers touching in the space under the door; clutching each other the best we could, but it was of little comfort to either of us.

In an instant, I knew what this meant. Our father wasn't a strong man, and he never had the guts to stand up to his wife, but his presence had lessened her cruelty. His presence brightened life for us, and we had a close relationship with him despite his inability to stop our mother's torments.

Everyone said I looked like our mother, but what I wanted was to look like him. Hours were spent at the mirror, looking for any glimmer of resemblance, but there was none. His eyes were the brightest blue and his hair a soft golden colour. He was such a contrast to the rest of us. *His dark girls.* Now he was gone and there was no one to lighten the day, no one to lighten the load that was our mother.

That night, I dreamt of him; in his car, the wheels spinning, unable to drive any further. He was wearing his jacket, but still his breath came out in thick puffs and his face was red with cold. He got out and tried walking back towards the city but was forced by the unrelenting snow to return to the shelter of his car. He tried to conserve what little gas he had, but it got so cold so fast that he had to keep turning the engine on for heat, until it wouldn't turn on anymore. A sea of cars surrounded him, unable to go any further; their interior lights turning on and off with each turn of the engine, like beacons in the storm. Fireflies lighting the path through the snow. Everyone trying to stay alive.

Then the banshee screamed, and I woke up. All night. Over and over again.

The grief over my father's sudden death should have consumed me, but it was overshadowed by the physical anguish I was in. No matter how hard I tried to concentrate on him, remember him, entirely feel the absence of him, my empty stomach tightened and rolled, my head ached with dehydration, and the heavy smell that filled the room made me dizzy with sick.

Daddy.

Chapter Ten

Each morning the sun rose again, and I was disheartened to find I had not yet woken from the nightmare I was sure I was having. Though heat now filled my room, I still spent most of my days huddled under the blankets, shivering against the horror of what I was feeling. I cried a lot, until the tears refused to fall any longer and an aching numbness filled me instead.

Those first few days, Mags begged me to let her tell Ben what was happening, and though I missed him desperately, I refused. If he found out what was happening to me, he would immediately come, and I knew for certain that would only make things worse for me, and for him. No longer sure what my mother was capable of, I didn't want to put him in danger or prolong my imprisonment.

Unless she planned to kill me, Mother couldn't keep me locked in my room forever; eventually she would *have* to let me out. Then I would really have my chance to run, and when I did, I would never return. Plus, I hadn't been able to tell Ben about the baby, and this wasn't how I wanted him to find out. I didn't want him to see me like this and have this be the memory of finding out he was to be a father. So, I told Mags to tell him our mother found out that I had been lying to her about where I was and that I had to lay low until it blew over. I told her to tell him I loved him and would go to him as soon as I could.

I knew I was doing the right thing, but I struggled against the small part of me that would risk anything to be with him, if only for a moment.

The thought of Mags going to his apartment to tell him he wouldn't see me for a while made bile rise into my mouth. Without me around, Mags could make a good replacement. She was me, but better in every possible way. I wouldn't blame him for choosing her, and *I* couldn't resist him, so how could I expect Mags to? It was a risk to send her there, but I couldn't just leave him without an explanation, so it was a risk I had to take.

"You aren't going to leave me for him, are you?" I cried to Mags through the door before she left.

"What? Are you insane? I have no interest in your boyfriend and I would never leave you for anyone or anything."

The word *insane* stung, but I knew she didn't mean it that way.

Each night before she went to bed, my mother unlocked the door and entered the room without warning. She never spoke to me or even looked at me. She came only to bring me water; just enough to keep me alive, just enough to keep me wanting more. At first, I begged and pleaded with her to let me out. I dropped to my knees and cried at her feet.

"Please don't leave me here, Mama. Please! I'll do anything, just let me out!"

Though she never reverted to the monster she'd become that first night, I could see it lurking behind her eyes, darting in and out of the darkness, hiding from sight. Waiting. But for what?

Eventually, I lost the energy to cry out to her. Eventually, I just laid in bed with my eyes closed, feigning sleep, until she left.

Weeks passed.

Mags came to me every night, when the house was asleep, and she was supposed to be in bed to push small bits of food under the door. Mother now watched all the food in the house very closely, but sometimes she was able to sneak a piece of bread or a slice of cheese into her pocket. By the time the food got to me it was stale or slightly covered in lint, but I ate it all anyways. Despite the tiny bump that now swelled just above my pubic bone, my clothes were loose on my body, and I took anything I could get.

We spent hours, late into the night, talking through the door. She told me of her classes and of ballet. I devoured any gossip about the girls at school, but it was nothing compared to the gossip circling about me. No one believed I'd just up and left for New York indefinitely. There was a rumour I was in jail; another I was actually dead; and then, that I was pregnant and had been sent away for nine months. What no one knew was, all those rumours were the truth. I was in jail. I was dead. I was pregnant. When she inevitably ran out of stories from the outside, she read books out loud to me, and if the books were thin enough to fit under the door, she slid them under so we could take turns reading to each other. Anything to make the time move forward; anything to ease the sting of loneliness I carried with me all day.

She urged me to keep dancing through it all. It was such a vital part of *her* that, if our roles had been reversed, it would be the one thing to have gotten her through it. Before she left for school each morning, she stopped at my door to slip me stolen pieces of her breakfast and to coach me from the other side on which warm up exercises to do and directed me through what Madame Caron had taught in class the day before. It was supposed to help keep my strength up, and she hoped that, when all this was behind us, I would return to the studio to dance with her again, but I knew it was hopeless. I wouldn't dance again. I didn't even want to. I'd always struggled behind the other dancers; now I would never be able to catch up. But the exercises and the routines did give me something to do, and doing them made Mags happy and filled her with a sense of purpose, which I was grateful for. So, I stretched my body, and I did the plies and the tendus. First position. Second position. Third. Fourth. Fifth. Over and over again.

At first, I savoured the soreness of my muscles and the aching of my feet because they told me I was alive and doing something of my own volition. I did it every day until I couldn't do it any longer; until my body was so weak I could barely move, let alone stand at the barre in my room. Still, Mags coached me each day and each day, I pretended I could still do it. It was all I could do for her.

I was definitely pregnant. If I'd had any doubts about it before, they were gone now. I could feel the life inside me; feel it growing; draining every ounce of energy I had; leeching the nutrients from my body bit by bit, so *it* thrived while I withered. I wasn't upset, though. I was happy to give it everything I had, whatever it needed. It was Ben's baby, and I would do anything for it, for him, for us.

By then, the snow had long melted and I spent a lot of time looking out the window at the road. There were days when I thought I could see Ben out there, standing in the street, watching the house. I imagined him, in the rain, waiting to save me. I was Rapunzel and he was the prince from the fairy tales we read as children.

Once upon a time there was a girl named Josephine who was locked away in a tower for years and years by an evil witch. Her sorrow and loneliness became so immense that she could put it out the window until it touched the ground. Ben, her prince and one true love, tried to take it on, every day, but the sorrow and loneliness was so severe it engulfed him, and he found himself unable to get up. One day, he overcame the sorrow and the loneliness because, on this day, it felt hollow and lifeless. Finally making it to the top, he found his love and unborn baby dead at the hands of the witch. Crushed by an immense grief, he threw himself out the window hoping to die. As he fell to the ground, the rose thorns ripped his eyes from their sockets. He didn't die as he had hoped. Surviving the fall, Ben now walks the earth crying from empty eyes for his lost love, dragging her sorrow and loneliness behind him.

Chapter Eleven

Life progresses as it does without any indication of what's to come next. We wake up each morning, believing that the day will be just like any other, and, usually it is. Usually, there are no surprises; but sometimes, everything changes, and the day is nothing like we thought. Our lives altered forever. It's always a surprise, a shock. It's always one moment that changes everything. One moment that could catapult you into what's to be your new life— unrecognizable from what it was before, from what you thought it would be.

The last day in my room started out exactly like all the others. There was no way to know it would be the last. Or the worst. If I had known it was the last day, after nightmare after nightmare, I would have been happy and excited. I would have been wrong.

As always, I spent the day in bed, huddled under blankets reading books, losing myself in the stories of love, mystery or fantasy. It was how I endured those long and aching days of solitude, forever waiting until night fell over the house, and Mags could visit. She went to the library everyday after school for me and filled her basket with books she knew were thin enough to fit under the door. Because they were all so short in length, I devoured multiple books a day. When Mags wasn't around, I almost always read them out loud to myself; partly to hear someone's voice even if it was only my own, but also so my baby wouldn't be as lonely as I was.

Later that night, Mother unlocked the door and came into my room, as she did every day, but I noticed right away that something was different. The glass of water I had been waiting for all day wasn't in her hand as it always was, and the despair that engulfed me was so sharp and acute it took my breath away. Her hand, which usually held the glass, was empty, and hung limply at her side, sheathed in a white glove. Not the lace ones she wore to luncheons or the long silk ones she wore to balls; it was the kind doctors wore. Her other hand was kept hidden from sight behind her back.

Without turning, she kicked the door closed behind her and strolled calmly towards the bed. Usually, she exuded a quiet anger, but today she seemed unusually happy. Relieved. Peaceful even.

Her smile reached all the way to her eyes. It was a smile that exposed a dimple in her left cheek I had never noticed before. This was the girl I saw in the framed photographs in my grandparent's bedroom —photos of a little girl in frilly dresses, beaming at the camera in the arms of her parents. If I hadn't seen those photos, she would have been completely unrecognizable to me now. Almost as much as she had been on the night my captivity started. The disparity between then and now was striking. How could one woman have so many different faces?

She sat down on the bed next to where I leaned against the headboard, her one hand still hidden behind her back. I tried not to show the fear that was growing at a steady pace inside me. She consumed fear voraciously and, at all times, I did my best not to give in to her. I tried not to show it, but my body trembled, and tears wet my eyes despite my efforts to hold them back. I was scared. I had never been more scared, and nothing could have prepared me for what was about to happen.

"Darling." Her free hand, gloved in cold rubber, grazed my cheek. Although I was completely revulsed, my body involuntarily moved towards the only real touch I had felt in what had to be months. "I know you're scared, but it's going to be okay. Your punishment is almost over. Soon, you'll be free. I know you've learned your lesson and you'll never disobey me again." Her smile widened and her lips pulled back tightly, showing all of her teeth. Her eyes were wide enough that the whites of them circled around the bright green of her irises. "I'm going to help you; I've found a way."

Then, she pulled her hand out from behind her back to expose a long metal stick with a sharp pointed end, which I recognised immediately as one of Nan's knitting needles. She placed it on my bedside table, the light from my lamp dancing off the sharp tip.

"What's that for?" I asked, shaking as I pressed myself back against the headboard, gathering my blankets around me like a wall as the panic built up in me.

Without answering my question, she moved towards me. In response, I tried to scramble from the bed and away from her, hoping to make what I knew would be a pathetic run for the unlocked and unguarded door. Before I could get far, she grabbed my wrist so fast and so hard I cried out in shock and pain. I tried to get away, I tried to fight back, but my strength was frustratingly low. Still, I kicked out my arms and my legs; I thrust my body back and forth, hoping to throw her off, but it was completely useless.

She overpowered me entirely.

She planned it that way.

She starved me for just long enough that I would survive but wouldn't be able to fight back.

"Let go of me!" I screamed so loud that my throat stung with the effort. No sooner had the words left my mouth, she punched me hard in the face, shutting me up instantly. My head rocked back, whipping my neck, and smashing the back of my skull hard against the headboard. A burst of pain erupted behind my eyes and warmth trickled down the front of my face. My nose throbbed and my eyes burned with tears.

Through my blurred vision, I saw her pull a long piece of cloth from her dress pocket. I blinked the tears away and recognised it as one of my father's ties; the one I got him for Christmas last year. Through my daze, my brain couldn't connect with why she would have it, but then she used the blue silk tie with the small black polka dots to tie my wrist to the headboard. When it was secured, the knot tight, she pulled more ties from her pocket— another blue one, a red one, and a yellow one with small, embroidered flowers. With them, she tied both my ankles and my other wrist to the bed. I kicked my legs against her and writhed my body away, but it was no use.

She overpowered me.

I was trapped.

"Help! Help me!" I screamed, tears streaming down my face, my voice gasping behind fear and blood. "Please, Mama, don't do this. I'll do whatever you say, whatever you want, just please don't hurt me. Please." I begged, the words falling fast and stumbling from my mouth. Unfortunately, I was trying to appeal to a mercy that, I knew, she didn't possess.

"I'm not here to hurt you, Josephine. I'm here to help you. I know it's hard to understand, and I know you think I'm just being cruel, but I'm not. You're my daughter and I'm just trying to help," she said in an unnaturally high, sweet voice.

Despite everything we had been through, I saw, in that moment, she really believed what she was doing was right. The certainty of it was clear in her eyes and that terrified me more than anything. If she thought this was right, there was no end to what she was capable of.

She put her hand to my cheek and continued in the same sing-song voice, as though she were a nurse talking to a small child before a simple immunization. "This will only hurt for a minute and then everything will be okay."

She picked up Nan's knitting needle, the sharp end pointing towards me and walked to the foot of the bed to stand between my tied legs. Everything about her movements was clinical, robotic even.

It was then I knew for sure what she was going to do to me. There were always stories about girls, even one from my own school, getting into trouble and attempting to "take care of it" at home. Sometimes, they died. *I* would die. I was sure of it. I didn't have the strength to survive, and the fear of certain death ripped through me, causing my body to rock back and forth with even more intensity, screaming as loud as I could. The instinct for survival overpowered the weakness of my body and I strained against the knots holding me. My scream got louder. Louder than anything had ever been before. I prayed that someone would hear it. Anyone.

She was just visible, through my tears, standing at the end of the bed, one hand grasping my knee and the other holding the needle. I closed my eyes tight against the horror. My body once again drained of energy. I thought that maybe I could just fall asleep, and when I woke up, it would all be over. Maybe I would be over too.

Her grasp on my knee tightened and my body stiffened when something sharp began to dig its way painfully inside me. I braced myself, but instead of more pain there was nothing but a heavy thump.

My mother was gone. The needle was gone. Everything was gone. Black. Shadows danced spasmodically behind my eyelids. The room spun. Tears spilled ice cold over my burning cheeks.

"Jo," a familiar voice said through the haze, pulling me back, but only for a moment.

Ben.

CHAPTER TWELVE

It was dark. The kind of dark that swallows you up so no one can ever find you again. The kind of dark that is cold, but also comforting, soft and velvet. It makes you want to surrender to it, let it support you until it consumes you completely. Painless, fearless, nothing.

I drifted in it for a long time, not sure which way was up or down. The dark pulsed around me, sucking me back faintly and then releasing me like the space around me was breathing. And then, the darkness flickered, oscillating between intense light and intense dark making my head ache in confusion. And then, everything became white, and I closed my eyes against the brightness.

White walls, white light, white sheets. My eyes opened again, bit by bit, adjusting to the light far too slowly as a hospital room came into focus.

A head of unruly blonde hair rested on the bed against my hip. *Ben.* How long had it been since I last saw him? I couldn't remember.

The air in the room was thick and my limbs felt heavy and detached from my body. I struggled to lift my hand to touch him but even that slight movement woke him immediately.

"Hey, you're awake!" He smiled at me, grabbed my hand, and pressed it softly against his lips, then held it against his rough and unshaven cheek. His dark eyes searched my face, concern so clear and raw my heart cracked at the sight of it. Why was he looking at me like that?

The room was so bright that my eyes burned, but despite the light, the edges of my vision were dark and blurred. I tried to blink it away, but the murky glare remained, and I suddenly had the feeling I was missing something, like I had forgotten something important. The feeling was so strong I could reach out and touch the dark patina of it, if only I could move my hand that far.

And then, like a dam being opened or a switch being flipped, the memories rushed in. The cold. The loneliness. My mother. The needle. My baby.

I gasped and sat up so quickly the room spun around me, my breath coming in ragged gulps, and I covered my face, struggling to hide my shame. My grief.

"Ben," I cried, "I'm so sorry." My face, feeling as

detached as the rest of me, crumpled and tears poured from my eyes. I wanted desperately to control it, to control myself as I had my whole life, but it was too great to contain.

"Hey, hey, hey," he said, taking my face between his hands so gently it hurt. "What could you possibly have to be sorry for?"

"Didn't they tell you?" I asked, searching his face for any sign of disappointment or anger, but there was none, only relief.

"Tell me what?" he asked, sliding his hands down until they held my own.

I hadn't wanted him to find out that I was pregnant while I was locked in my room, but now being in the hospital, it didn't feel better or easier to say the words. I was about to turn his life upside down and all I wanted was to be able to do it on my own terms.

Too late.

"About the baby." At that, I began to cry again, afraid his initial response would be like Mags's. Or worst of all, my mother's.

"Of course they told me, and I think it's great." He squeezed my hands even tighter and pressed them to his lips.

"You do?" I knew he loved me; he told me every chance he got, but we had only known each other a few months and we were so young. Too young to have a baby. I grasped at my belly, remembering the needle once more. Remembering what my mother had intended. "Is it okay? The baby, did she——"

He nodded, stopping my words. "They said the baby is doing fine." He smiled even brighter and held my hand tighter to his heart. "The doctor should be in to talk to us soon, but I'm sure everything is just fine."

Relief flooded through me just as another wave of memories crashed in, breaking the relief into pieces. It was too much. Too much to bear and I crumpled under the weight of it.

"She locked me in there." Tears poured from my eyes again and I was sure they would never stop. In the room, I had to survive, but now that I was out, the reality was too gruesome to face.

"I'm sorry I wasn't there to protect you. I didn't know." He buried his face into my lap. His shoulders heaved slightly. Though silent, I knew he was crying but trying unsuccessfully to hide it. After a few moments, he composed himself, lifted his head and continued. "When Mags told me you couldn't see me for a while because you had gone to visit some relative, I didn't believe her. I knew something was wrong. I knew you would've called if you were really going somewhere. So, I started walking past your house multiple times a day, hoping to see you. But I never did. I never saw anyone. Then, last night as I was walking by, I heard you screaming. I didn't know what she was doing to you up there. I'm so sorry." He choked. "I should have done more. I should have banged on the door the minute you went missing, but I knew how scared of your mother you were, and I didn't want to make things worse for you."

I thought back to the boy I thought I saw standing outside all those times and my heart ached, knowing that it *was* him and not just my delusions.

Just like my relationships with Mags, I understood that only one of us could fall apart at a time and I tried to pull it together enough to comfort him, to tell him it was okay, that everything was going to be okay. Suddenly the realization someone was missing from the room dawned on me. "Wait, where's Mags?" I asked, feeling the absence of her so completely. I knew that, for her to be anywhere else but in that room with me, meant something was very wrong.

"She's at the police station." He hesitated before continuing. "They are just questioning her about what happened."

His eyes avoided mine and I knew he was keeping something from me.

"What do you mean?"

"Jo, you were locked away in there for more than six weeks. When Mags saw your mother enter your room with a knitting needle behind her back and then heard you screaming, she took a hammer from under the sink in the kitchen and hit her over the head with it to stop her from hurting you."

Six weeks. Had it really been that long? Had it only been that long?

"Is she okay?" I wasn't sure if I was asking about Mags or our mother.

"Like I said, Mags is at the police station. She is being taken care of. Your mother, well, she's gone. She can't hurt you anymore."

I noticed he didn't say she was dead, only gone—whatever that meant. But I decided to believe that, no matter what, she was dead. At least to me. At least to us. Ben was right, she couldn't hurt me anymore.

Every day, I waited to see my sister dance into the room. Every day ended without her. When I asked Ben about her again, he told me to just be patient and to focus on getting better, but how could I do that when half of me was missing? How could I, when the shadows were starting to creep into the edges of my vision despite Ben's presence? I needed her there to help me fight them.

But I tried. I tried to push the fear from my mind and focus on the baby.

After a week of observation, I was being released from the hospital. Ben left some clean clothes for me in the bathroom adjacent to my room. A loose wool dress taken from his aunts closet, which I'm sure was meant to mask both my pregnancy and the thinness of my body.

I hadn't yet found the courage to look at myself in the mirror. While locked in my room, I'd covered my only mirror with a blanket when the shadows under my eyes grew so dark and my lips became so dry and cracked, I hardly recognised the face looking back at me. I'd begun to look like I was already dead—like a corpse.

Now, I was starting to feel better, and I hoped that meant I was starting to look better too. Someone came every day to help me wash or brush my hair. It was just enough to help me feel human again, but I still hadn't looked.

Bent over the bathroom sink, my fingers clutching the sides of the counter, I gathered the strength to look up and face myself for the first time in weeks. *Months*. I knew it was best to do it this way —privately. I couldn't bear the thought of accidentally catching a glimpse of myself in a window or a decorative mirror in the hall on the way out. Like some funhouse illusion. Mirrors reflecting distorted versions of yourself back at you, only this time, the reflection would be true, and the monster reflected back would actually be me.

Feeling as ready as I was ever going to be, *too late*, I looked up. When my eyes met the dull ones in the mirror, my stomach dropped. My hand covered my mouth in horror. Even after a week in the hospital being fed, hydrated, and cared for, the effects of my imprisonment were so much worse than I thought. I had wasted away to practically nothing. I *was* nothing. My hair was thin and dull, as was my skin. My face looked sunken in, and the skin around my eyes was so bruised, I was surprised it didn't hurt when I pressed my fingers against it. Even without the help of mirrors, I knew I had lost a lot of weight, but facing myself, my bones showed against my skin, looking as though they were ready to rip clean through. It was surprising what six weeks could do to a person.

I looked down at my belly. Despite my weight loss, my tiny little bump remained. I put my hand over it protectively, took a deep breath, and knew I was going to be okay. I was ready to put it all behind me.

The doctor came to talk to us before we left the hospital. He was a much older man, and he didn't look directly at us when we talked to him, giving me the feeling we were keeping him from someplace he actually desired to be.

"We suggest you continue to see a doctor for weekly checkups, as we won't know the full effects until the baby is born." He spoke reading from a clipboard, then nodded at us and started for the door.

"Wait," I said, holding one hand out to stop him as the other went instinctually to my belly. "What do you mean 'full effects?'" We had seen him a few times in the past week, but this was the first time he mentioned anything about something possibly being wrong with the baby.

"Surely you understand that you are suffering from numerous nutritional deficiencies, not to mention the prolonged dehydration and the physical trauma you sustained. Because of this, there could be problems throughout your pregnancy, or with the baby once it's born," he said as if it should have been obvious to me.

"What kind of problems?" Ben asked, his fingers winding into mine, calming me, if only slightly.

"Miscarriage, preterm birth or even birth defects, but we just can't know yet," the doctor said, tapping his pen on his clipboard as if he were marking a checklist. Then he wished us luck before leaving us alone.

I didn't move or make a single sound, but Ben pulled me to him and hugged me tightly, holding all the pieces of me together. I thought I'd escaped the prison of my room and what had happened there, but it was becoming increasingly clear I never would. I lost something there, and the trauma of it was going to follow me, and possibly my child, forever.

Sitting in the passenger seat of Ben's truck, a deep sadness crept inside me as we turned onto my street. Everything and everybody I knew was gone. Everyone else in the neighbourhood was living their lives as they always did. As if nothing had happened. I saw Mrs. England through her window, rocking her baby in her living room. Mr. Donahue was washing his driveway with a hose despite the almost constant rain. Our neighbour, Evelyn, let her dog out into the front yard, just as we pulled into my driveway, and she waved at us from her porch just like she would any other day. I gave a small wave in return as Ben put the car in park. Then, we sat in silence staring at the darkened house.

"You don't have to do this," Ben said, turning in his seat to look at me. "I can go in, pack you a bag, and then take you home with me. Hell, we can forget your stuff altogether and get you new stuff when we get to Halliswell."

"I already told you, I can't leave without Mags," I responded, not looking away from the house.

"We've been over this, Jo. They can't release her until the case is closed. It may have been in defence of your life, but she still hit someone with a hammer. Her lawyer said that, given all the evidence, she should be released very soon, but for now she has to stay in the foster home. When it's all done, we can petition the court to release her to us."

I understood everything he said, but moving to another town without her was unthinkable. It was a betrayal of the unspoken commitment we made to each other, the one we were born with. The guilt of the knowledge that I had been willing to break it before made it all the more unspeakable. I was all she had. How could I leave her now?

"Can't we just stay in town until then?" I asked, though I already knew the answer. It wasn't the first time I'd asked, but I asked again anyways, hoping another answer would present itself.

"Aunt Meredith is home from the hospital; there isn't enough room in her apartment for all of us, and we just don't know how long this is gonna take."

I nodded but couldn't say anything else. The house loomed above me, filled with rooms. Could we stay here? I briefly wondered if I was strong enough to sleep within its walls again. The thought made my stomach boil but maybe I could stand it for her.

I got out of the car and walked slowly up the stairs only faintly aware that Ben followed silently behind me. Standing on the front porch, staring at the front door, I knew this place was no longer mine. The house I had lived in my entire life was no longer my home and it felt wrong to just walk in. Like I was an intruder. So, instead of putting my key in the lock, I took the heavy knocker and knocked loudly, three times. Of course, no one answered, and I was absolutely sure no one ever would again.

Ben cleared his throat behind me and put his arms around me, squeezing me tight against him. Then, taking the keys from my shaking hands, he unlocked the door and swung it open.

I half expected Mrs. Bachelder would be on the other side to greet me. She would herd us into the kitchen to hug us and feed us cookies like she did our whole lives. My eyes filled with tears at the realization I would probably never see her again either. I wouldn't even know where to look for her now. Was she worried about me? Had she heard about us on the news? I had no way of knowing. My tears of grief were quickly replaced with ones of revulsion as a horrible smell slapped me hard in the face, forcing me to cover my nose.

Only the police had been inside all week, and they hadn't prepared us for what we were walking into. The house was evidence all the staff had been long let go and that my mother had completely lost her mind. Everything was absolutely filthy; the carpets caked in mud; the windows streaked with grime. All the furniture was moved haphazardly around each room as though there had been a struggle, but we knew there hadn't been. Not down here anyways.

When we opened the door to the kitchen, the hot smell of rot was overwhelming, but other than dust and an unusual number of flies, the kitchen was actually cleaner than the rest of the house, looking as though it hadn't been used at all in months.

"God, where is that stench coming from?" I said, swatting a swarm of flies away. I circled the island where the cooks prepared the food. I opened all the cupboards, revealing only stacks of china and various kitchen tools. I opened the door to the pantry to find jars, cans and sacks of various dried and preserved foods lining the shelves as always. It smelled slightly stale, but nothing was rotting in there.

Then I opened the fridge and right away wished I hadn't, for I'd found the source of the smell and the flies. The fridge was full of rotted food. It must have been full before the staff left. It must have been full before the power went out. Without people to serve her, my mother had simply closed the door to this room and forgotten it completely. Inside, whatever hadn't liquified was wriggling and flies poured out around me. I slammed the door shut again, but it was too late.

Ben grabbed my hand and pulled me from the room, quicker than my weak legs could move. When we were through the swinging door, the worst of the smell and the flies trapped behind it, we bent over, breathing in deep the slightly cleaner air.

"I'm sorry, I didn't even think," was all I could say, but he just hugged me against him.

"No harm done," he replied, though he looked as green as I felt.

We made our way up the stairs, eager now to get my things and just get out. It was obvious we couldn't stay here, and I kicked myself for thinking it was even a possibility. We hadn't yet made it to the most horrifying room of all, and it was already clear we had no choice but to leave town and return to Ben's life, leaving mine behind. I had no choice but to start over somewhere else.

This place isn't mine anymore, I reminded myself. It never really had been.

At the top of the stairs, I stood in the hallway lined with three closed doors—behind one was our shared bathroom and behind the other two, our bedrooms. I wanted badly to go into Mags's room and stay there. I wanted to crawl into her bed to feel close to her again, but I also knew I couldn't linger or I might break. I had to pack up my things and leave this place forever.

I walked past her closed door, brushing my fingers along it as I went, and then stopped before my own. With my hand hesitating on the door handle, I just stood there, afraid of what would happen when I turned it; afraid of what I would see when I walked inside. I stayed there for what felt like a long time, but Ben never rushed me, never said a word.

When I was as ready as I was ever going to be, I took a deep breath—*too late*—and opened the door. It was exactly as it had been that night. The only immediate difference I could see was a dark stain on the carpet by the foot of my bed, and I felt sick at the sight of it. The stain would never come out. It probably sunk through the fibers all the way to the original wood beneath. It would forever be a stain on this room, as it was a stain on me.

The smell in there was almost as bad as the kitchen, except here it came from my own humiliation. It was a smell I knew came from my body, unwashed for weeks, and from the bucket I had been forced to use as a toilet. Despite the coldness of the room, hot shame shot through me, and I couldn't stand to be there any longer. Sweating and dizzy, I turned to leave, but not before seeing Ben's horrified face. The shame burrowed even deeper. I ran next door to Mags's room, crawled into her unmade bed, and buried my face into her pillow, feeling the tears coming against the smell of her that still lingered there.

Ben followed silently and sat on the edge of the bed, patient, letting me cry uninterrupted. Then he brushed the hair from my wet eyes and said, "Jo, we can't stay here," his voice shaky with emotion.

He had been there that night; I was sure of it. I remembered hearing his voice in the dark. But his face now revealed that, if he had been there, he hadn't seen anything but me and though he tried to hide the shock, it was ingrained in him now and he couldn't run from it any more than I could.

I nodded. Even if I could get Mags back, I couldn't bring her back here. Even if we cleaned it up, it wasn't the same, and it never would be again. We didn't belong here.

With Ben's help, I quickly packed some clothes from my dresser and filled the chest my father made me when we were born with the few things that were important to me—the fairy figurine from Nan, my ballet slippers, photos of me and Mags—and left everything else behind.

When I locked the door, I knew without a doubt I would never return to that house. Though I grieved for the loss of my father, and I missed Mags so much, the thought that this part of my life was over was thrilling, and I was surprised by the relief and the closure the locked door provided.

As we drove out of town, I watched the city fade behind us in the mirror with an odd sense of peace

I wasn't expecting. The old me peeled away in layers, and with each passing kilometer, I became lighter and lighter.

We drove north for hours without stopping. The warmth of the approaching spring was replaced with a clean, bright cold, but it wouldn't be long until spring's warm fingers reached their way up here too. Ben held my hand the entire way and as the sun started to set, I fell into a deep, dreamless sleep, lulled by the vibrations of the truck.

Ben shook me awake when we drove into Halliswell so I wouldn't miss it. It didn't take long to pass through the small coastal town; it was one street along the sea, lined with a tiny grocery store, a hardware store, a gas station and a restaurant on one side and a marina filled with boats on the other. The streets were dark and silent, all the residents home on that cold Sunday evening. The town was small, but well cared for, and it was evident the people who lived there loved it very much and took pride in what they had.

We drove through the town and made our way up a steep hill winding through the trees until the pavement fell away to a narrow dirt road lined with birch. We passed a few houses along the way but they were so much further apart than I was used to growing up in the city. It was bizarre to imagine living so far removed from the rest of the community. Not that we spent a lot of time getting to know our neighbours but we did know them and in some ways they were the only semi meaningful contact I had with anyone outside my house.

That feeling in my gut, the one I felt so strongly the day I met Ben returned as we drove. Like someone was pulling, hand over hand, on an invisible rope attached to my navel.

At the end of the road, Ben turned the truck into a short driveway and stopped in front of a white two-story house with large bay windows and a front door painted a bright emerald green. For a moment, I saw my mother's eyes peering at me, but I blinked the thought away. She wasn't welcome here.

When Ben said that he lived in a small fishing town, I guess I assumed that he lived in a small fishing house, but this was truly a home and it was beautiful. I rushed out of the truck and stood before the house, illuminated by the glow of the headlights.

Ben came up behind me, wrapped his arms around my waist and pulled me into him. Though the night was cold, the heat from his body and the familiar smell of the sea close by warmed me. "Welcome home," he smiled into my ear.

And I smiled too. This was my chance to start over, to be my own person. The last few months had forced me to grow up, and it was time to leave the stories of my childhood behind.

CHAPTER THIRTEEN

"Do you like it?" I stepped back from the freshly painted yellow wall and admired my work. "I read somewhere that yellow is calming to babies. Do you think that's true?"

"Of course, it's true." Ben laughed. "I love it; it's brilliant." He kissed me on the cheek and the prickle of his unshaven face against my bare skin made me laugh.

"I know I'm getting a little bit ahead of myself; we still have so long to go," I said, rubbing the small bump beneath my shirt, "but I just don't know what to do with all this free time!" I turned into him, put my arms around his neck and kissed him playfully.

We had been home for three weeks. After being locked away for so long, I was grateful for the freedom, but the reality was that without school or

Mags, I didn't have a lot to fill my time. I knew that I needed time to recover, but the only way that I could contribute to our life was to take care of the house. I cleaned everything top to bottom in those first few weeks, but it didn't take long to run out of things to wipe down. While the house was perfect for us, nothing had been changed since Ben's parents passed away. It was still very much his childhood home, and I hoped to spend the rest of my pregnancy making it into our own space to fill with our own memories.

I'd started small by cleaning and rearranging the furniture in each room. Eventually I cleared away old knick knacks Ben's mom had collected over the years, packing them neatly into boxes to be stored in the small attic above our bedroom. Ben couldn't bring himself to get rid of anything, and having just lost everything myself, I understood how he felt.

Once I was finished with the basics, I turned my focus to the room which had been Ben's when he was a boy. The walls were originally a well-loved blue, but I thought our baby deserved a fresh start too, so now they were a bright, warm yellow, which made the room glow in the warm afternoon light of early spring.

"I can think of one thing we can do with the free time," he said, swinging me effortlessly into his arms. He carried me down the hall into our bedroom as I laughed. He placed me gently onto the bed and held himself above me, taking care not to put any weight onto my still frail body. "I love you," he said.

"I love you too." I looked up at him, and for a moment I felt so happy; happier than I thought I would be capable of ever again.

He bent down as if to kiss me again, but instead tickled my ribs gently with his fingers and my neck with his lips. A great laugh erupted from deep down in my belly. It was a sound I hadn't heard for a long time, not since *before*. Instead of taking it any further, he settled down on the bed next to me, our heads touching.

"Maybe you need to make some friends. You're alone all day while I'm at work, and I think it would be good for you to have someone else to talk to." The way he said it made me think he had rehearsed it beforehand. His words stiff but awkwardly casual.

The carefree feeling of moments before swept away, anxiety creeping into the empty space it left. The shadows came closer, and my wall started going back up, brick by brick. My throat tightened, constricting my breathing. My heart beat even harder in my chest. The darkness took over like a switch being flipped and I was powerless to stop it.

"How exactly would *I* make friends? Look at me! I'm a freak."

"You are not a freak," Ben replied, his jaw set but his eyes soft. I knew that, though he had hoped for a better reaction, he had braced himself for this one.

"I know you don't believe me, but Mags was the

only friend I had, my whole life. And she isn't here! You think I didn't try with the other girls? They didn't want me. No one does!"

The emotion in me grew so strong, I couldn't face it. I wasn't really sure if it was anger or shame or fear, but whatever it was, it overwhelmed me. I tried to turn my back to him, to get up out of bed, anything but face him. But he pulled me back, his hands on my cheeks.

"Jo, listen to me! What happened to you was not your fault! What happened in that room, what happened in that house your whole life. It wasn't your fault."

I laid there for a long time, facing him, my eyes closed. My breathing was slow and deliberate as I concentrated on slowing the hammering within my body. Cell by cell. Breath by breath. Calming every part of me before I could even fathom speaking again. Ben, always patient with me, stayed silent, waiting for me to be ready though my silence filled the room so much that it felt thick and heavy.

"I know... that... it's not... my fault." The words sounded foreign coming from my mouth and I had to physically force each one from my body. "It wasn't my fault, but it changed me." My words came faster because I knew I had to say them before they disappeared. "It changed me and what if everyone can see it?"

That's what I was really afraid of, though it wasn't a matter of *if* they could see it. Of course, they could. It had been about a month since I got out, but I hadn't recovered completely. My hair was still thin, my skin bruised. My eyes looked too big for my face and my belly too big for my body. Like a monster, grotesque and jutting.

He leaned forward and kissed both of my eyelids. "Love, the only thing people can see is your strength and your goodness," he said, resting his forehead against mine. "I have a friend; her name is Ami, and she lives down the road. Remember I told you about her?"

I did remember him talking about her that day we met in the diner, as well as a few other times over the weeks we spent together before my confinement. Even then I had felt jealous of their friendship and that feeling did not lessen over time. Instead, it grew with the comprehension that I was such a mess and she was so dependable.

If Ben sensed my discomfort, he did not show it and continued. "She just got back from school. I could—"

Before he could go any further, I jumped up from the bed, faking a sudden recovery. "I don't think so. I'm fine. Really." I held my arms out as if to prove it to him.

"Let me invite her over for dinner tomorrow night," he said, ignoring my display as he climbed off the bed behind me. "I think you two would really get along."

"Really? Why do you think that?" I challenged him. My body was still worked up and I needed a fight to help dissipate the anxious energy vibrating under my skin.

He thought about it, then said, "Well, she likes to read, and so do you."

"So, because we both like reading, a generally solitary hobby, you think that means we will get along?" I was being petty, and I knew it.

"Well, yeah."He visibly deflated and I knew I had won, but seeing the slump of his shoulders as his smile disappeared brought me back to that moment and I felt awful for how I was treating him. It wasn't fair.

Of course, it would be good for me to make a friend, but meeting someone new meant telling the story, and I never wanted to tell that story again. But Ben was so good to me and I knew that he was only trying to help me. I had to be better. Not only for him but for myself and for our child. I reached down into myself and took hold of the desperately stubborn part of me and pushed it aside. "I'm sorry," I said, reluctantly. "You're right. I do need a friend. I'm just scared." Instead of facing him, I picked the laundry basket up off the floor and started putting away the laundry I had haphazardly folded earlier that morning. It was an obvious way to deflect his attention, but he continued speaking anyway.

"Ami is a great friend. I'm sure you will find you have more in common with her than just reading. At the very least, it would be good for you to have someone to go to if you ever need help. You don't have to hang out with her everyday but it would make me feel better leaving you here alone if you had some kind of relationship with her. She's our closest neighbour. Give her a chance. For me."

Despite my anxieties, I knew he was right and I agreed with a slight nod. I was still facing the dresser and I wasn't sure if he saw it, but when I turned to him, the smile that stretched across his face told me everything I needed to know. It made it worth it, and I swore I would do better from now on. I promised *myself* I would be better.

The next night, Ami was set to come by at six for dinner. Having grown up with chefs and housekeepers, I'd never once had to cook for myself before moving to Halliswell. I was learning slowly, but this was the first time I had to cook for someone other than Ben, and I was terrified. So, I chose something relatively simple—roast chicken with potatoes and green beans. And, simple it was, because everything turned out the way I intended. More or less. The chicken was a little dry and the beans were overcooked, but it was passable as a meal.

I was lighting the candles on the table when I heard a knock at the door. My spine stiffened and my heart skipped at the sound. I looked up at the clock hanging on the wall above the table. She was fifteen minutes early. I wasn't ready. "Ben!" I called out, but instead of a reply, I heard water running in the bathroom upstairs.

The thought of being the one to open the door to someone I never met before made my palms sweat. I looked up the stairs, hoping that, if I stalled long enough, he would come down and take this responsibility away. But then the knock came again, and I knew I had to be the one to open the door.

I took off my apron, smoothed my skirt down and walked to the door, flinging it open—*too late*—with a smile I hoped didn't look as forced as it felt.

"Hi! I'm Amita, you must be Josephine," the beautiful woman standing on the porch said, with a shy wave and a kind smile which was warm and genuine in the same way that Ben's was.

I wondered if it was a small-town thing, or if it was something they had picked up from each other over the years. And I wasn't sure what I'd been expecting, but this wasn't it. Perhaps it was the country setting, or the fact she had been such close friends with a boy her whole life, but I realised I'd expected she would be wearing flannel and work boots. Instead, she wore a simple black wrap dress with matching black kitten heels, and she looked incredible. I suddenly felt underdressed in my nicest outfit, which was a white summer dress in a print of small purple flowers that was completely inappropriate for the cool spring weather. I fingered the hem and felt stupid for not going shopping before the dinner.

"Are you going to let me in?" she asked, with a crooked smile and a raised eyebrow.

"Oh gosh, I'm sorry. Yes, yes come in!" I ushered her through the door, taking her jacket and hanging it in the hall closet as slow as I could without it being obvious I was stalling. "Ben!" I called again up the stairs. "He should be down any moment." I laughed nervously.

"Are you okay? You seem a little anxious," she said, amused.

"Yes… I mean no." Willing myself to get it together, I took a deep breath and tried again. "Yes, I'm okay. No, I'm not anxious. I'm just a bit tired, I'm sorry." I suddenly had the feeling I was acting as though I were in a movie, and shuddered at the thought that maybe she saw it too. I willed myself to just be natural. Be myself.

Whoever that was.

Amita walked through the house with confidence, as if she had been there hundreds of times before. I suppose she had. She sat down on the sofa, with her legs curled beneath her, as I sat on the chair across from her; my legs crossed in front of me as though this was her house, and *I* was the guest.

"So, how do you and Ben know each other?" I asked, though I already knew the answer. I was just desperate to fill the silence.

"Well, we went to school together." Her voice was deep and gravelly. "And we have been neighbours our whole lives." She tucked her dark hair behind her ear as she spoke. "My family moved here from India when Ben and I were in kindergarten. I hardly spoke any English, and I was so scared my first day, but I remember getting on the school bus and seeing this little blonde boy with the worst bowl haircut I'd ever seen. His stop was the first, and right before mine, so he was the only one on the bus. I could have sat anywhere, but he waved to me like we were old friends, and now here we are." Her smile changed her whole face as she remembered, and it was so sweet that my heart ached for both of them.

"That's a nice story," I said.

Ben had told me a similar story when I asked about Ami, but his was that he lived far out from town and there weren't many houses around, and the ones that were had no kids, so he spent a lot of time playing by himself. Then he heard a family with a girl his age had moved in around the corner. Her parents had gone to Ben's and asked them if Ben wouldn't mind looking out for their daughter. They were worried they hadn't taught her enough English before the move and she was going to struggle, but they didn't want to hold her back any longer. Ben, kind-hearted even as a child, of course agreed. He told me how, when he saw the little girl get on the bus with her missing front teeth and what sounded like an equally bad haircut, he was so excited to make a friend that it never even really occurred to him he was doing a favour for someone else.

"You don't have much of an accent." I said and it was more of a statement than a question.

"I do if I'm around my family and also if I have too much to drink. I learned English pretty quickly and then I worked hard to drop the accent. It wasn't easy being the only brown kid in school. I just wanted to be like everyone else. Now, I know better, but I have been talking like this so long…" her voice trailed off.

I wanted to tell her that I understood what it meant to be different and to want to be like everyone else, but I was trying so hard to control what she saw that I remained quiet.

Suddenly, I realized that Ami was still talking, and I was too embarrassed to admit that, while contemplating my own differences and admiring the perfect straightness of her hair, I hadn't actually heard what she'd said. I struggled to form a response that would make sense when her full lips curved up into an expectant smile. It was starting to get a bit awkward, but I was helpless.

"Ames!" Ben bounded down the stairs into the living room. Ami jumped up from the sofa and into his arms, which folded around her comfortably. "It's so good to see you," he said as he hugged her tightly, her feet lifting slightly off the ground.

"It's good to see you too, we've both been gone a long time," she responded. Setting her feet back on the ground, she turned and gestured towards me. "I was just meeting your bride."

"Oh, we aren't married," I said. "I mean, maybe one day. Only if you want to or don't want to." I rambled as Ben and Ami looked on incredulously. My skin burned with embarrassment. I had never been good with people, but for some reason, this was going worse than usual.

"I'm sorry, it was just a joke," said Ami. "We obviously have a lot of catching up to do."

"It's okay; why don't we go into the kitchen and eat?" Ben said with a chuckle. Turning to me, he asked, "Are you okay? What's wrong with you?" He meant for it to come off as teasing, but he didn't realise it was the same question I had been asked by so many people my whole life, and it stung more than it should have.

"I don't know," I said, trying to force out a laugh that sounded more like I was choking.

"Come on," Ben said. "Let's eat, I'm starved."

I was grateful for the distraction dinner provided, stumbling over minor small talk as though I had never talked to a person before. With Ami's dark eyes on me, my brain couldn't seem to make the proper connections it needed for conversation. Luckily, she and Ben had so much to catch up on, they didn't seem to notice I'd stopped talking. I was almost offended, but it was better this way.

They talked about everything that happened in the months they'd both been gone—Ami's midwifery training, Ben's aunt's accident, how we met. They talked about everything except what had happened to me. If she noticed my frail and haggard appearance, she didn't mention it or ask questions. The only explanation was that Ben must have told her everything before she came. Prepared her. The thought of her knowing something so personal overwhelmed me and burrowed even deeper into the silence I was already holding.

When we finished eating, the two of them offered to clean up so I could rest, and I excused myself, saying I needed some air. I put on my boots and jacket and escaped out the front door. I sat on the front step and a sigh of relief heaved from my chest in a puff of warm mist against the cold night air. Resting my head on the handrail, I relished in the silence and the dark.

But, after only a few minutes of peace, the door opened and Ami emerged, holding the grey and white afghan from our couch in her arms.

"Thought we might need this," she said as she sat down beside me, covering both of our legs with the blanket. The heat of her body began to warm me immediately.

I smiled but said nothing, looking out over the yard, the stars flickering overhead.

"Look," she said, interrupting the silence. She hesitated before continuing, her voice growing quieter with each word. "I know you have no reason to trust a stranger, and you shouldn't, after what you have been through."

Surprised, I turned to her, my face hot with embarrassment. So, she did know.

"Ben told me," she confessed, seeing the question on my face. "He didn't go into a lot of detail, but he thought I should at least know what to expect before coming over. I'm sorry if that upsets you."

She sat next to me in an oddly comfortable silence, much more comfortable than the talking that had happened inside the house. She seemed so genuine, I couldn't find it in myself to be angry, but the shadows threatened regardless.

"It doesn't upset me," I finally said, forcing each word out. "It embarrasses me, but it doesn't upset me." I don't know why I felt she deserved any kind of explanation, but I felt the need to give one, nonetheless.

"What do you have to be embarrassed about?" she asked, her dark eyes wide in disbelief.

"It's personal," was all I could say, and I looked back up at the stars to avoid looking into her eyes any longer.

"Is that why you acted so weird in there?" she asked, pointing back towards the house, sitting so close to me I could feel the length of her body pressing against the side of my own.

"I don't know." I wanted to leave it at that, not say anymore, but at the same time, I was tired of keeping everything inside. The force of it was exhausting, but the words in my throat were invigorating, and I said them with the full knowledge that they weighed more than they seemed. "When I opened the door and *you* were there, you were so beautiful."

"Well, thank you," she said. "But, why would that make you act weird?"

"I was surprised."

"Surprised by what?"

Too late.

"That I noticed."

CHAPTER 14

A WOMAN'S VOICE, singing softly, rose through the night outside our bedroom window. Though I couldn't make out the words, it was a tune I recognised, floating up through the murky darkness of my memory.

Unable to ignore my curiosity, I left the warm comfort of our bed to follow the melodic voice down the stairs, out the front door and all the way down to the beach, with only the light of the full moon to show me the way. The path was unkempt and uncared for. Branches scratched at my skin and tangled in my hair. But no matter how deep I went, the voice never grew closer, the words never clearer.

When I finally reached the end of the path and broke through the trees, there she was, the singing woman, kneeling on the rocks at the shore, washing something in the dark water. Her hair, black as the night surrounding her, fell in curtains over her shoulders, concealing her face from me.

Now that I was this close, the song became clearer, and I recognised it as a lullaby my nan had sung to me when I was really little and scared of the monsters under my bed.

"Hello?" I called out to her.

She continued to sing the beautiful, haunting melody, her hands submerged beneath the water. I called out again and still got no response. As I neared the edge of the water, I noticed the small pieces of fabric being scrubbed between her hands. Not only were they baby clothes, they were the very ones I'd bought our own baby earlier that week.

She pulled a small sleeper from the water and looked at it. It was horribly stained, and the water that dripped from it was not just dark but red.

"What are you doing?" I cried. "Where did you get those?"

Absolute fury erupted inside me and I took a step forward, grabbing the washing woman's shoulder. Finally acknowledging my presence, she turned towards me, and I gasped. I recoiled in horror, stumbling backwards before falling to the ground.

I'd expected her face to be every bit as beautiful as her voice, but instead it was twisted and grotesque. A monster. Before I was able to scream, her grey, sagging jaw fell open to reveal a mouth filled with rotting stumps where teeth had once been, and she wailed three loud piercing cries into the night.

The sound of my own screaming melted away the macabre scene and I awoke with my face buried deep into my pillow. I knew I was safe in my own bed, but the sound of the mournful cries still rang loud in my ears.

Ben woke with a start and immediately reached for me. "Hey, hey it was just a dream. It's okay," he soothed as he tried to gather me into his arms.

"It's the Bean Sidhe!" I cried, sitting up in bed. I shoved Ben and the blankets away from me, unable to handle the sensation of anything touching my already crawling skin.

"Jo, what's going on? You're scaring me." He put his hand into mine and held it hard, willing me to come out of it and back to him.

I'd had nightmares almost every night since coming to live with him and he was used to it, but they were never like this. He was *always* able to bring me out of it fairly quickly, if he needed to at all. This time, however, I just stared into the darkness of the room, unable to shake the fear of what lurked there.

"I heard her scream," I said, my voice dull and lifeless. It was as though all the energy had drained from my body.

"Heard who scream?" he asked, his concern visibly growing as he looked around the room.

"The Bean Sidhe."

"Honey, what-?"

"The Banshee!" I shouted at him, so loud he flinched away from me. "She's coming for the baby. I saw her. She was washing *our* baby's clothes in the water and they were—" I sobbed, tears flowing from my eyes, "—they were covered in blood."

"Love, is this another one of the stories your nan told you?" There was a hint of something in his usually kind voice that sounded a bit like exasperation.

It surprised me, but it didn't discourage me. I knew what I saw.

"The Banshee is the harbinger of death. She visits when there is to be a death in the family."

"That's just an old story, Josephine. It isn't true." He sighed and squeezed my hand a little tighter in his.

I looked him dead in the eye. "How do you know?" When he didn't answer right away, I repeated myself, this time yelling, "How do you know?" and shoved him hard in the chest. He looked so hurt that I immediately regretted it, but the fear and the dark boiled together inside me and I couldn't stop. "She came to me before my father died as well. Did you know that? I heard her in the night, and I thought it was nothing but then the next day, he was dead! Something's wrong, I know it is." A sharp and piercing grief cut through me, folding me in half as I cried into my open hands, and I wasn't sure if it was the grief from the loss of my father or everything I currently had to lose.

"If it'll make you feel better, I'll call the doctor in the morning and make an appointment to get you and the baby checked out." Somehow his voice was perfectly calm while I felt something akin to a storm raging within me.

Though Ben was always sympathetic, it was clear he didn't believe me, but it wasn't his fault. He didn't know what I knew. He hadn't grown up with the stories like I did. He didn't know what to look out for.

"It's too late. Once she visits, there's nothing you can do to stop it," I said through sobs.

He wrapped a soft blanket around my shoulders and drew me in close. I let him, surrendering my exhausted self to the comfort of him. He held me until I fell back asleep and was still holding me when I woke in the morning.

I recalled the nightmare clearly, and although I felt uneasy about it, the light of the morning chased the darkness away and eased my fear enough that I was able to move it from the forefront of my mind to a corner where I hoped I could forget it altogether. I put my hands to my belly and was certain I still felt the life inside me. Certain my baby was okay.

"Hey, I'm sorry, I must have dozed off. Are you all right?" Ben said, lifting his head from my shoulder. His eyes searched my face, looking for any trace of what he saw in me last night.

"Yeah. Yeah, I'm sorry about what happened—how I acted towards you. The dream was so real, and it terrified me, but I feel better this morning. You were right, they're just stories."

He kissed me on the forehead and then on each of my eyelids. I nestled into him, burying my face into his shoulder.

"You don't have to apologize to me," he said. "You've been through so much, and it'll take a while for you to fully recover. As long as you're okay now, that's all that matters to me." His look was so sincere it made my throat ache. "Why don't I go and make you some breakfast? I think we deserve a break from your burnt toast, don't you?" He laughed and ducked out of the way before I could smack him playfully.

After he'd gone downstairs, I stayed in bed a little longer, thinking of the night before—of Ami, and of the dream. The daylight always changed my perspective on things. Why was it that at night, in the dark, my mind played such cruel tricks on me? I remembered my surprising reaction to Ami and the terror I felt after encountering the Bean Sidhe, and it all felt so far away, like it happened to somebody else, somewhere else.

The smell of coffee brewing was my cue to head downstairs. I wrapped myself in my robe and made my way to the kitchen, where the Bee Gees were playing *You Should be Dancing* on the radio. When I peeked around the corner, Ben *was* dancing at the stove, because how could you not when that song played? He looked so cute, absentmindedly using the spatula as a microphone. It made me laugh so hard that I snorted, alerting him to my presence.

"Hey! What are you laughing at?" He turned to me, still bobbing to the music, a goofy smile across his face. "I love this song, it's so catchy."

"You're a horrible dancer." I laughed and settled in at the table, which was laid out with eggs, toast and sliced strawberries. "Thank you for breakfast," I said, filling my plate, starving as always.

Ben bent down to kiss me and as I lifted my chin to meet him, there was a knock on the door. "Who could that be?" Ben said, walking down the hall to answer it.

I followed close behind him, feeling equally self conscious about my appearance *and* curious about who was there. The door opened to reveal Ami standing on the porch with a large black lab sitting obediently beside her.

"Hey, I'm sorry, I know it's early," she said to Ben, before looking past him to me. I felt her eyes drill into me, and I pulled my robe closed even tighter around myself. "I'm sorry, I should have called."

"What? No, of course not. We're just having some breakfast, wanna join us?" Ben asked her, gesturing towards the kitchen with the spatula still in his hand.

"Oh… no. I couldn't," she answered. Her eyes

flicked back and forth between us but lingered on me slightly longer than on Ben, though I was sure he hadn't noticed. "I was just walking Luna and thought I would return the container you sent me home with last night." She held out the plastic margarine tub Ben had filled with leftovers, which I definitely hadn't expected, or even wanted, back.

"Thanks," he said, taking it from her. "You really didn't have to bring it back so fast, or probably at all." He chuckled.

"Yeah, I guess I couldn't wait," Ami said, looking at me again. "I better go." She gave a little wave before turning and walking down the driveway.

"That was kind of weird," Ben said. "She never brings back my containers. Oh well, let's eat!" He pulled me back to the table, where I ate every bite of the food on my plate, but I didn't taste any of it.

After breakfast, I hurried upstairs to change into jeans and a warm wool sweater. For the first time, I couldn't comfortably button my jeans up. Though a little frustrating, it made me smile to leave that button undone. I glanced in the mirror quickly, smoothed my tousled hair the best I could, and wished I had time for a proper shower, but I didn't want to lose my nerve.

Back downstairs, Ben stood at the sink whistling quietly as he washed our breakfast dishes without complaint. I leaned against the door frame to watch him, suddenly feeling so eternally grateful for him and everything he did for me. The appreciation ignited guilt within me as well, and the two sentiments ran parallel, fighting against each other.

"Hey, I think I might take a walk," I said, disrupting his melody.

"Do you want me to come with you?" he asked over his shoulder.

"No, I'll be fine. I won't be gone long," I called, already starting towards the door.

He said nothing else and resumed his whistling, so I slipped into my jacket. Once outside, I walked in the direction Ami had gone. I didn't know where she lived, but as I turned the corner, I saw her dog, Luna, sleeping in front of a small green house. I took a deep breath before turning up the driveway and walking right up to the front door.

Too late.

I knocked. I heard shuffling sounds and then footsteps, before the door opened. And there she was, just as she was the night before, just as she was this morning. Captivating. Her long straight hair, parted down the middle, fell over her shoulders. When she saw me, she tucked both sides behind her ears, her skin warm and flushed despite the chill of the morning air.

"What were you doing at my house this morning?" I blurted before she was able to react to finding me on her doorstep; before she was able to say anything. The anger I held was unexpected and it wasn't why I'd come, but it boiled inside me, nonetheless.

"I told you, I was returning your container." She smiled, raising one eyebrow, unaffected by my outburst, which made me feel like a child in the midst of a tantrum.

"Don't lie to me," I said, taking a step closer to her.

"Okay," she challenged. "Why do *you* think I came over this morning?" She leaned her shoulder against the frame of the door, crossed her arms over her chest and waited for my answer. Her nonchalance infuriated me even further.

"I don't know." I couldn't think. I couldn't work out why she was there this morning or why I was here now. Nothing made sense to me. Really, I had hoped she would be able to provide some answers, to shed some light on how I was feeling.

"Why did you come *here*? To yell at me?" she asked, a touch of hurt tinging her last few words.

I didn't have an answer to her question, just as I didn't have an answer to my own, so instead, I turned and walked away from her as fast as I could. I couldn't get out of there fast enough, but the questions continued to flash through my mind. Why was I there? What was I doing? I felt like I was losing what little mind I had left.

That morning when I woke up, I felt completely normal. Now, after seeing her, I was right back where I was last night. Ami didn't follow me, but I felt her eyes on me until I turned the corner and fell from her view.

That night, I dreamed again of the Bean Sidhe. The dream was the same, but with one significant difference. Instead of screaming three times, she only screamed twice.

"She's counting down," I cried to Ben when he woke to my screaming the second night in a row. He pulled me to him, and I cried myself to sleep against his chest.

The next day, I couldn't forget the dream, and the light of morning didn't chase away the fear or darkness as it had the day before. I was terrified and chose to spend the day in bed resting, just in case. Ben tried to get me to come down, but I refused, and in the end, he brought my meals and stayed with me, deciding to make a "date" of it. It was light for him, but dark for me.

The next night, as I feared it would, the dream returned. The Bean Sidhe screamed only once this time. One more day. The short countdown was almost over.

Just as I had the day before, I stayed in bed the entire day, waiting. Waiting for the day to be over. If I could make it through until morning, then I would know Ben was right and it really was just a dream. That the stories I heard as a girl were just that, stories. I watched the hours tick by on the clock, feeling like a prisoner in my own bed again. As my room began to darken and night fell, my eyes became heavy, and I let myself fall asleep.

The room was completely dark when my eyes

flew open. Feeling a warm rushing between my legs, I instantly knew what was happening.

"Ben, something's wrong!" I clicked on the lamp, throwing the blankets away from me. Then I saw it, the blood on the sheets where I had been sleeping. "No. No. No. No. No!"

Ben woke up confused and disoriented at first, but then he saw it too. He watched speechless as I gathered my long nightgown up over my thighs, revealing more blood pooling underneath me.

"No. No. No. No. No." Suddenly, I doubled over in pain so severe I could hardly breathe through it.

After a few seconds, the pain subsided. I covered my face and felt the tears hot and wet against my skin. I had only a few seconds before another wave of pain ripped through me and I screamed in agony, feeling like my abdomen was being squeezed and twisted from the inside.

"I'm going to call an ambulance," Ben said as he ran from the room and pounded down the stairs.

The space in between pains was the oddest sensation, like nothing was happening at all. There was no pain, and in those brief moments, I thought maybe I was just imagining it, but then another shot of pain would rock through me.

Ben's voice, loud and panicked, made its way up the stairs. "It's my..." Ben hesitated before continuing. "...wife," he said, instead of 'girlfriend.' "She's pregnant. Oh, god. There's a lot of blood and she's in a lot of pain." There was a pause before he gave the dispatcher our address, and then he was rushing back up the stairs to me.

Each stair that he took felt like a beat of my own heart. I could hear it thrumming inside me. What once was two heart beats, now only one.

"The ambulance is on its way," he said, running into the room.

But his voice was so far away, and I couldn't keep my eyes open anymore. He grasped my shoulders and shook me, but I couldn't come back. The darkness was so thick and warm. His hand slapped against my face gently, urging me to come back, to wake up, but I couldn't. My eyes wouldn't open. I was locked inside my mind with nothing but the waves of pain to keep me company.

"Please, Josephine, wake up. Wake up!"

His hands released my body back onto the bed and his footsteps faded from the room once more; I wanted to cry out for him not to leave me. I was so scared, and I didn't want to be alone, but no matter how hard I tried to call out to him, nothing happened. No voice. No movement.

"What happened?" Ami's voice broke through my haze, bringing me back a little but not enough.

Had it been minutes? Hours? Days? Hands were on me again, but not Ben's familiar ones. These hands were delicate but sure and left my skin hot wherever they touched. They went first to my forehead to check for fever, and then to my wrist for my pulse.

"I don't know. She woke up bleeding and then she was in a lot of pain. I called an ambulance, but then she lost consciousness, so I ran to get you. You can help her, right?" Even after everything we'd been through, the fear in Ben's voice was unfamiliar and jarring.

"Ben, I'm a midwife, not a doctor." Ami sounded just as, if not more, scared than Ben.

"But you deliver babies; this is your job!" From fear to anger. The transition was so swift and so unlike him. I wanted to reach out to him, but he was getting farther and farther away.

"Yeah, I deliver *healthy* babies, but if things start going wrong, I call a doctor."

"Please, just help her."

She took my wrist again. "Her pulse is weakening, and she's still losing blood. We need the ambulance to get here," she said, her voice hopeless, useless. "Come on, pick her up. We'll meet the ambulance."

Without another word, my body was lifted from the bed. I shivered violently when the cold air touched the warm wetness of the skin beneath my soaked nightgown, before a blanket was wrapped around me. Ben carried me down to the car carefully and laid me down in the backseat. My head settled back on something soft, and warm hands ran through my hair.

"It's going to be okay," a gravelly voice whispered, before the shadows consumed me completely.

CHAPTER 15

WHEN MY EYES opened again, an odd sense of déjà vu washed over me. I knew with certainty nothing would ever be okay again. White room. White walls. A hospital. Again. Ben was there, as he was before, his head in his hands.

I called out his name, but my voice was still small and far away, so I tried again. "Ben?"

This time he heard, and he looked up at me, his eyes red and swollen.

"What's wrong?" I asked, but I already knew. Before he could respond, every cell in my body cracked in half. I covered my face with my hands, turned away from him and cried harder than I had ever cried before.

The next morning, the nurses sat me in a chair by the small window of my hospital room, while

Ben finished filling out the paperwork so we could go home. I couldn't look outside though; the sky was blue, and the sun was shining—the opposite of the storm raging inside me. Doing my best to ignore the beautiful day, I focused my attention instead on the far corner of the windowsill, where dirt had built up and a dead fly lay dry and crisp from the sun. I imagined that, if I looked at it long enough, it would buzz to life and fly off. Maybe death wasn't real at all. Maybe it was all a lie.

"Hi," Ami said from the door, interrupting my thoughts.

Despite my grief, the sound of her voice made my heart beat a little faster, and that further loss of control infuriated me.

"What are you doing here?" I snapped, not looking away from the fly. Away from the death.

"I came to see if you're okay," she said, clicking the door shut behind her as she stepped into the room.

"I'm not."

She pulled up a chair next to mine, took my hand into her own and held it tightly but didn't say another word. It took everything I had to keep it together, but every second that passed between us, I felt my walls breaking down. Brick by brick, they crumbled under the weight of her unwavering patience.

After a few moments, I couldn't hold it any longer and I stirred just slightly, breaking the spell I was under, and Ami turned to watch me. She lifted a shaking hand and wiped a tear from my cheek with her thumb. My lower lip trembled. I tried to stop it, but I couldn't. I breathed in and out slowly, trying to regain control of myself, but after just a few shaky breaths, I lost it completely. Tears flowed freely down my cheeks and sobs ripped from my chest.

"I don't know why I'm so sad," I cried, my breathing ragged and forced. I paused and took another shaky breath before I crumpled all over again. "I had a baby. Nobody would believe me now, but I did. I don't have a baby, but I *did* have one." I held Ami's hand tighter, resting it against my heart while my other hand covered my mouth, trying to hold it all in.

Ami turned her chair to face me, took both of my hands in hers and said, "It's okay to be sad. You had a baby. You had one and it was yours and now it's gone." My heart rose and fell with her words. "That baby was *everything* to you. It wasn't just a fetus. It was the life that you had planned out. It was all your hopes and dreams. It was everything to you."

"It was a boy."

"I'm so sorry for your loss. We will not forget him. I promise."

My eyes met hers. I hadn't expected to find anyone who would be able to understand how I was feeling. I knew Ben was sad, but the look in his eyes looked more like pity for me rather than grief for what we'd lost. Plus, he was able to distract himself by filling out the forms and getting the proper instructions from the nurses, while I was left with my own thoughts, my shadows closing in tighter and tighter. But Ami, her empathy shook me.

I searched my mind for something to say back to her, something to convey how grateful I was, but it was empty. I was empty.

After a few more moments of silence, she said, "I'm going to go find Ben and then we're going to take you home." Her fingers brushed my cheek again before she walked away, closing the door softly behind her.

Home. I wasn't really sure what that meant anymore. I wasn't safe anywhere.

It was hospital policy that I had to be wheeled out in a wheelchair, and I never felt more on display than I did rolling down those halls. People looked at me as I was pushed by, and I knew they could see it all. They knew I was empty inside. Each face turned towards me as we passed, and their eyes followed me down each and every hallway. They followed me into the elevator. They followed me out of the hospital and right to Ben's truck. They didn't say anything; they didn't have to. I could see the disappointment and the blame in their eyes reflected in the glass beside me.

CHAPTER 16

THE DRIVE HOME was long; the silence unbearable, but the thought of talking or turning on the radio was equally excruciating and absurd. I didn't deserve anything that might ease my discomfort. Instead, I stared out the window, my body turned away as the impenetrable forest soared past behind the foggy glass. Then, as we drove down our street, something caught my eye that, somehow, I hadn't noticed before.

"Stop!" I yelled, breaking the silent spell we had all been under as I sat up straighter to see better through the window.

Alarmed, Ben pulled over to the side of the road and I jumped out before we had even come to a complete stop. He and Ami called my name, but I didn't turn back. I ran off the road and stopped at a wood fence, astonished by the lone maple tree, standing ancient and tall in the middle of the property directly adjacent to our own. The base of its thick trunk was surrounded by a ring of large stones and its branches spread out wide and far above them.

Unmistakable. A fairy tree.

"That tree…" I started to say as Ben and Ami came to stand beside me. I didn't look away from the tree—I couldn't—but I could sense the worried look shared between them.

"What about it?" Ben asked, confused.

"I've seen it before." It was like a dream. A dream I'd had many times but couldn't remember. It was there, but just out of reach.

"Of course, you've seen it, it's right next to our house, we've driven by it tons of times," Ben said

Yes, of course that made sense, but why didn't I remember seeing it before? Why hadn't I recognised it for what it was at once?

"It's a fairy tree. Why would there be a fairy tree here?" I asked, looking around as though I expected the answer to just present itself to me.

"I'm not sure, honey." Ben was obviously trying to keep his voice steady and encouraging, but I could hear the doubt behind his words. I could hear the pity that now stained everything he said.

"I've seen it before," I repeated. My memory reached back to the stories Nan told me of the fairy trees in Ireland; back to the books she showed me, each photo a different tree in a different field but somehow each looking identical to this one.

Ben put his arm around me and led me back to the truck, and I let him, but my mind continued to turn the stories over and over, trying to make sense of it all.

He parked in front of our house before realizing that Ami was still sitting between us. "Oh, sorry," he said to her. "I forgot to stop at your place." He laughed. It sounded rotten.

"That's okay, I can walk from here." She put her hand on my arm. The feeling of it made my skin crawl. "If you need anything, just call me. Come over. Whatever you need." She gave my arm a squeeze before sliding out of the truck behind Ben. Then, she gave him a long hug. Too long.

I watched from my seat.

When Ami finally walked off in the direction of her own house, Ben ran around to the passenger side and opened the door for me. He put his hand out to help me, but I didn't take it. Instead, I said, "I'm going to take a walk. I'm not ready to go in yet."

"Okay," was all he said, his eyes sad and searching.

I pushed past him and walked off without looking back. My arms wrapped tightly around myself to keep the cold spring air out and my insides in. Though only silence followed me, I didn't have to look back to know that Ben was watching me go and I walked faster than needed to escape his eyes.

Never once, in my entire life, did I go to my mother for advice. The few times I even tried, when I was still very small, she'd laughed and called me weak or stupid. Maybe I was. Women lose babies all the time. That's what they told me at the hospital. That it was natural and for the best because it probably meant something was wrong with him or her. As if that would make me feel better. I knew I could never count on my mother for help, but despite everything, I longed to have a mother to talk to. I longed for my nan. For Mags. For anyone.

I stopped walking and leaned over the fence bordering our neighbour's property, feeling the strong pull of the tree drawing me towards it like a magnet. All the leaves had long fallen away, leaving it barren. Lonely. Familiar. Though it hurt to do so, my body slid reluctantly through the gap in the wood fence. With each step towards the tree, the air grew colder, and I shivered under my jacket despite the thick red sweater Ami had brought to the hospital for me.

Really, I wanted to turn back. Something wasn't right about the tug I was feeling; I knew it right away. But I wasn't ready to enter our house yet, the place where it happened. I wasn't ready to see the blood erased by unfamiliar sheets and a new mattress. With each arduous step forward, the loneliness of the tree combined with my own made the heaviness almost unbearable. Still, I went on.

Under the protection of its immense branches, I laid my hand upon its cold, rough bark and heard something, very faint and out of place, like a groaning or a rumbling coming from deep inside the wood. At first, I thought the tree was standing its ground against the wind, but when I looked up, the branches were still, the air still. Stepping even closer to the tree and leaning over the large stones surrounding the base of its trunk, I pressed the length of my body against it and slowed myself, trying to hear the sound again.

"What are you doing?"

Startled by an unfamiliar voice behind me, I jumped, my heart pounding, and turned towards the stranger, my cheeks burning. A pretty young woman with bright blue eyes stood close behind me, so close I could catch her scent. Cinnamon, soap and rich earth, like she had just made an apple pie and then worked in the garden. She had long brown hair wound into a low bun at the nape of her neck, with delicate tendrils, fallen from their pins, framing her face. Her grey shapeless dress was a little old fashioned for my taste, but it suited her, and reminded me of photos of my nan when she was a young woman.

"What are you doing on my property?" she asked, in no way unfriendly, but I got the feeling from her crossed arms and impatient stance that I wasn't exactly welcome there.

"Oh, I'm your neighbour," I said pointing in the direction of our house. "I… I was just taking a walk."

"You really shouldn't be here," she said, leaning in slightly towards me, her tone darker than it had been. "It's bad luck," she whispered, so low I almost missed it.

"What do you mean?" I asked, inspecting her face, taking in every inch of it. There was something familiar about her. Maybe I had seen her in town somewhere. I couldn't quite recall.

Like a shade being drawn, blocking out the sun, her bright blue eyes darkened abruptly.

"I mean, you shouldn't have touched it!" she screamed , the fear plain in her wild eyes.

I flinched away from her, tripping over the stones and falling back against the tree.

Then, as quick as she lost it, she softened, and her eyes went from indigo to bright blue again. She composed herself, straightened her dress and checked her hair before saying, "You look cold, do you want some tea?"

Without waiting for a response, she turned and started up the hill towards a small house, which I also hadn't noticed before.

"Come on," she said without turning around again.

I hesitated at first, my eyes wet with tears, my heart pounding, but eventually followed her. My curiosity far surpassed the concern of any possible danger I was getting myself into. Despite her overreaction, I didn't think she was planning to hurt me. There'd been fear in her words, but not anger. Although, as I knew all too well, sometimes fear could be far more dangerous.

Her house was small, but very well taken care of. The yard surrounding it was perfect, the gardens overflowing with flowers and vegetables. The building itself was two stories, with a small deck much like our own. The entire thing looked as though it had just been freshly painted. In fact, it looked a little bit like it had just been built.

"Who else lives here?" I asked, hesitating on the porch.

"Just me," was all she said, glancing over her shoulder at me before disappearing into the house, leaving the door open behind her.

My head was screaming at me to turn around and leave, but something warm and comforting whispered in my ear that I should go ahead and step inside. Unable to resist, I listened to the voice and followed the woman.

The inside of the house was even nicer than the outside. Polished wood floors gleamed under my feet as I followed her down a short hall and then to a living room directly off the foyer. Two beautiful sofas faced each other before a roaring fire. The room was a little too warm; beads of sweat prickled under my arms and across my brow.

She sat on one of the sofas and motioned for me

to sit on the other. Two cups of steaming hot tea were waiting on the table between us, as if she had been expecting me all along.

"What's your name?" she asked, taking a sip of the tea, and nodding towards me to do the same. I picked up the cup but couldn't quite bring myself to take a drink, so I held it in my hands, letting the warmth spread into my cold fingers.

For some reason, I found I wanted to lie to this stranger, to tell her a fake name, but in her blue eyes, there was something genuine. And, again, familiar, so I couldn't bring myself to do it. "Josephine," I said, telling the truth.

"My name's Iris, Iris Bower." She reached her hand out over the table. Her handshake was gentle, but her skin was hardened and rough, and it was clear she worked hard around the house and in the gardens out front. "Now, what were you doing down there huggin' my tree?" The stark fear in her eyes earlier was gone and in its place was a wry amusement.

"I wasn't hugging it." My cheeks burned as I imagined what I must have looked like to another person.

"Looked like huggin' to me," she chuckled.

"I was listening to it," I said, defending myself, though I wasn't sure that sounded any less crazy than hugging it did.

Her face grew noticeably more serious at my comment. "What were you listening for?" she asked, so quiet it was almost a whisper, but her eyes never left mine as she waited for my answer. Though she remained calm and collected, an impatience vibrated from her, and I knew she was holding something back.

"I'm not sure, exactly," I answered honestly. "You do know, it's a fairy tree?" I was testing her; there was something she was hiding, something I needed to know. I could feel it, just as I felt the strong pull of the tree that had brought me here.

"I don't know anything about that," she said, standing brusquely and walking over to the fireplace. She knelt before the fire and pretended to busy herself with stoking the already lively flames with a sharp iron poker she took from the holder beside the fireplace. Like everything else, it looked brand new.

"My nan told me the fairies use them as gateways between our world and theirs," I said, pushing it a little further to see her response. Other than an almost imperceptible pause, there was none, so I continued. "You said touching it was bad luck. What did you mean by that?"

She stood up and stared into the dancing flames for some time before taking a deep breath and making her way back to her seat on the sofa. Her calm, friendly demeanour was gone, replaced by something I couldn't quite pinpoint. Something between grief and dimmed elation. She hugged her arms around herself.

"Look, I can't explain it," she finally said, "but all I know is, bad things have happened around that tree, and that's how I know to leave it be."

"Like what?" I asked.

She got up from her seat once more and went to stand before the window, looking out at something in the distance. I didn't have to get up and look to know that it was the tree. When she spoke again, her voice was far away and sad.

"When we first bought the land, we set to work clearing it to make room for our crops and animals." She paused. Her breathing grew deeper, louder. "My father died while trying to cut that tree down. He was only trying to help us out. He was always trying to help us out. He had hardly made a cut in the trunk when he had a heart attack and died, right there in front of us." Iris reached into a hidden pocket in her dress and pulled out a cigarette. She lit it, blowing the curling smoke towards the window, obscuring her reflection. "We were all so heartbroken that we didn't think anything else of it at the time, but then——". She choked on the words and raised her smokeless hand to cover her mouth, giving herself a moment to compose herself. "——my husband died the exact same way in the exact same place. After that, I piled stones around it, to protect it, and to protect us."

"You think the tree killed them?" I asked. Part of me thought she was insane, but it was a very small part, because I also knew I wasn't surprised.

"Maybe, maybe not; but it's not something I'm willing to risk being wrong about." Condensation from her warm breath fogged the window and she took the chance to draw the simple shape of a tree with a person standing beneath its sprawling branches. From where I sat, it looked as though the person was floating in the air above the ground. Hanging.

"I can't explain it," I said, "but the moment I saw it, I felt drawn to it. Then I found myself standing in front of it, and I could *hear* it."

Although her back was still to me, her head turned just slightly. She knew what I was talking about. She understood what I meant, and she could laugh and make fun all she wanted, but now I knew I wasn't alone. I stood to go to her, but some photos on the wall caught my eye. A mother, a father and two blue-eyed children—a girl and a boy.

"Oh, you have kids? Where are they?" I asked, looking around.

But the house seemed completely devoid of anything that indicated children. No toys. No laughter. She turned towards me with a smile so artificial it made my mouth sour. It was especially grotesque with the cigarette smoke swirling around her head. The clock ticked loudly as I waited for Iris to answer. She took a long drag of her cigarette, took her time blowing out the smoke, and then looked me right in the eyes.

"They're upstairs, sleeping. You should go." A

deep sadness flashed behind her eyes, and she frowned as she put out her cigarette in an ashtray on a small table next to the window. Against the beauty of the room, it was sorely out of place, and overflowing, as though she stood in that exact spot smoking cigarette after cigarette. Day after day.

"I thought you said you lived here alone," I said, wondering why she would lie about something so straightforward.

"Yah, that's right. I live here alone with them," she corrected herself, but something in her eyes said she wasn't telling the entire truth.

"I have a son." I said it to see how it felt and immediately I wished to take it back. I didn't want this woman to have any piece of him.

"You keep him away from that tree, ya hear?" Her eyes met mine, hard.

"I touched it, the tree. I pressed my whole body against it. Do you think something will happen to me?" The question that had been nagging me since stepping foot in the house.

"Looking at you," she said, lighting another cigarette, "I get the feeling something already has."

My heart slammed into my ribs. For that small amount of time, I had been able to forget everything and lose myself in a story outside of my own, but what I had suspected at the hospital was true. Everyone could see there was something wrong with me.

"How did you know I was coming here?" Anger

and shame built up in my chest and I had to relieve the pressure.

"What d'ya mean?" she asked, one arched eyebrow raised.

"You had a cup of tea ready for me. How did you know I was coming?"

"What tea?" she scoffed, shaking her head.

I looked down and saw the steaming mug I had held in my cold hands only a minute ago was gone. "What? Where did it go?" I looked around the table, around the room, confused.

"Where did what go?" The tone of her voice once again was rougher, and darker, than it had been.

I looked away from the empty space where my cup had been and up at Iris. The young, pretty face I had seen only moments before had turned grey and dead. Her skin hung off her sunken cheekbones, her eyes were gaping black holes and the flesh around her neck was dark and bruised. I gasped and stepped back, accidentally kicking the table. The impact caused the single cup of tea—hers—to fall to the wood floor, sending water and shards of china flying in all directions.

The thing that had been Iris came towards me with its neck bent slightly wrong and its hands out, trying to stop me. Before I could get away, it took my hands and squeezed them tight. Its skin was so thin and colourless, like paper.

"Please don't go. Please don't leave me," it

begged; desperation etched into the lines of its face. I wrenched my hands away from the monster and ran.

"It's too late! You'll never get away!" It cried.

When I looked back to see if the thing was following me, I saw only Iris, as she had been before, looking after me, an expression of concern on her face. It didn't make me stop, though. I ran from the house, past the tree, all the way down to the road, where I ducked under the fence once more.

"Jo!"

Startled, I turned to see Ben running up the road towards me.

"Thank god, I have been looking for you everywhere." He gathered me into his arms, lifting my feet from the ground.

"Ben!" I hugged him tight as tears stung my eyes. I breathed in the familiar scent of him and calmed slightly. *It wasn't real. It wasn't real. It wasn't real.*

"I was so worried about you." He pulled away and looked at me right in the eyes, searching for the answer to a question he was too afraid to ask.

"I'm sorry, I… I…" I stuttered.

I couldn't get the words out. I couldn't tell him what had just happened to me. Instead, I burrowed myself into him and let him hold me until my heart quieted and my breathing returned to normal. When I was calm, he took my hand and started to lead me back towards our house. At first, he was silent, and there was a sharp tension coming from him I'd never sensed before. Despite his relief in finding me, for the first time ever, he was furious with me, but he was trying his best to control it. The realization of it was so unexpected, tears stung in my eyes once more.

"I know you are going through a lot right now, we both are, but you can't just take off for hours and hours," he said, slow and controlled.

"Hours?" I stopped walking. "What are you talking about?" I looked around and realised he was right. It had been midmorning when we arrived home, and now, the sun was setting behind the trees.

"You've been gone for almost eight hours," Ben said, trying to steady his shaking voice. "I have been looking everywhere for you! I was about to call the police. I thought something had happened to you or that you had—"

"Had what? What did you think I had done? Killed myself?" I accused, my arms outstretched, unable to believe what he was saying.

"No," he sighed. He took off his glasses and rubbed his eyes, obviously exhausted. "I was just worried about you." He stepped closer to me and took my hands in his. "You've been so sad since we lost the baby, and we didn't really get the chance to talk about it at the hospital."

"All right, let's talk about it!" The rage had built up inside me and I couldn't stop it. It started in my heart, where it rolled and undulated like tar threatening to boil over and coat the rest of me in sticky unrelenting blackness. I was stuck there, always. The pain of the loss and the confusion of what was happening to me compounded, and I shattered.

"Jo, not like this," Ben pleaded.

"No, exactly like this. Let's talk about it. Our baby is dead. And what? I'm supposed to be just fine now? Well, I'm not!"

I saw him flinch at the harshness of my words. Saw that I hurt him, and even though I knew it wasn't fair, I needed to be sure he felt just as bad as I did. When he didn't bite at the fight I was trying to start, I walked right up to him, and I shoved him hard; harder than I knew I was capable. He stumbled back from me, his mouth open in shock. Still, he did nothing, said nothing.

His weakness infuriated me, so I turned and ran from him. I ran all the way home and, without thinking, I ran straight through the front door and right into the house I had been trying so hard to avoid all day.

The smell of tomato sauce and garlic was strong. Ami emerged from the kitchen, drying her hands on a towel as if she lived there. The sight of her stopped me instantly.

"Oh, I'm so glad you're okay. We've been so worried," she said walking towards me with her arms outstretched as though she were coming in for a hug.

"What are you doing here? What are you *always*

doing here?" I wasn't mad at her, it wasn't her fault, but I yelled anyway. I was tired of being constantly on display, like there was always someone watching me.

Even worse, Ami's eyes watched me too closely and it was like she could see right into me. I didn't want her to see what was inside.

"I'm so… sorry," she stammered, surprised and obviously hurt by my outburst. "I was just trying to help. Dinner is on the stove. I'll go." She grabbed her jacket from the back of a chair and hurried towards the door.

"Ames, wait!" Ben called as she rushed past him. Turning to me, he yelled, "Why do you have to treat her like that? She's only trying to help!"

"Help!? Help who exactly? She's only here to be close to you!" I knew what I was saying was ridiculous, but I had to try to make myself believe it, because the alternative, what I *knew* to be true, was too confusing.

"Are you insane?" He didn't notice, and I know he didn't mean it, but the word hit me hard. "Ami is my oldest friend! There's nothing even remotely romantic between us; there never has been!"

"Insane? If you think I'm so insane, why are you even with me?" I yelled back, my arms outstretched.

"I didn't mean that. I'm sorry," he said, though his tone was icy and tired.

I was breaking him down. Bit by bit. I kept going. "Oh, you didn't mean it? Of course you didn't." He shook his head. "Answer my question, Ben, why are you with me?" He put his hands against his forehead and turned, struggling. "The baby is gone. You have no reason to stay! Why are you still here?"

"Because I'm responsible for you!" He yelled, his whole body tense.

Even though I had pushed him to this point, I flinched at his words. His face crumpled as he realized what he'd said, but it was too late.He yelled out my name as I pushed past him, stormed up the stairs, slammed the door to our room, locked it, and sat on the bed, heart pounding. I knew I was being unfair. I knew he deserved better than this, but I didn't know what else to do, how else to be. I couldn't stop.

Ben's words replayed in my mind on a never ending loop and each time the loop restarted the sting of pain remained the same.

Because I'm responsible for you. Because I'm responsible for you. Because I'm responsible for you. Because I'm responsible for you.

Of course he felt responsible for me and I felt stupid that I'd actually believed that he loved me. If I hadn't been pregnant with his child, would he have let social services take me? Where else would I go? I had no one and he knew it. He was trapped, just like I was.

A few moments later, Ben knocked gently on the door. When I didn't respond, he didn't knock again.

CHAPTER 17

The clock ticked on. Time passed. The shadows in the room grew deeper and deeper until blending together entirely.

It was well after midnight when I heard Ben outside the bedroom door again. He stood there for a long time, unmoving, the shadow of him darkening the illuminated space under the door. Probably thinking I was asleep, he unlocked it slowly and slipped into the room in total silence. Without undressing and without touching me, he laid down on the bed and curled away from me. Soon, his breath grew shallow and long. I lay there next to him, completely still, knowing that if I were to move even just a little, I would fall apart. I had to stay perfectly still to keep the pieces of me together.

Unable to find the respite of sleep, silent tears

flowed steadily down my face and onto my pillow. I struggled to stay quiet, still, and in control. I didn't want to wake Ben; I didn't want him to know that I was dying inside. Completely still on the outside, my breath steady, my eyes closed; I probably looked as though I was in a deep, heavy sleep, but what I hid neatly was the storm raging within me. My throat was closing up and it became hard to breathe through the hard lump, but I didn't mind. The drowning feeling was a welcome relief from the searing pain in my heart.

Unanswerable questions tore through my thoughts, consuming me. Why did this happen to me? Was it my fault? What had I done to deserve it? What would my baby have been like? Who would he or she have been? Who would I be now, without him or her?

The pretty yellow nursery in the next room haunted me with its empty crib and unworn clothes in the dresser. How would I ever face it? Rationally, I understood that I didn't have the right to feel this sad; to be this destroyed; to treat Ben so badly. I didn't know the baby. I never even had the chance to hold or touch him or her. These facts were so obvious to me, and yet, tears continued to pour from my eyes and soak the pillow beneath my cheek. No matter what I told myself, nothing could ease the devastation. Still, through the entire storm that raged, I never moved. Never made a sound. I stayed that way until my muscles ached and my throat was raw.

Days passed and I only left my bed when I absolutely needed to use the bathroom. I took mere bites of the food Ben brought up to me, to make him happy and to make up for what I'd done to him. But the truth was, I liked the feeling of hunger gnawing at me. It was something simple that, this time, I could control. In the moments when the hunger was the most intense, it was almost able to overpower the sadness entirely. Almost.

Usually, I didn't let myself sleep long enough for dreams to come. I was too afraid of what nightmares my mind would conjure as it tried to process what had happened. Then, one afternoon, I fell into the kind of deep sleep I had been avoiding and surrendered myself to the comfort of the dark.

Whatever I was feeling while awake was dull and lifeless compared to what was happening inside me. Stepping through the veil into my mind, a literal storm raged. Rain poured from above, but when the drops ran down my cheeks and into my mouth, the water tasted warm and salty. Thunder boomed ahead and lightning flashed, illuminating the area but revealing nothing. I spun around and around, looking for some kind of landmark to let me know where I was. The lightning lit up the sky again just as my gaze fell in the direction of the tree.

I knew I was dreaming, and I kept telling myself to wake up, but I had been so long without sleep that I couldn't bring myself out of it. I knew it was a dream, but the sensations were real. My skin was wet and ice cold. My hands shook and my teeth chattered, and I really felt like, if I stood out there in the open, I was going to die. I ran for the only shelter I could see: the tree.

In this world, it had a full canopy of green leaves and I was able to hide from the rain beneath its branches, but I couldn't escape from the crackling sensation that filled the air around me as though I were surrounded by electricity. Then, a loud crack shattered the world. The sound was so loud it made my heart stop and my ears bleed, and I felt the power of it split every atom that was me. Breaking me down, bit by bit. When the lightning flashed again, I saw the tree, its trunk split down the middle, blackened by fire. I ran my hand over the wound, my fingers coming away black. Then I heard something, a voice reaching through the mist. It was my own voice, but touched with a brightness I could never muster. The voice came again, louder and more urgent, calling my name. "Jo. Jo. Jo."

Mags.

Her voice sparked an energy in me that had been forgotten, and I waded through the thick darkness towards her. I longed for her. I searched for her. Every direction I turned, I was alone, but I could feel her. I could see her brightness shimmering as if underwater. When sleep and the darkness finally slipped away, I opened my eyes, and there she was, her face close to mine, laying in the bed next to me, one hand under her cheek.

"Mags?"

"Hey, sis," she said, using her other hand to brush the hair from my eyes. "I'm here now. I'm here for you."

I let her body surround me, pulling me in, protecting me from everything I had been running from. "Is it really you?" I whispered through a shaky breath, my eyes full of tears. I looked up into her face, a face as familiar as my own, and studied it, looking for a clue that this too was only a dream.

"It's me," she said and held me like that for a long time, until I was ready to let go. "I'm sorry I couldn't be here sooner. I'm so sorry."

And I cried. I thought that I had no tears left, but they fell freely. Fell for myself. Fell for her. Fell for everything we'd lost.

She waited patiently until I was done and then she told her own story , her words so matter-of-fact; so unlike her. Removed.

"When I saw what she was doing to you, I couldn't just stand there. I ran to the kitchen and got the hammer from under the sink. I'm not even really sure how I knew it was there, or how I thought of it. I just did. On the way back upstairs, Ben burst through the door. I think he heard you screaming from the street, and I guess he followed me, because after I hit her, he was there. The police believed me when I told them what happened and that I was just defending you, but they said they couldn't just release me without an investigation. Ben told them he was your fiancé , so they let you go with him, but I guess you can't hit your mother with a hammer and then just walk free. Anyways, the investigation is over, and the case is closed. Mother is locked away and won't ever be released."

The truth hit me hard.

Locked away. Not dead.

"She's alive?" My voice sounded steady, but I wasn't.

"Yes? Wait, you didn't know?" she said, incredulously.

"I knew she was gone. I wasn't sure what it meant, exactly, and I never asked," I confessed. "I hoped she was dead—that you'd killed her—and I left it at that."

"I thought I did. There was so much blood. She was in the hospital for a long time, but she was recently released from there and moved to Riverview. You know, the psychiatric hospital in old Essondale. The police said she isn't fit to stand trial for what she did to you, so she'll stay there until she is, though it's likely that will never happen."

My mother was alive. I thought her hold on me had been broken, but this explained why I still felt the suffocating presence of her. I imagined my mother in a mental hospital, her slim body wasting away under a blue hospital gown, her long hair tangled, her green eyes vacant. It was impossible.

"Jo." Mags's voice brought me back. "It's time to

get up and out of this room. Ben's so worried about you. We both are."

I knew she was right, and I knew it was time. I wasn't alone anymore. With her here, I could do it. I could be better. So, I nodded in agreement and released a long, shaky breath. "Okay," I said.

She took my hand in hers and led me into the bathroom. I let her help me get undressed and into the bathtub. We didn't speak. We didn't have to. I was grateful that, although she saw them, she didn't comment on the bones pushing against my thin skin.

Dried and dressed, I looked in the mirror and saw in the reflection the shell I'd been in the hospital before coming here. Bruised, hollow. I hadn't wanted to go back there, and I was disappointed in myself for walking down that path again willingly. It wasn't my fault then, but it was now. I did this to myself.

When I was ready, we went downstairs together. Ben sat on the couch, leaning forward, his elbows on his knees, his hands clasped in front of him. When he heard us enter the room, he jumped up with relief evident in his eyes. He rushed towards me and pulled me into him, hugging me for a long time, and I let him.

"You're back," he smiled.

I wished I was back, but I didn't have the heart to tell him I wasn't. Not really. But, with Mags around, I could try. I would try.

That night, Ben cooked a roast to celebrate. At first, he insisted I sit down and rest, but all I had been doing was resting.

"I want to help," I told him as he started pulling ingredients out of the fridge.

"I don't want you to push it," he replied, with a sweet smile he flashed from behind the open fridge door. He still had the joy and optimism that was so completely "Ben," but his shoulders were hunched and there was a tightness to his jaw that wasn't there before. These were the things *I* had done to him, and I had to do whatever I could to make it up to him.

"Hey," I said, taking a bunch of celery out of his hands and placing it on the counter. "I'm sorry." I wanted to say more, to explain myself, but apologizing was all I could manage.

He took my hands in his, brought them to his lips and then pulled me into an intense hug. I wanted to pull away; the feeling of being touched so completely felt impossible, but I held my breath and let him take what he needed. He released a shaky breath before pulling me away from him. "There is nothing you need to be sorry for. Not now, not ever, not about any of this."

I nodded. "I just need to get back into my life and to feel like I have a purpose again. So, please don't treat me any different." I squeezed both of his hands in mine. "Now, show me what to do." I smiled, just as Mags walked into the kitchen. She always had a way of coming and going at precisely the right times. She could read a situation and know exactly where she needed to be and what she needed to be doing in that moment.

Now, she bustled around the kitchen with us. Ben chopped carrots; Mags checked the roast like she knew what she was doing, not that she had ever checked one before. Ben showed us how to mash potatoes and how to make gravy the way his mom did. Mags was comfortable there—laughing at his jokes and moving around the kitchen with confident ease. As I watched them, I saw what we might have looked like, Ben and I, if we had been given the chance at a normal life. He could easily replace me with her. She wasn't as broken as I was. I thought, maybe, that would be better for him. For everyone. Though I pushed the thought away quickly, it still made me feel dark and alone.

When they were both turned towards the stove, I walked out of the kitchen and left the house, closing the door softly behind me.

Outside was cold and dark, but I preferred it to inside, which was stuffy and too bright. Without another thought, I started out into the darkness, following the light of the quarter moon towards Ami's house. When I passed by the fairy tree, it was illuminated by the stars, just barely visible in the dark. It called out to me as it had before, but this time, I was able to resist.

As I approached Ami's house, her dog barked

from inside, alerting her of a presence in the yard. The porch light turned on and her front door opened just as I began to climb the steps. When she saw me, surprise flickered over her features, and she closed the door quickly. I imagined her leaning her forehead against the other side, not sure what to do. The last time she'd seen me, I'd basically told her to stay out of my life and I wouldn't blame her if she wouldn't talk to me, but moments later, the door opened again. She stood before me, her eyebrows raised, her dark hair loose around her shoulders. And though she leaned forward slightly, I got the feeling she didn't want me there.

"What are you doing here, Josephine?" she asked, her voice harsh.

Josephine.

Because of the way I'd treated her, we had taken so many steps back from each other that I was surprised to find us almost back at the formality of having never met at all. I had never been Josephine to her. I hadn't been Josephine to anyone since my mother, and the name was a slap in the face.

"I just had to get out of there," I answered, pointing in the direction of my house. "I didn't know where else to go."

"So, you came here?" she said, anger flaring up behind her eyes. She took an aggressive step towards me. "You know what, you have made it obvious over and over again that you do not want me around. What is it about you?" Frustration grew loud in her voice.

I took a step back, almost losing my balance on the stairs. "What do you mean? What about me?"

"Ben told me how, when he met you, he couldn't help himself. He saw you sitting across that diner, and even though you sat there with your twin sister who looks exactly like you, there was something different about *you*, something he couldn't ignore. Couldn't resist. He told me the thought of letting you walk out of there that day was so terrifying, he *chased* you. He said he couldn't get enough of you. That, no matter the risk, he just kept coming back. Why? That's not Ben. Ben is careful and calculated. He thinks before he acts. And then you move here, and I find you've done the same thing to—" She stopped talking then, closing her mouth into a tight line to keep the words from flowing through her lips so freely.

Her cheeks darkened and I felt mine do the same. I had been trying to deny there was anything at all between us, and then she went and almost said it out loud. But, to her, it was as if I'd put her under some kind of spell. As if I had that kind of power.

"What do you mean? I haven't done anything. You're the one who keeps coming around, injecting yourself into our lives!"

"You think I want this!? Ben is my best friend!"

Want.

Suddenly, my body was pressed against hers. Her lips were on mine. There was a thought in the very back of my mind telling me I should stop, go home, but I couldn't listen to it. I couldn't control myself. I had to be there, with her. The door slammed closed behind us as I pushed her backwards into the house. She turned me and I slammed back against the hall table, knocking books to the floor. I couldn't breathe. The air in my lungs was growing stale, but I couldn't pull away from her. I was starved for her. My fingers wound through her long hair and ran over her soft body. She led me into her bedroom as her hands found the hem of my shirt. Her fingers felt like fire as they grazed the bare skin above my jeans. She pulled my shirt over my head and then quickly removed her own. She was soft and warm, and it knocked the breath out of me.

Just as we collapsed onto the bed, her dog barked at something outside. We jumped apart, not speaking; the spell we were under broken in an instant. We pulled our shirts back on and rushed out of the bedroom. We made it to the entryway just in time for there to be a quick knock on the door before Ben opened it and walked in.

"Ami, have you seen– " he called out before seeing us standing there. "Oh, there you are. I was worried about you." He walked towards me and hugged me. "Are you okay?"

If he suspected anything had happened, he didn't show it. He looked genuinely relieved to find me safe with his best friend. Mags followed him into the house, and from the look on her face, she wasn't so easily fooled. I caught sight of myself in the hall mirror and could see why. My hair was tousled, my lips swollen, my face red. I looked guilty.

"Yah, I'm fine. Sorry I didn't tell you that I was going out. I just needed some air and I wanted to apologize to Ami for snapping at her the other day."

He kissed my swollen lips, grinned and said, "Thank you," so sincerely that the guilt almost cracked me in half.

"We just finished making dinner. Join us?" Ben asked. Without waiting for Ami to answer, he put his arm around her and led her out of the house.

She looked at me, eyebrows raised in concern, and I started to follow behind them.

"We'll be right there!" Mags called, grabbing my hand and holding me back. She turned on me. "What are you doing?"

"Be quiet," I said through my teeth. "They'll hear you."

She looked over my shoulder and waited for Ben and Ami to round the corner. "They're gone. Now, tell me what you think you're doing?"

I had always told Mags everything, but I could see the disappointment and confusion in her eyes, and I knew I couldn't tell her this. "I don't know what you're talking about," was all I could think to say.

"Oh, come on, Josephine!"

Josephine.

"What!? I didn't do anything."

"Look at you!" She gestured towards me, looking me up and down. "You think I can't see what you've been doing over here? What if Ben could see, too? This isn't fair to him and it's not good for you. It's not *you*." She spun away from me, but not quickly enough to hide the tears in her eyes.

"You don't know me! You did once, but not anymore. I am not the same."

She turned back towards me, taking my hands, "You *are* the same. I *do* know you. I see you. I see that you need help. Let me help you."

I ripped my hands from hers. "Help me? Really? You expect me to believe this is all about *me*? You think I couldn't see what you were doing over there with Ben?"

"You can't be serious. I'm here for you, Jo. I am here for *you*."

I knew she was telling the truth, and the magnitude of what I'd done crashed into me. I sat down on the sofa, defeated, and let my head fall into my hands. "You're right." My voice cracked. "I know. What's wrong with me?"

Mags sat down, put her arm around me and rested her head on my shoulder, squeezing me against her.

"I love Ben, I do. But the sight of him, when he touches me. It makes me want to crawl out of my skin," I admitted.

"What exactly is going on with this Ami woman?" she whispered.

"Nothing, not really, not yet. I don't know. The moment we met, she knocked the wind out of me, and I have been struggling to get it back ever since. I've been trying to stay away, to keep her away but…" I struggled to find the right words to explain how I was feeling. "I have felt… dead, and today, she made me feel alive." I sighed. "This was the first time anything like this has happened, I swear." I looked at my sister then, expecting disappointment, and saw only sympathy.

"You can't let it happen again," she said, looking me straight in the eye. "You've got something good here. Ben loves you, and you need that more than ever. Let him take care of you. Let me take care of you."

Hand in hand, we hurried back to the house. As we passed the fairy tree, I watched to see if Mags would notice it, if she would feel the pull of it as I did, but she walked on seemingly unfazed. My hand slipped from hers as I turned to look at it in the dark.

CHAPTER 18

Despite everything, dinner went smoothly. Somehow, Ami and I were able to put aside what had happened between us to get through the evening. The easiest way to do that was to avoid each other as much as possible. So, Ami spent most of the night with Ben, helping him serve dinner, helping him clean up, avoiding me, and I kept close to Mags. Who, thankfully, had been doing a good job at keeping what she saw to herself.

After we finished eating, Mags and I went outside and settled in on the porch swing Ben had hung for me shortly after I first arrived. We swung back and forth, bundled under blankets, my head on her shoulder, while she told me about the foster family that had taken her in during the investigation. Their names were Matt and Annie Jenkins—a kind, elderly couple who had treated her well. They never had kids of their own and they didn't have any other foster kids with them at the time, so she had her own room on the second floor of their large house. During that time, she was able to continue her ballet lessons at the studio but had enrolled in a public school in the Jenkins' neighbourhood. They offered to keep her in our old school, but she begged them to let her switch. She didn't want to hear the gossip about our family floating down the halls after her.

"How'd you get them to let you come here to stay with us? What about school now?" I asked. We were technically only a few months away from graduation, but I hadn't even considered school since arriving in Halliswell. Besides, there were rules against pregnant girls attending school. But I wasn't pregnant anymore.

"When Ben was finally able to call me, he told me you weren't doing well." She squeezed my hand and kept rocking the swing. "I knew it. I could *feel* it. Things were hard for me too, of course they were. But there was a dark lump in my chest that wouldn't go away, and I just knew it was you. So, I ran away."

"You did what? How did you get all the way here?" I imagined her hitchhiking along the cold, dark coastal roads. I thought of her walking along the highway where three women had recently gone missing.

"I went straight to the bus station before they

even knew I was missing. They might come looking for me, but I will fight it. I doubt they will though. I age out in a few months. It's hardly worth their time. As for school, Ben enrolled me in the one here and I start classes on Monday."

I swallowed against the lump in my throat and said, honestly, "I'm so glad you're here. I've missed you so much." I turned and hugged her tightly. She was always the only one who understood me, and I hoped, even though *I'd* changed, that hadn't. "Mags?"

"Hmmm?" she responded.

"I think there's something wrong with me," I whispered.

"What do you mean?"

"I see things sometimes. I hear things." They were words I had wanted to say out loud my whole life, but was too afraid she would see me differently. Now, after everything, I knew she wouldn't. She would understand and maybe she could help me.

"Oh, Jo, you've been through so much. You still need time to heal."

Just then, the door opened, and Ami stepped out onto the porch. She looked at us, uncertain, as if she was interrupting something.

"Goodnight," she said with a little wave as she started down the stairs.

I watched her go, but she didn't look back. When she turned the corner, Mags stood suddenly and ran after her.

"Wait!" I called. I considered following, but her legs were strong from dancing and there was no way I could catch up.

I didn't like the thought of them together, in the dark, where I couldn't see them, but she was gone for only a few minutes before she returned to the porch and sat down beside me as if nothing had happened.

"What did you say to her?" I asked, the annoyance in my voice obvious.

"I just let her know that what happened was a mistake, and it wouldn't be happening again. She agreed."

"She did?" Obviously, she was right, but it stung hearing it from Mags's mouth.

"Yah. She's Ben's best friend. She feels terrible about it, and agrees the best thing would be to try to stay away from you as much as possible." She piled the blankets on us once more.

She was right, though the thought of not seeing Ami again settled deep in the pit of my stomach. I did not love it, but I settled against my sister and told myself she was all I needed.

That night, something roused me from a deep and comfortable sleep. It was still dark, the light of morning not even stirring the edges of the near complete darkness that fell over Halliswell at night. I remained in bed a while longer, hoping to fall back asleep, and though I was not quite able to bring myself to cuddle up to Ben, I laid close next to him, letting his warmth and closeness comfort me. It was nice being there next to him, and again I felt guilty for how I had treated him since coming home from the hospital.

A ring of pointless thoughts circled around my mind, and whenever I tried to control them, they eluded me—always darting just out of reach. Eventually, I decided it was useless. Careful not to wake Ben, I got out of bed, padded to the door, and closed it softly behind me.

The hall, usually dark, was illuminated by a dull light spilling from under the door of the nursery. Someone was in there. Ben was asleep, so it had to be Mags. What the hell did she think she was doing? I stormed to the door and threw it open, only to find that not only was the room empty, but it was just as I had left it. The walls were painted in the calming yellow I had chosen, and other than the white crib in the center and the small dresser in the corner, the room was completely bare.

The near empty room mirrored the near emptiness of myself, and the sight of it was like a punch in the stomach. Tears filled my eyes, and I bit my lip to keep them from falling. Just as I was about to turn the light off, something caught my eye. A small pop of blue. Something *was* different. It wasn't exactly as I had left it. There was a blanket in the crib I had never seen before. A soft blue one. We hadn't had the chance to buy very much for the baby, and I knew for sure that I hadn't gotten a blue blanket. Where had it come from?

Curious, I approached the crib. The blanket was old, worn and slightly dirty around the edges. Before I could even wonder where it had come from, I noticed there was something beneath the blanket and I gasped. It looked like a small body below the fabric though it was misshapen and bumpy. Inhuman. I closed my eyes tight against the vision of what my baby would have looked like being born twenty four weeks early and reminded myself that there was no way he could be here. I wanted to run. I wanted to pretend I hadn't come in here at all, but I knew I couldn't walk away without knowing for sure. So, I pulled the blanket back slowly, only to reveal a bundle of sticks hidden beneath. Looking closer, they weren't just sticks; they had been tied together with a rough twine to mimic the shape of a person about the size of an infant. Two arms. Two legs.

All at once, I knew exactly what had happened. I couldn't help but scream and scream. It didn't take long for both Ben and Mags to rush into the room. Ben took me in his arms immediately and squeezed me tight. The screaming stopped, but I couldn't stop shaking.

"Oh my god," Mags said, turning away from the crib when she saw what it contained.

"What is that?" said Ben, trying to get a better look without letting me go.

"They took him," I whispered. It was so clear

now. Why hadn't I seen it before? Everything had been going fine. I knew I didn't do anything wrong.

"Who took who? Jo, what are you talking about?" Ben asked, his voice fuzzy and far away.

"The fairies," Mags and I whispered at the same time. She'd grown up with the same stories I did. She knew what it meant when a baby was replaced with something else.

"The fairies, right," Ben said, releasing me and massaging his temples. "I'm sick of hearing about these damned fairies!"

He never understood why our nan told us such scary stories when we were only children, but what he didn't know was that these stories were ingrained in us and in our culture. They weren't just scary stories to be told around a fire; they were real.

"It's true!" I cried. "Our baby is alive somewhere. They took him and tried to replace him with this... thing to trick us!" I grabbed the stick figure from the crib and smashed it onto the floor.

Both Mags and Ben flinched away as the splintered pieces of wood scattered around the room.

"Jo, those were just stories. They aren't true," Ben said, stepping towards me with his hands out in front of him as if I were a wild animal he was trying not to spook.

"Then how do you explain this?" I pointed at the pile of broken sticks. "Did you put it there?" I pointed at Mags. She didn't answer. I turned to Ben,

"Did you?" I asked him.

"Of course not. No one's been in here since it happened," Ben answered.

It.

"Then how did it get here, if it wasn't either of you?"

Neither of them could answer, and by the looks on their faces, I could tell what they really thought: that I had done it. They thought I had gathered all of these sticks; made sure they were all the right size. They thought I'd tied them together with twine to imitate the baby I lost. They thought I came in here and put it under the blanket, and then proceeded to scream.

I stormed from the room, and when Mags tried following me, I turned on her. "You, of all people, should understand," I growled, before entering my own room and locking the door behind me.

And there we were again, her on one side of the door, me on the other; so close to each other, but at the same time, not at all.

CHAPTER 19

IN THE COMPLETE dark of early morning, the house lived around me. The creaks and groans and drips filled the silence left behind by the events of that night. The cold wood of the door held me back gently, caressing my face, as the slow steady breaths of the house calmed me when I slowed my own to meet them.

Despite their whispering, I could still hear Ben and Mags's muffled voices rise up the stairs, from where they had retreated to talk about me and what they thought had happened. They thought I was crazy, and they believed they understood what was happening, but they didn't. At times, Ben's voice grew louder, raised in fear or anger, but the words remained distorted and unintelligible, and by the time they reached me, they were nothing at all.

It wasn't long until a single set of footsteps ascended the stairs and then paused outside my door. Even before she called my name softly, I knew it was my sister; I could feel her there, so close to me. My breath hitched in my chest when her fingertips slipped under the door, barely missing my own. I curled my fingers away from hers, the harsh reminder hurling me through the dark, right back to my old bedroom, to which I'd sworn never to return. A hard lump formed in my throat, tears stung behind my closed eyes, and I bit my lip to keep myself from crying out. Without a response from me, she was forced to pull her hand away and continue down the hall, leaving me alone again.

The sound of her closing door broke the silence around me, and I released the shaky breath from my burning lungs. It destroyed me to hide from Mags when my entire self longed to reach out to her. But more than I needed the comfort of her, I needed her to leave me tonight.

I wiped the tears from my cheeks with the palms of my hands and stayed where I was with my ear against the door until the inhale and the exhale of the house became steady and quiet again, and I knew that it and everyone in it was asleep.

I slipped out the door and padded down the hall, my bare feet hardly making a sound against the worn wood of the old floor. Pausing outside Mags's door, I listened for any sign of her being awake, but was met with only a thick silence. I continued down the hall and snuck into the nursery, not turning the light on until the door was closed tight behind me. Plunged into darkness again, my hand felt along the wall for the light switch until I found it and immersed the room in a golden light. I was both surprised and grateful for what I saw. The baby remained broken into pieces and scattered across the floor. Neither Ben nor Mags had returned to clean it up.

I dropped to my knees and combed the floor, gathering every piece of broken stick—every splinter of wood I could find—knowing that I needed to find them all; knowing it would need to be complete if there were to be any chance of it working.

Once I had them all, I went to work putting the baby back together. Despite the chill in the room, sweat prickled under my arms and along the back of my neck. I pulled the hair away from my face and tied it back with an elastic from around my wrist, took a deep breath, and continued rebuilding what had been broken. Because its body was so badly damaged, I was forced to weave many of the pieces together with my shaking fingers to get them to stay in place, but once the twine was tied tight, it looked almost perfect. Two arms. Two legs.

I'm so sorry I hurt you. Failed you.

I stroked my fingers over the baby's reknitted body and as I did, an abhorrent wrongness emanated from it, burrowing deep into the pit of my stomach and flushing me with sick. Bile rose up into my throat and the sweat that had only begun to bead upon my skin now ran in rivers. Inside, my body burned, but my skin felt cool to the touch. I wanted so badly to lay my head down on the cool wood floor next to the baby.

It was obvious what was happening, what was wrong. There was a piece missing and I needed to find it, or I wouldn't be able to go on.

Using all my strength, I crawled around the room on my hands and knees, checking every inch, but it was nowhere. Hopeless, shaking with fever and about to give up, I noticed the crib standing alone in the middle of the room, sharp and clear against the haze and shadows that had begun to creep into the edges of my vision and I knew. I laid down on my back, pushed myself underneath it and sure enough, there it was. A small stick had gotten wedged underneath. I pulled it loose and wove it into the bundle. Instantly, the feeling of hot sick that had invaded my body receded.

It was complete.

With the baby cradled in my arms, I leaned against the wall, rocking it back and forth gently, catching my breath and relishing the hope that this nightmare could finally be over. I squeezed it to my chest, not minding at all when the sharp ends of the sticks pushed hard into my skin. Feeling something, anything but the shame and the loss that had overwhelmed me for too long was welcome.

When I calmed down a little, I was able to see it all from a different perspective. This meant losing the baby hadn't been my fault. Now, I knew the truth.

Nan said that when a Fae child became ill or died, the Fae replaced it with a healthy one from our world. In place of the stolen baby, they'd leave their own sick child, or, if their child had already died, another object. Such as, a bundle of sticks bewitched to look like a baby. In our case, because no one had gone into the nursery for a while, the charm had worn off, revealing the truth.

My baby was alive somewhere.

It wasn't my fault. I hadn't done anything wrong, but I had the chance to make it right. I could get him back.

The sky outside the window turned from black to a deep blue as dawn approached. I was running out of time. Careful not to make a sound that might wake Mags, I carried the baby from the nursery. Downstairs, Ben, covered with a thin blanket, was deep asleep on the couch and I paused at the door for just a moment, to be sure he wouldn't wake up at my presence.

In the kitchen, I laid the baby on the counter next to the stove, took a carton of eggs from the fridge, and cracked three of them into the sink. The eggs, free from their shells, ran towards the drain, so slow it was almost hypnotising. When they reached it, I watched them as they slipped out of sight, as though they had never been there at all. Then, I filled each half shell with water and leaned them against each other in the bottom of a small pot.

Through the window over the sink, the sky lightened further, turning from deep blue to a light grey. The sun would be up soon, which meant Ben and Mags would also be up soon. I had to hurry.

I turned the knob on the stove and heard the familiar hiss of gas being released. It wasn't often that I had to light the stove on my own, so it took a few tries, but finally there was a whoosh. Frightened, I jumped back, but the ball of fire vanished as quickly as it appeared, leaving behind a small flame barely licking the bottom of the pot. Expecting to hear stirs from within the rest of the house, I held my breath until my chest burned, but the house remained silent.

The baby lay still next to the stove where I'd placed it, unmoving under my unwavering stare. Seconds ticked by, and then minutes, but nothing happened.

It was supposed to be simple—to get the fairy to reveal itself and to force it to return the stolen baby, all I had to do was make it laugh. I had to do something so completely ludicrous, like boiling water in eggshells, that it would be unable to resist telling me so. It was supposed to appear before me, scoffing. Instead, only the baby remained, silent, still, and wooden.

Tears of frustration and disappointment filled my

eyes, threatening to spill over. I pressed the palms of my hands to them to get them to stop. I had been so sure my plan would work. Anger and humiliation built up inside me. Without thinking, I picked up the pot and threw it forcefully into the sink, which almost instantly stirred the simultaneous sounds of Ben moving on the couch and the floor creaking above me. I hated myself for being so careless with my anger.

I had to hide the baby before they could see what I'd done; before they had a reason to think I was even more crazy than they already did. With only seconds to decide what to do, I took the baby from the counter and shoved it under the sink next to the cleaning supplies and then covered it with old newspapers.

The coffee was set up and ready to brew as it was every morning, so I flicked the switch to turn it on just in time for Ben to rush into the kitchen, looking even more dishevelled than he normally did.

"Jo, are you okay?" he asked, looking around the room for the source of the sound that had woken him so suddenly.

"Yeah, I'm so sorry I woke you up," I said, pushing the dark feelings down where he couldn't see them. "I was trying to make breakfast. I was going to boil eggs the way you showed me, but I knocked the pot into the sink, and the eggs broke."

My quick lie worked. He didn't question it at all.

"That's okay," he answered, absentmindedly

looking at his watch. Looking anywhere but me. "I'm going to be late for work anyways, so I'll probably just take a coffee and go."

He worked at a store called Normann's Books, though people went there to buy everything from books to car parts to packs of gum. The store was lined with floor to ceiling bookshelves, but tucked in between the rows of books, you could easily find a pair of faded blue jeans that needed a new home, or a set of hammers no one could find a use for. Mr. Normann loved books and believed everyone should have access to them, but not everyone in town could afford the luxury; so, years ago, he started to trade items for books and the items traded would be put on the shelves for sale if he had no use for them himself, which he usually didn't.

The coffee finished brewing and I hurried to pour Ben a cup, wanting him to leave the house just as badly as he wanted to leave it.

"Thank you," he said, taking the mug from me.

Everything was so formal. Polite. Sad.

"About last night," he started shifting awkwardly from one foot to the other. "I guess I don't really know what to say, but I'm sorry I upset you. I'm not sure how those sticks got there, but I promise it wasn't me. I don't know what happened. I can't explain it."

He still struggled to make eye contact with me, and I knew what he was getting at. He still thought it was me.

I wasn't worried though, because soon, I would prove to them it hadn't been me either, and that I wasn't crazy.

"It's okay, I understand," I said, to appease him.

He put his coffee down and stepped towards me and I willed myself not to step back away from him. He put his arms around me and kissed me on the cheek before saying, "I gotta go." And then he was gone.

There wasn't enough time to carry out the second part of my plan before Mags came downstairs, so I sat down on the couch and waited patiently. As soon as I had the chance, I would try again.

CHAPTER 20

MAGS DANCED IN through the front door after spending all morning using the porch balustrade as a barre for her ballet exercises—effectively avoiding me and keeping an eye on me at the same time. It wasn't odd; she did spend most mornings out there. But when she came downstairs just moments after Ben left for work, I expected her to start in on me about what had happened last night. She only gave my hand a gentle squeeze before taking a cup of coffee outside with her.

First position. Second position. Third. Fourth. Fifth.

"It's really warming up out there," she said, smoothing back a few tendrils of dark damp hair that had escaped her tight bun. "Why don't we go down to the beach for a picnic? It would be good to get out of the house."

"Sure, that sounds great," I said from the couch, where I had sat all morning. Waiting.

"Are you okay?" she finally asked, leaning against the door frame. "I'm sorry about last night. I don't really understand what happened."

"Yeah, I don't know either. I didn't do it," I said, looking up at her.

"I know," she said, pushing off from where she leaned to sit with me on the couch. "And you're right, I should understand. I know what this looks like. But, I just never really bought into the stories Nan told the way you did. It was more *your* thing with her, and I'm just having a hard time believing it now. But I do believe that you didn't do it."

Her eyes were still full of concern and her smile only reached her lips, as she bounced off to the kitchen to make sandwiches to bring with us down to the beach.

As soon as she was out of sight, I called out, "I'm going for a walk!" and left before she had the chance to say anything or come after me. I hurried down the road towards Ami's house.

The tree.

Her front door opened as soon as I knocked, almost as though she was waiting for something. For me. Her demeanour was a stark contrast to what it had been when I found myself at her door the day before. Then, she was fiery and full of emotion, but today she was resigned. From the way she looked at me, it was clear she had accepted it. She had accepted there was something between us that couldn't be ignored. We either had to act on it, which definitely wasn't an option, or just accept we could only ever be friends. And though the truth was exhausting, she held the door open and let me inside.

She opened her mouth to speak, but I cut her off before she could say anything. "We are going down to the beach for a picnic, wanna come?"

I didn't want to talk about it. I just wanted to be around her, and I needed a buffer between me and my sister.

She stared at me; her brown eyes steady. "I don't think it's a good idea to spend so much time with you anymore. Ben's my friend, my best friend, and this isn't fair to him."

"Please," I begged. "I had a really bad night, and I know this is hard and confusing, but I really need a friend. Just friends?"

After a moment she sighed and simply said, "Okay."

I helped her pack a lunch and we worked together in a comfortable silence I was grateful for. It was nice not having someone ask me how I was all the time. It was nice not having someone constantly watching me, waiting for me to snap. We packed a few sandwiches, apples and a big bottle of water into a backpack, along with a small blanket, and set out towards my house.

The tree.

We walked in the same comfortable silence that we had worked in before. I reached out and took her hand and was surprised when, despite what she'd just said, she didn't pull away. It felt right, but when we rounded the corner and my house came into view, Mags stood on the porch, waiting. At the sight of her, Ami dropped my hand and stepped slightly away from me. She stayed behind as I ran ahead to meet Mags.

"Please, just trust me," I said. The disappointment in her eyes was obvious. As was, I'm sure, the desperation in mine. "I need her here."

She hesitated, but could never say no to me, not really, and as her eyes flicked between the two of us, she eventually nodded. "Fine. Let's go. I'm assuming you know the way?" she called to Ami, as if the conversation between them last night hadn't happened at all.

Our house sat slightly back from a cliff edge and the waves pounded against the water below though the weather was mild, the wind barely blowing for once. It was a short, but surprisingly tough hike down to the water's edge. The trail was rocky, steep, and unkempt. I struggled more than I thought I would, more than the others, though I was determined not to show it. They were both strong, healthy women, while I was weak and used up. It was humiliating.

Soon enough, we came to a small bay tucked

into the side of the cliff. It was breathtaking. I'd always loved the ocean and I was grateful that my journey hadn't taken me inland. The water stretched out as far as I could see; there was no end to it though I knew a series a of islands lay just beyond the horizon. They were something tangible and tucked just out of sight. But just because I couldn't see them, it didn't mean they didn't exist.

The air was still cool, but the sun shone brightly and unobstructed, reflecting off the water, illuminating the beach and warming the rocks. We laid out our blankets, then leaned back to bask in the sun on what had to be the first really nice day I had seen since moving to Halliswell. It was cathartic , melting away the fear and the shame that had been hovering around my edges all morning. All year. For just a little while, I was able to relax, forget and enjoy myself.

I didn't have to look to know my hand was close to Ami's. I could feel the heat of her body beside me. Without hesitation, I placed my hand on hers. Again, I expected her to flinch away, but her fingers relaxed beneath mine. Mags turned towards us slightly and I knew she had seen, but for some reason she kept quiet. I figured that I would hear about it later, but for now we just sat that way for a long time, relaxing and being together.

As the sun moved higher in the sky, we set out our food and ate lunch. Between the three of us, we'd brought enough to feed a large family.

Sandwiches on freshly baked bread with roast beef and spicy mustard; crisp veggies and a soft, sharp cheese; a bag of salty chips, and chocolate chip cookies Mags had made the day before. It was perfect.

We chatted about nothing in particular, and laughed at each other's jokes. It was easy being together. The absence of Ben meant I could fully be myself, as I was *now*. He was always looking for the girl he met before, the one he loved first. I thought again back to the time he said he was responsible for me. He never said it or anything like it again, but the longing was there, unmistakable in his eyes. When I was with him, I had to be careful. I had to calculate the amount of space I took up and make sure it added up properly, allowing enough room for both versions of me. With Ami, there was only one version of me, because she didn't know me before. And with Mags, I knew it didn't matter. She would always take me as I was. So, without the weight of my former self, I could breathe.

After such a tranquil day, we were reluctant to go home, but Ben would be back from work soon and he'd wonder where we were. So, we packed everything up and set off.

A few minutes later, once again struggling up the path, I realised I'd left my sunglasses on the beach and told them to go ahead; I would catch up.

"We'll come with you," they said in almost perfect unison.

"I'm capable of going by myself," I said, smiling at their protectiveness. "Really, Ben will be home any minute and he'll worry if we aren't there. You go ahead and meet him, and I will be right behind you."

They looked at me, planting their feet firmly on the ground to become a united front. Taking in my feeble appearance, it was clear they believed I couldn't do it, that I wasn't able to do something as simple as walk on my own.

"I am not an invalid!" I snapped. "I don't need you following me around all the time!" The words poured from my mouth, uncontrolled.

Ami put her hands up in front of her, in apparent surrender. "Okay, okay. I'm sorry. You're right," she said, while Mags stood silently beside her, the hurt plain on her face. "We'll meet you at the house."

As quickly as the anger rose, it subsided, leaving behind the debris of their pain and shock. "Okay, see you in a few," I said with a wave over my shoulder as I skipped away.

When I stepped through the trees again and onto the beach, the scene was a lot different than the one I was expecting. A lot different than it had been only moments before. The clear blue sky was replaced with dark clouds, completely blocking the sun and casting the once warm beach in cold and shadows. The wind howled and the waves hit the shore with furious intensity.

I combed the beach looking for my glasses, but they were nowhere to be found. With each wave, the water grew higher and higher, reaching towards me, calling out to me. I told myself that it was only the tide coming in. I hadn't been in town long, but even *I* knew that the timing wasn't right. I tried to ignore it, but it wound its way around my ankles. I expected the frigid chill to shock my bare skin, but instead it was warm and inviting.

I stepped towards it, into it. Another step. It beckoned to me. Tugged. The sky darkened further, and I felt so tired, like I could sleep. I was sure that, if I were to lay down, the water would engulf me and carry me away. Then, maybe, I wouldn't be so tired anymore.

I was about to take another step when I heard Mags calling my name. The water released its grip on me and retreated—sucked back to where it belonged.

"Coming!" I called, forgetting to be annoyed that she hadn't listened to me.

I turned and walked off the beach. As I approached the trail, I looked back over my shoulder. The sun was still beaming as it had been, and when I looked at the beach, everything was normal. No clouds, no waves.

"What are you doing? What took you so long?" Ami asked.

"I couldn't find my glasses," I said.

"You sure looked for them for a long time," Mags

said, her eyes wide with unease.

"We got all the way to the house and waited, but got worried, so we came looking for you," Ami said.

"What do you mean?" I asked, confused. "I wasn't gone *that* long."

"We were waiting for at least thirty minutes," Mags said, looking down at her watch.

I stepped back from her, struck hard by the realization that it had happened again. There was no way I had been on the beach for more than just a few minutes. Was I truly losing track of time? Or was it being taken from me?

"I'm sorry; I don't know what happened," I said, feeling the weight of Ami's gaze bore into me. No one could know what I saw at the beach, or that I was losing time. They wouldn't understand. They would think I was losing my mind. So, I put on a big smile and forged ahead with a forced casualness I hoped they didn't notice. "Well, better get back before Ben worries."

The short walk back to the house was silent. No one spoke. No one had to. I knew what they were thinking. When we got to the house, Ben's truck was parked in the drive. I half expected him to come rushing out the door to fuss over where I'd been. Instead, he was on the phone when we walked through the door. When he saw us, he jumped up and said, "Oh, here she is." He cupped his hand over the receiver. "Jo, it's for you."

There was a dismal excitement vibrating in the

space around him and his eyes were full of apprehension. I couldn't imagine who he could possibly be talking to. Who would want to talk to *me*. Everyone I knew was in this room.

Mags watched me take the phone from him, a crease forming between her eyes. She could sense it too. Something wasn't right, and she was worried.

"Hello?" I asked in barely a whisper.

A woman on the other end responded, "Is this Miss Josephine Auclair?"

"Yes, it is," I said. "What is this about? Who are you?"

"My name is Nora Blake. I am calling on behalf of Richard Hanover, the attorney of Chris and Caoihme Auclair—your parents. He is handling their estate and affairs in the absence of any other living family except for yourself and your sister—" She broke off and I could hear the rustling of papers on the other end. "A Miss Magalie Auclair who according to our records has been missing from her foster home for a few weeks. Would you happen to know anything about that? Do you know where she is?"

I looked up at Mags who looked even more confused than I felt. "No, I haven't seen her," I said, fully aware that my level of concern did not match what it should be when being told your sister is missing, but I just couldn't fake it. What was this really about? Why would a lawyer be calling me? Maybe with Daddy dead and our mother locked up, possibly for good, we were going to get some money. I looked around the room with its dull curtains and outdated furniture. I don't think we *needed* money but it would sure be nice.

"Mmhmm," Nora responded, clearly not buying it. "Look, we've had a call from Riverview Hospital about your mother."

My heart stopped. "What about her?" I asked, my voice steady and cold.

"I'm sorry to say, she's not doing well there, and they are suggesting she be transferred to their high security wing. We need you to meet with the doctor as well as Mr. Hanover, to make some decisions about her care and to sign some papers." She spoke completely matter-of-factly.

"No, I can't do that," was all I said in response to the actual nightmare presented to me.

"I'm sorry, Miss Auclair, but this is something that just needs to be taken care of." Her tone implied she wasn't really sorry at all. "It says here that you are under the care of a Mr. Benjamin Ellis until the day of your eighteenth birthday on June nineteenth. He has given his consent for you to come here and help make these decisions under his supervision. Really it's not ideal, but the difference of a few months is negligible and we need this done now."

"Okay, okay. I will be there as soon as I can," I said, then hung up.

I stood with my back to Ben and the others for a

while, composing myself and planning what I was going to say, and do. Finally, I turned to face them, and, with a false cheerfulness, filled them in.

Though I did know that my mother was alive, I had planned to never see her again. Yet, here I was, finding myself actually *wanting* to go. I needed closure. I needed to see her, and I needed to know that she understood what she did to me. Facing her and saying goodbye could close the door on this chapter forever. I could finally get the fresh start I so longed for.

"Absolutely not," Mags said, stepping between Ben and me after I relayed to them what the woman on the phone had said. "I don't want you anywhere near her after what she did to you."

"I have to do this. I have to face her." I looked Mags in the eye, unwavering. She had to see how important it was to me. "I need this. Please."

"We can all go. We can all take care of her. " Ami stepped forward to put her arm around me . "This might actually be good for her," she said to Mags , with a look that said more than just what her words conveyed. Mags was the only one who truly understood my relationship with our mother, and she knew what this would do to me. Somehow Ami understood what it would do *for* me.

We all looked at Ben, waiting for his response. I expected him to say no, but he looked relieved, almost. Happy to not have to go through this alone with me.

"Okay," he said. "Let's all go. If it's really that important to you."

It was more important than he could know.

CHAPTER 21

WE DROVE THE entire way in near silence. For four hours, the only sounds were the radio, which was turned down so low I could hardly tell which song was playing, the windshield wipers going at full speed, and Mags's soft snore from the back seat where she slept propped up against Ben's shoulder. Again, the sight of them together, turned my stomach and I looked away.

I'd told her that she should stay behind. That they were looking for her and it wasn't safe for her to come to the hospital with us, but she wouldn't listen. She wouldn't let me face our mother without her; even if that meant she was caught and sent back into the system. She promised that if it happened she would run away again and again. It wasn't worth the risk for me, but she'd gotten into the back seat of the car anyway and refused to move.

Up front, next to Ami, I was too nervous to say anything. With every kilometer that passed, the hole in my stomach grew bigger and bigger, until it was so big I worried it would swallow me up altogether.

The hospital was located on a stretch of the Lougheed highway that ran through Coquitlam. The immense building came into view gradually, offering glimpses of red brick and white trim through the dappling of the trees. When we finally saw the whole place, it had an ominous air. Though the grounds were beautifully manicured and the hospital itself was magnificent, the large colonnaded entrance felt menacing.

Ami turned down the driveway marked with a sign that said, "Riverview Hospital" which took us around to the back of the building. Without looking into the backseat, I knew Mags had woken up; her reflection stared back at me from the side view mirror. Our gazes held steady, but we remained quiet.

We parked in the spot closest to the building, the visitor parking eerily empty, but none of us moved to open our doors. The rain beat hard against the car, and without the wipers on, the scene before us was completely obscured. I looked out the window at the warped hospital and dreaded going in.

I was utterly terrified to see my mother again. My entire body shook as I questioned what I was doing there at all. But, just when I thought I couldn't do it, just when I thought I would ask Ami to turn the car around, Mags's hand touched my shoulder, and her presence gave me the courage I needed. I didn't have to do it alone.

Too late.

"All right, let's go," I said, abruptly reaching for the door. Before I could open it, Ami's hand grabbed mine.

"Do you want me to come with you, or do you want me to wait here?" she asked.

She would have been happy with any answer, and I knew she would support me no matter what I decided, but I could see that she wanted to be there with me, for me.

"Please come," I responded with a reassuring smile, squeezing her hand tight within my own.

Mags started to protest from the back, but I turned to look at her, and whatever she saw in my face made her stop whatever she was going to say.

"I think the more people who are here to help the better," Ben said in a flat voice from the back as he opened his door and stepped out into the rain.

Was he mad at me? He had hardly said a word on the drive, but I couldn't think of anything I'd done to upset him. I wouldn't worry about that now though. I had to focus on what I'd come here to do.

We rushed through the rain to the entrance with our jackets over our heads and entered into a small foyer and waiting area, furnished with the type of uncomfortable chairs that inhabited all doctor's offices. A large counter lined one wall. Next to it, a locked door guarded the rest of the hospital. Was it meant to keep people in or out?

Mags went ahead, taking charge of the situation like she always did.

"We're here to see our mother, Caoimhe Auclair," she told the nurse through a hole in the glass.

The nurse checked a clipboard, her polished red nail trailing down the list. "Of course," she said in a flat voice. "Before you see her, Dr. Hayes would like to speak with you." She handed another clipboard through an opening at the bottom of the partition. "Please fill this out so I can sign each of you in as visitors. And if any of you have a purse, please put it in the drawer below so I can check it."

We opened the large drawer, placed our bags inside, and then she pulled the drawer open from her side to take our bags out. She checked each of them thoroughly, pulling out every item. After finding only the normal things—wallets, keys, lipsticks—she pulled the lining out of each one and inspected the stitching, looking for places to hide things. Finally she put the purses back in the drawer and returned them to us.

"If you have anything in your pockets, it's best to tell me now," she said. We pulled our pockets inside out so she could see that they were empty. When she was satisfied, she slipped the visitor badges through the opening. "Stick these to your shirt; if they aren't visible, you *will* be mistaken for a patient." She summoned another nurse to show us to the doctor's private office, and pushed a button to open the locked door.

The halls of the hospital had probably once been painted a bright white but were now a dull yellow. Everything felt hushed, yet I thought I heard distant sounds. A laugh. A cry. A scream. I looked at the others to see if they could hear it too, but they seemed unfazed.

We walked on, through an endless labyrinth of closed doors and barred windows. I expected to see patients roaming the halls, or rocking back and forth in chairs, but there was no one. Where were they?

Finally, we stopped in front of a door with a name plate engraved with "Dr. Kent Hayes Ph.D, Psy.D". The nurse knocked once and then entered without waiting for a response from within. "The family of Mrs. Auclair is here, Dr. Hayes."

A deep male voice responded, "Thank you, Grace, show them in."

The nurse motioned for us to enter and then hurried down the corridor back in the direction we'd come. The office was brighter than I expected, with tall windows and freshly painted walls. An elderly man sat behind a large wood desk covered with various stacks of papers. He stood when we entered and came around to greet us.

"Miss Auclair." He shook my hand and then did the same to Mags. "And who is this?" he asked, looking at Ami and then Ben.

"This is our friend, Amita and this is Benjamin Ellis. My..." I didn't know what to call him. Everything felt so formal here and the word "boyfriend" was ridiculous. Plus, he wasn't here because he was my boyfriend. He was here because he was my..."guardian." I finished the sentence though the word tasted bad in my mouth.

Dr. Hayesshook Ami's hand first and then did the same to Ben. Then he turned back to Ami and said, "Unfortunately, I can only discuss a patient's care with members of their immediate family."

"Oh of course, I'll wait outside." She leaned in to whisper, "If you need me, I'll be right in the hall."

"I'll be okay."

Then I noticed that there was another man in the room I hadn't noticed before. He sat casually on a small leather sofa along the wall, one ankle resting on his knee. When we were done introducing ourselves to the doctor, he put down the folder he'd been leafing through, stood and walked towards us, his right hand outstretched. "And I am David Hanover, your family attorney." And we all took turns shaking his hand as well. When he came to Mags he said with a smirk, "I'm just gonna go ahead and pretend that I didn't see you here

Magalie. But I'm glad you're safe." Mags looked at me and I shrugged slightly. I thought for sure that a lawyer would turn her in, but then again, whose side was he on?

I sat in one of the empty chairs facing the desk and Mags sat down in the other while the lawyer took up his position on the sofa again. Having run out of places to sit, Ben stood awkwardly behind me with his hand on my shoulder as Dr. Hayes moved around the desk to his own chair.

"Well," he started, "the reason I asked you to come is because I wanted to inform you that I am recommending your mother be moved to our high security facility. To do so, I need both police involvement and the family's permission. I've already spoken with the police and they agree."

"High security? What do you mean?" Mags asked.

"It means that she'll be moved to a wing of the hospital with a higher guard-to-patient ratio. She will be in full lock down, and allowed very few guests." Mr Hanover answered before Dr. Hayes could. He leaned forward on the edge of the seat, his hands folded between his knees. "Technically, we don't need your permission. You are still a minor and can't actually make legal decisions but we find that in cases like this, it's usually best to involve the family members anyway."

"Why does she even need to be moved?" Mags asked.

I couldn't speak.

"Your mother has clearly been through a great deal of unresolved trauma in her life. Now, it's boiling over as you well know," Dr. Hayes answered. He glanced at me, but quickly looked away. "She's been violent with the nurses and the other patients, and has become increasingly difficult to manage. She tells horrible stories to our most delicate patients, sending them into complete fits."

"Stories like what?" I asked. I had to ask.

"Her favourites include one about a group of boys following a young girl into the woods, and another about a baby-snatching fairy."

"What did you say?" I looked at Mags. Her eyes were wide, but she remained looking forward, avoiding my gaze. Ben now put both hands on my shoulders and squeezed gently to let me know he was still there.

"They're only stories," Dr. Hayes began, putting his hands up to calm me.

"What did she say about the fairies?" I demanded and Ben stiffened behind me.

"Miss Auclair, I really don't think…"

"Tell me," I said with a force that surprised me. I wanted to yell at him. I wanted to pull him from his desk and scream at him, but this was not a safe place for an outburst. I might never get out.

"Josephine, calm down." Mags reached for my hand, but I pulled it away before she could take it.

Josephine.

I looked back at the doctor and waited until he relented.

"She said that when her babies were born…" He paused, clearly uncomfortable. "When you two were born, a fairy took one, switching the baby with one of their own—a sick fairy child."

All at once, I couldn't breathe. The air was sucked from my chest, from the entire room, from the whole world. My heart pounded against my ribs so hard I could hear it. Feel it slamming through my entire body.

Ben came around the chair to kneel before me. "You don't have to do this. You can go and I can do it."

I shook my head. *One of us.* My mother thought one of us was a changeling, and I didn't have to imagine which one. I struggled to be still, to appear calm.

"Look, all of our patients have their stories," he said. "They tell them to make sense of the things they've done and the things that have happened to them. That's what she's doing here. She knows what she did was wrong, but this story takes the accountability away from *her* and places it on something she couldn't control."

Taking something that happened to *me* and making it into something that happened to *her*.

"I want to see her," I said.

"I don't think that's a good idea. The trauma paired with the head injury…" Mr. Hanover shook his head and picked up some papers from the sofa beside him. He stood and placed them on the desk between Mags and I. "Now, if you could just sign these papers, we can get her transferred and you can go home. All of you."

"Mr. Hanover, we came all this way, and I want to see my mother. Dr. Hayes, please take me to her," I repeated myself, letting my tone make it clear I wasn't leaving this building otherwise.

He looked at me and knew I wasn't going to back down. "Very well, but I will warn you, Mr. Hanover is right, she is not the woman you remember."

"Good."

"Let's get these signed, and then we'll take you to her." He placed a black pen on the papers in front of us and we all signed them without reading them.

"All right, let's go," I said.

"Wait here a moment; I'll make sure she's ready." Dr. Hayes left the room and Mr. Hanover picked up the signed papers from the desk, put them in his briefcase and turned to us. "I'll be in touch soon. We are working out the details of your parents' estate. It's a bit more complicated since your mother is still alive and we don't know how long her current metal state will persist. Regardless, there is some money from your father's will that has been put into a trust for both of you to access on your eighteenth birthday. I'm sorry I couldn't have everything worked out before this meeting but getting your mother moved took precedent." He shook our hands again before leaving the room as well.

As soon as the door closed behind him, Ami opened it up again and stepped inside the office. She knew right away something was wrong, and she hurried towards me but stopped when Ben stepped closer to me and put his arm around my shoulder. It felt weirdly possessive. Was he jealous? Did he know? Instead of wrapping her arms around me like I knew she wanted to, she stood back a little. I wanted to lean in and lose myself in her, break down. I wanted to scream and cry, but I couldn't. Not yet. Not here. I focused on keeping myself still on the outside. Mags stood behind Ami, looking at me, her eyes worried. She knew what I knew.

"What happened?" Ami asked Mags, avoiding me and Ben completely. She sensed Ben's jealousy as well.

"They just want to move our mother to a more secure wing of the hospital, so we had to sign some papers," Mags said for me. "They're gonna take us to see her, and then we can go." Mags smiled and clapped her hands together in a gesture that was far too jaunty for the situation.

Just then, a different nurse opened the door and motioned for us to follow. The labyrinth continued deeper into the hospital, until she stopped in front of a door with a tiny window woven with wire. Through the glass, I could see only the same yellow walls that lined the halls. Using a ring heavy with keys, she unlocked the door and then turned to us.

"She might not talk to you. She might not remember you. She has good days and bad days, but we never know moment by moment how she's going to be."

She ushered us all into the room, not enforcing the "immediate family only" rule.

Ami was about to see my mother.

I was about to see her.

The room held only three pieces of furniture: a bedside table holding a plastic cup of water, a wooden chair, and in the middle, a small metal framed bed, to which my mother was strapped.

It was a shock to see her tied down much the same way I had been the last time she saw me.

Cuffs were fastened around her wrists and ankles, and although they were lined with fleece, her skin was ringed with dark bruises from struggling against them. Belts were strapped across her chest, her waist, and her knees to keep her still. She was completely incapacitated. Only her head was able to move, and it was turned towards the wall.

She looked so small. She had lost weight, her hair was thin, her skin loose.

I walked ahead of the others, and when her face came into view, I flinched, stunned. I thought back to the day in the hospital when I'd finally looked at my reflection and saw what a monster I had become. That same monster lay tied to the bed before me. Everyone had always said we looked alike, and it had never been more true.

I felt like I was going to be sick, so I clamped my hand over my mouth and turned away. Ami, Ben and Mags stood to the side and let me compose myself. They understood this was more for my benefit. Mags had nothing to say to her; she had decided that our mother was dead the moment she hit her over the head with the hammer.

When I had control of my stomach again, I pulled the chair up to the bed and sat down. The sound made her head turn in my direction. Her green eyes stared past me, through me, unseeing. I leaned in close, close enough to smell the stink from her unwashed body.

I wanted to say, "You are nothing to me. I hope you rot in here, awake just like this, forever." That's what I planned on saying, but in the moment, all I could say was, "Mama?"

She took in a breath, not quite a gasp, but a reaction. Her eyes met mine.

"Changeling!" she screamed, struggling. "Get away from me!"

A long wail poured from her open mouth, unending as she tried to arch up from the bed, straining against the straps that held her down. Mags pulled me away from her. Ben and Ami stood back in shock as she continued to scream, not knowing what to do. Nurses rushed in and injected something into her arm, almost instantly making her stiff body go slack. Her head lolled to the side, and she was quiet again.

"I think it's time for you all to leave," one of the nurses said as she guided us through the door.

Once back in the car, we sat unmoving as the rain continued to pour around us —the sound both muted and deafening. This time I sat in the back with Ben and Mags was up front with Ami. It felt forced and awkward and obvious.

"What does 'changeling' mean?" Ami asked, breaking the silence in the car.

I cringed at the sound of the word coming from her mouth. I'd hoped she hadn't heard it or would just ignore it.

"Um." I hesitated. "It means she believes that, when we were born, a fairy stole one of her healthy babies and replaced it with me, a sick fairy baby, a changeling."

Ami giggled for just a second and then slapped her hand over her mouth when she realised that neither of us were laughing. "I'm sorry, I shouldn't laugh, but… that's absurd!"

Ben squeezed my shoulder, "Yah, Jo, just forget about it okay. It doesn't mean anything."

I had been trying to hold it together. Especially with Ami there, I didn't want to lose it. I didn't want her to see me. Really *see* me. She had already seen enough. It was too much though. I couldn't do it anymore. I couldn't hold it in. The shadows moved in.

"It's not *absurd*; it's true! We are *twins*, we are supposed to be the same, but I was always different!" Mags turned in her seat to look back at me. "I heard the stories all my life; she never let me forget! I cried all the time as a baby. Nothing could stop me. No one could soothe me. I walked late. I didn't even speak until I was almost four years old! *Everyone* thought there was something wrong with me!" My breathing was ragged, and my throat raw from keeping it all in.

"Jo," Mags leaned back over the seat. "There's nothing wrong with you. There never has been." She cupped my face in her hands, trying to ease my panic.

Tears burned behind my eyelids, but I wouldn't let them fall. I pulled away from her, buckled up my seat belt, and kept my eyes open until they dried up.

It was a long, tense, uncomfortable drive. We arrived home around dinner time. I wasn't hungry so I walked straight into the house and went up to bed. Ami stayed and I hated the idea of them talking about me, but I hated the idea of staying down there even more. When they were done talking, Ben came upstairs and sat beside me on the bed. "I'm sorry that was so hard. I wanted so badly to know what to do and how to help you. I think I failed though. I'm sorry." He put his around me, and it was comforting in a way his touch hadn't been for a while. The pressure of his body against mine calmed me, but it wasn't enough. I needed more. I needed the entire length of him pressing into the entire length of me. I snuggled in closer to him and tilted my head up to kiss him, gently at first, but then more urgently. Now that I knew what I needed, I needed it right now. Not sex, but I would give it to him to get what I needed.

His breath hitched, and he wasn't able to mask the aching shock. I had hardly let him touch me since coming home from the hospital. He never complained, but I could see now how much it hurt him to keep his distance.

Desperate for the sensations within my body to stop, I hurried to undress him and then myself. We fell into bed and the weight of him comforted me immediately. His bare skin against mine heated me all the way through and calmed the buzzing in my nerves. When it was over, I held him hard against me and when he tried to pull away, I held him even tighter. Only when my breathing calmed did I finally release my grasp. He rolled to the side and gathered me into him. I'd pushed him away for so long that I forgot what it was like to be close to him.

Until now, I'd been under the belief that, if my baby wasn't in the world I didn't deserve to be happy. I couldn't even fathom happiness without him, but it was okay now. I was going to get him back. After seeing my mother, I knew I wasn't crazy. It didn't just happen to me; it happened to her too.

It was real. It was all real.

CHAPTER 22

THE FOLLOWING WEEK, Mags was to return to school to finish out the year and graduate. Though I found myself jealous of her leaving the house with purpose, I was also relieved I didn't have to go.

Mags, though, was excited. She flourished when presented with something new, and getting people to like her was never a challenge. She could walk into any room and walk back out with everyone following behind.

"Will you really be okay here without me?" she asked from across the table, as we ate breakfast.

"I'll be fine," I said. "I've been feeling a lot better. I know I scared you before, but I'm okay now, I promise."

The truth was, I needed her out of the house to carry out my plan without her eyes on me, without her constantly telling me what she thought.

"Are you sure that you don't want to come with me? You should finish school too; you're so close to graduating!"

"I can't imagine ever stepping foot into a school again. You know what it was like for me," I reminded her.

"This isn't Shaughnessy. No one here knows you. It might be a good way to make new friends."

Ah, there it was. It wasn't so much about graduating as it was about trying to get me away from Ami.

I watched her take small bites of her cereal and imagined I was her, getting ready for my first day of school without a care in the world. I picked up my own spoon and mirrored her movements. Small unhurried bites. Careful deliberate chewing.

Maybe it was *that* easy. Maybe, if I just acted a certain way, I could move easier through the world like she did.

Before leaving for work, Ben popped into the kitchen to say goodbye, and for the first time in a long time, I kissed him long enough for Mags to clear her throat behind us.

I laughed and he smiled down at me, happy to have me back. I was happy too, I really was, though I did have my own reasons.

Eager for them both to leave, I waved from the porch until they were out of sight and then I remained there watching the bend in the road, just in case they decided to turn back. When the road remained empty, I hurried back into the house to get started.

I was worried the baby wouldn't still be under the sink where I'd hidden it, but when I opened the cupboard and pulled the newspapers away, there it was, exactly where I had left it only a few days ago. Relieved, I pulled it from its hiding place and checked it over. When I was certain all the pieces were there, I zipped it into my backpack along with the newspapers and a pack of matches before heading out the door.

At the beach, with the morning sun low in the trees casting shadows over the calm water, I paused for a moment to absorb the silent tranquility of the bay.

The perimeter of the beach, where the rocks gave way to forest, was scattered with small logs and sticks washed ashore. I gathered them together and stacked them inside a circle of rocks left behind from an old beach fire, and stuffed newspapers between the gaps in the wood. When I lit a match and held it to the paper, the flames consumed it quickly, burning away the advertisements—including one for Normann's. I continued to light the paper from all sides until the wood caught, and the heat of the flames reached out to warm my face.

When the fire was going strong, I pulled the baby from the bag and faced it.

This was it. When this baby died, the delicate

balance between the fairy world and ours would be uneven and they would be forced to return my baby to me. I stepped closer and placed the baby on top of the fire, slowly enough that the flames licked my fingers as I did so. The sticks were dry, and the baby caught fire instantly. The flames consumed it, the outline of it bright with heat, until the middle of the fire collapsed and engulfed it completely.

It was destroyed. Gone. Dead.

I waited patiently, staring at the flames until my eyes burned from the smoke, but nothing happened. The stories never told details of what to expect when a baby was returned. I didn't know if it would just appear before me, or if perhaps a winged creature would walk from the woods with a blanketed bundle in its arms.

The woods surrounding me remained quiet, there was no one. I was alone.

I sank down to my knees on the rocks and continued to wait in front of the still burning fire until the sun was high in the sky. Until the fire burned down to nothing and I was certain it hadn't worked. I was too late. Maybe, if I had found the baby sooner, if I hadn't been too scared of the pain of walking into the nursery, it would have worked.

Disappointment rose inside me, so high I couldn't keep it in. It was a crushing, burning distress and I cried. I cried for myself and for my baby and for my failure. Tears dripped onto the rocks beneath me, but the sun dried them almost immediately. They were so temporary, like they meant nothing at all.

When my tears finally ran dry and I found the strength to stand again, the water lapped at my feet, wetting my shoes. I looked down in surprise. It didn't make any sense; I had built the fire closer to the forest than to the shore. But, somehow, as I sat there and cried, the water had reached all the way up the beach towards me, to wind its fingers tightly around my ankles. Each wave that pulsated forward pulled me back with it, drawing me further out. I let it. It filled my shoes, soaked my jeans, made my shirt cling to my cold skin.

Far enough in that I balanced on the tips of my toes, my head hovering just above the surface, I still felt it urging me to take just one more step. What would it feel like to slip below the waves and disappear? Would everything be erased? My failures? My pain? My life?

I didn't need it to pull me any further. I took that final step.

When my head went under, the bottom opened up beneath me. The water was endless. Though it was a sunny day, below the water was completely dark. There were no fish, no plants, nothing but me.

My hair fanned out around me, undulating in front of my face as my heavy, wet clothes dragged me further into the depths. My lungs fought against the lack of air as the instincts of my body tried to take over, but my limbs didn't respond. My legs didn't kick towards the surface. Soon, the remaining air left my lungs, bubbling out of me. I sank even further. Despite the burning in my chest, I was comfortable, with the weight of the sea pressing down on me.

Just as I felt as though I could fall asleep forever, a familiar voice spoke, warming the water around me.

"Josephine," the voice said, like a knife in my heart. " Don't give up."

I wanted to call out, but my lungs were filled to the brim with water, and I couldn't say a word. I reached into the darkness, feeling for a touch, but found nothing. There was no one.

Fight.

As quickly as it came, the warmth receded and the cold water rushed back in. I broke the surface, my lungs aching, and I gasped, desperate for breath. When I eased my feet down, they touched the bottom, as if it had been there all along. I coughed the water from my lungs until my throat was raw. Instead of making my way to the safety of the shore, I just stood there shivering, willing the voice to return.

My patience was met with only the sound of the waves and the wind in the trees. I wasn't sure how long I stood there, but eventually I walked back to the still empty beach. Drained of all energy, I laid down on the rocks and closed my eyes. I'd never intended to go into the water, I didn't make a decision to do it at all, but I ended up there in the end. It was like someone else was guiding me, tugging me towards what would have certainly killed me had I let it.

They disguised it so beautifully, death. They made it seem so easy. Like it was nothing more than slipping away and maybe that's exactly what it would have been had I relented. A sigh into the abyss instead of the ripping, screaming, clawing death of grief that slaughtered me from the inside out. I wanted to lay there on cold rocks forever, never get back up, but Ben or Mags would come looking for me, and I couldn't bear to answer their questions about this. I didn't even know what I would say.

Back at the house, I took a scalding shower and changed into dry clothes. The warmth returned to my body, but my voice was hoarse from crying, from screaming, from drowning. Later, when Ben got home, I told him I'd caught a cold, and he believed me. He always did.

CHAPTER 23

THE NEXT FEW weeks passed by easier than I
expected. Lying to Ben by telling him I was sick was
a good excuse to lay in bed for a few days and it
gave me time to think and to grieve in peace. What
happened at the beach had torn me to pieces but it
also gave me closure. My baby was gone, and he
wasn't coming back. I had to accept that. I was
ready to accept it, though I knew without a doubt I
would carry the empty feeling in my chest around
with me until the day I died.

Every morning after Ben left for work and Mags
left for school, I walked over to Ami's house to
spend most of the day with her. She was still in the
midst of midwifery training, so there were days
when she had appointments with expectant
mothers, and there were times she had to leave

suddenly when one of them went into labor, but our community was small and there weren't a lot of women needing her services.

One morning, Ami and I were sitting on her front porch throwing a ball for Luna when a sudden flush rose in my body, followed by an urge to be sick so strong I barely made it to the toilet. Ami followed me into the bathroom just as I flushed the toilet. I leaned against the sink and splashed some cold water on my face, then rinsed my mouth out with water from the tap. I felt better but was still a little dizzy.

"What was that about?" she asked. "Are you okay?"

"Yah I'm fine, sorry. I don't know what happened there. I haven't been feeling very well lately; it just comes out of nowhere." I dried my hands and face with a towel.

Her eyes met mine in the mirror. "Wait, could you be pregnant?" she asked with a small smile.

The thought hadn't even crossed my mind. "Is that even possible?"

"If you've had sex, of course it's possible." She squeezed both my hands in hers. "I'll be right back, wait here."

She disappeared down the hall to the room at the back of her house she was preparing to be her clinic when she was finally ready to practice on her own. She returned moments later with a small box labelled "e.p.t" and handed it to me.

"What's this?" I asked, turning it over in my hands.

"It's a home pregnancy test," she responded.

"I can test at home?" I tried to recover from the whiplash between a few moments ago when we were sitting out on the porch and now when I was taking a pregnancy test.

"Yeah! They're pretty new. I got a few to keep at the clinic for women who didn't feel comfortable going to their doctor or a pharmacy. "

I followed the directions inside the box and added three drops of urine to the test tube of liquid. Ami set a timer for two hours and we waited.

"Do you want it to be positive or negative?" Ami asked as I paced back and forth from one end of her house to the other.

"I don't know," I said, shaking my hands in front of me as I walked back into the living room. "It's so soon. Am I supposed to get pregnant again so soon after…?" I couldn't finish the sentence but I didn't need to.

"It's actually really common. Like your body kind of remembers what to do and just picks it right back up," she called out to me as I turned and walked back down the hall, glancing into the bathroom each time I walked by.

"I'm so young and it was an accident last time. I should have been more careful this time. I can't have two accidents in the same year." This time I walked back into the living room with my hands on my head. Ami nodded in understanding but she didn't know that last time wasn't exactly an accident and maybe this time wasn't either.

"Jo! It's okay." Ami jumped up and grabbed my arm, swinging me back towards her before I could take off down the hall again. "We still have at least an hour and a half before that timer is going to go off. Let's get out of here and go for a walk."

She was right of course. I would go mad if I walked up and down the hall for the full two hours. It was better to get out and at least try to take my mind off it. I agreed to the walk, but only if she agreed to not talk about pregnancy or babies and if she made sure we were back in plenty of time to check the test.

We took a path into the woods that began at the far corner of her backyard, past an old wood shack, a rusted boat sitting directly on the ground and other piles of nondescript scrap metal. She noticed me looking and offered a quick explanation. "My dad." As we walked, the woods closed around us though the path remained clear. "He always loved collecting things. Even before we moved here. We've always had piles of junk around our houses. I guess I'm used to it." She laughed lightly, but there was also a hint of sadness in her voice. "They moved back to India last year to look after my Nani. They said that the house is mine and I can do whatever I want to it, but I haven't gotten around to clearing away all their stuff yet. It kind of makes it feel like they're still here and I'm not all alone."

"You aren't alone?" I said. "You have Ben and me. Mags kind of." Ami and Mags had not grown close, but they were friendly and Mags understood that she was important to me so she tried.

"I know. But I don't really belong with your family, Jo."

I wanted to protest. To tell her that she was wrong, but I understood what she meant because I felt it too. I wasn't sure *I* belonged there any more than she did.

"Hey…" I started, but broke off. Unsure how to start what I'd been wanting to say for so long. "We never really talked about what happened the day that Mags got here." We'd spent a lot of time together since that day we'd kissed in her house and although we hadn't talked about it, it was always hovering in the room with us.

"Yeah, I'm really sorry it happened," she said.

"It was completely my fault," I spit out before she could blame herself any more.

"No. You were vulnerable and Ben is my friend. I don't know. I meant what I said that day. That there is something about you. Something that makes me want to keep you here."

"You said that Ben said the same thing? He's ever said anything like that to me."

"Well, it sounds a bit crazy."

She was right. There was nothing special about me.

"I'm starting to think that everyone *I* meet has something about *them*. Like maybe I latch onto anyone who is even remotely nice to me." First Ben, then Ami. I knew that it wasn't normal to fall in love with everyone so quickly, but it didn't make the feelings any less real to me.

"You've been through a lot, it's expected that you would be looking for safe places," she said, taking my hand in hers. It was true that we hadn't kissed again, but we'd held hands lots of times since that day. I liked the feeling of being tethered to someone. Like they really could keep me here with them and without it, I might float away. Into the darkness. I was always reaching for Ben's hand or my sister's so it didn't feel wrong to reach for Ami's too.

I nodded. It did make sense and I was grateful to have people in my life who could at least try to understand the harsh reality I came from.

"The kiss shouldn't have happened. I should have stopped it, but I got caught up in the moment." She paused, slipped her hand from mine and crouched down to pick some wildflowers blooming along the path. "I don't know who I am exactly, but I do know that Ben is all I have here. And now you. I can't do anything to jeopardize that."

If someone like Ami didn't know who she was, what chance did I have? But I think I knew what she meant, even if she didn't want to say it out loud. When I'd asked if Ami was seeing anyone, Ben told me that she never had boyfriends while they were in high school and as far as he knows, she's never dated anyone. He always thought that it was because of her parents because their own marriage had been arranged, but nothing changed once they left. I thought back to my own mother and her expectation that I would meet a "nice boy" in our community and how impossible that felt for me. In this way, Ami and I were the same. Bound by expectation but never quite living up to it.

The trail followed a loop through the woods and came out on the road between our houses. We walked in silence back up to her house where the timer showed that we had another ten minutes to wait. Ami went to the kitchen to put the kettle on and I proceeded to pace.

After a few minutes, she put a hot cup of chamomile tea in my hand and said, "Are you ready?" I nodded though I wasn't ready at all, but then the timer went off and we couldn't avoid the topic any longer.

In the bathroom, I couldn't bring myself to look at the test. I still didn't know what I wanted the result to be. A part of me knew I wouldn't be able to heal until I got a baby, but another part was full of fear, and I didn't know which part held a more prominent space inside me. When I asked Ami to check for me, she didn't resist or hesitate. I tried to interpret her expression as she read the results, tried to prepare myself, but her face gave nothing away.

"It's positive," she said, then beamed, and any doubts I had disappeared.

"What? Are you sure?" I looked at the test as if I knew anything about telling whether it was positive or negative.

"I'm sure." She gathered me into a tight hug just as a choked sob escaped from my throat.It hit me then, all at once, what had happened.

It had worked.

The fairies had given my baby back after all. It was so obvious. The baby they took from me hadn't been born yet, so they couldn't just return it after I burned the changeling they had left in its place. The more I thought about it, the sillier I felt for expecting it to just appear on the beach that day. No, this made so much more sense, and I relaxed into Ami, finally able to breathe deeply.

CHAPTER 24

When I rushed through the door of Normann's Books, a bell chimed above my head, signalling my arrival.

"I'll be right there," his voice called out from the back room.

I wandered down the aisle labelled "Nonfiction and Car Parts." A guidebook for Ireland was wedged beside a nondescript piece of metal. I pulled the book down from the shelf and opened it to a random page. Although the book was full of pictures, maps and anecdotes from other travellers —where to go, what to see—the page I opened to had just one picture spanning both pages. It was of an empty, deep green field and right in the middle, cracked in half by the pages meeting at the spine, was a large tree. Under the photo in tiny print were the words "Fairy Tree".

"Hey, what can I do for you ?" Ben said as he walked out of the back room, wiping his hands on a dusty apron.

I snapped the book closed and stuffed it back onto the shelf feeling as though I had been caught looking at something forbidden.

"Jo?" he said, concerned when he saw that it was me. "Are you okay? Is something wrong?" He rushed towards me, closing the gap between us in two large steps.

"No, nothing's wrong!" I laughed. "I have some news and I couldn't wait another second to tell you."

His eyes squinted, curious. "What news?" he asked, examining my face for any clues.

On the drive over, I had imagined all the different ways I would tell him, but standing there with him thinking something was wrong, I couldn't wait any longer. "I'm pregnant," I blurted out, and subsequently watched his eyes move through confusion and surprise before landing on happiness. He picked me up and twirled me around. "Are you happy?" I asked when he put me down again.

"Of course, I am!" he said, and I could see in his eyes that he meant it. Ben, always so full of light, had been infected by my darkness in the last few weeks. Though he handled it better than me, anyone could see that the light had gone from his eyes. With this news, he lit up again, pushing my darkness further away than ever before.

Behind me, Ben noticed Ami waiting patiently for her turn to congratulate him, so he pulled her into a tripartite hug. I couldn't be happier either, with both of them so close; it was everything I ever wanted.

After hearing the good news, Ben didn't want to let me out of his sight. He was so excited, and every time we went to leave the store—his shift didn't end for another two hours—he began talking again, and making plans for the baby. Eventually, we were able to leave, with the promise that we would meet him at home with dinner.

When we pulled into the driveway, Ami said, "I'm gonna go grab a few things from home and then I'll be right back."

Mags watched us from the porch and then made her way down the steps as Ami drove away. "What's wrong?" she asked, meeting me in the driveway.

"Nothing's wrong," I laughed.

"I'm not stupid, Jo; I know when something's up," she countered, hands on her hips.

As with Ben, I couldn't wait another second to tell her, so I blurted it out. "I'm pregnant," I said, smiling so big that my cheeks were starting to hurt.

But she didn't smile back as I expected her to. Instead, she looked away from me and shook her head.

"What?" I asked.

"You aren't ready for this," she whispered,

turning to avoid my eyes.

"What do you mean?" I asked, pulling her to face me once again. I was surprised to find a familiar fear in her eyes. Familiar, because I'd seen it so many times in my own identical ones.

"You aren't ready to have a baby. It's too soon."

After the anticipation and happiness of the day, her reaction was a slap in the face that I wasn't expecting, and I felt the sting of it deep within me. A pulsing darkness pushed away the light I was holding onto, and my skin began to prickle painfully beneath the weight of it.

"Too soon?" I sneered. "How could it be too soon? I thought you would be happy for me."

"I'm always going to be happy for you when it's what's best for you, but this *isn't*. You shouldn't have this baby," she said, her voice diminishing to a whisper by the end. If I thought her poor reaction to the news of my pregnancy was a slap in the face, this was a punch in the stomach, and it knocked the breath out of me. "What? What did you say? After everything that I've been through? I can't believe you would even—"

"Josephine. You aren't well," she interrupted, her voice firm. Now she looked right into me, and I knew she meant it.

"What are you talking about?" I asked, though I knew what she was going to say. While I thought I was being so careful to cover up what was going on inside me, she could see it all. She always could.

"Ami, for starters. You can't bring a child into the world when you are not only having an affair, but having one with a woman. Then there was that bundle of sticks in the crib, which still hasn't been explained. Where did it come from? And then it just disappeared? Where did it go? Something happened a few weeks ago, too, didn't it? Your clothes were wet and smelled like fire. I didn't say anything, because you seemed more at peace than I have seen you since… before. But something did happen that day, didn't it? What? What happened?"

"I don't know what you're talking about," I said. I tried to walk away, but she followed me into the house. "And I'm not having an affair!"

"You think that, just because you aren't sleeping with her, what you're doing over there isn't wrong? There are more ways than one to have an affair!"

"We are just friends, Mags!" I responded, pulling random ingredients out of the fridge, unable to focus on what to make for dinner.

"Josephine, I can see you. I know when something's wrong. Please, talk to me."

"Nothing's wrong!" I yelled. "You're just jealous. You've always been the center of attention, but now it's my turn and you can't stand it!"

The hurt in her eyes was obvious, and she recoiled as if I had hit her. "That's not true," she said. Her stance and the position of her hands in front of her were not affectionate, but protective. And not protective of me, as they usually were, but of herself. She was scared of me.

"Leave me alone!" I stormed upstairs, slamming my bedroom door behind me.

She didn't follow.

I leaned against the door and wondered in what world my own sister was afraid of me.

Was she right? Maybe there *was* something wrong with me.

A few minutes later, there was a knock on my door. Thinking it was Mags, I didn't respond, but then another voice spoke. "Jo, are you in there?" It was Ami. From the tone of her voice, it was clear that she knew at least something about the fight I'd just had with Mags.

"I'm okay. I'm just not feeling very well. Can you tell Ben that I went to bed early and apologize for me? Maybe we can celebrate tomorrow."

Ami agreed and made me promise to call her if I needed anything.

Later that night, I heard voices rising from below, so I left my room and sat quietly at the top of the stairs to hear what they were saying. Mags and Ben were arguing, and it sounded very similar to the argument I'd had with her earlier that day.

"I only want what's best for her," she said. "She hasn't been well since… what happened. If not before that."

Before? What did she mean?

"You don't think I want what's best for her?" Ben said, defending himself. "She was devastated when she lost the baby; this could help put her back together. I know you think you know her, but you're wrong about this."

"I'm not wrong. I don't know what's going to happen, but I just know this will end badly."

"It's too late; it's already done," said Ben. His voice was muffled a little, as though his hands were in front of his face.

"Abortion is legal now, remember? We can take her down to Vancouver, to a doctor, and convince them that having this baby would be detrimental to her health. Then we can get her some help. When she's better, really better, then you guys can start a family."

I jerked back as if I had been slapped. I'm not sure I had ever felt so betrayed as I did in that moment. How could she even suggest I kill this baby, after everything I'd been through? When I'd worked so hard to get him back?

It was quiet for a long time.

"No, you're wrong. We can do this. I'll help her," Ben finally said.

"I wish I was wrong," Mags said, so quiet I almost didn't hear her at all.

"I can't talk about this anymore," Ben said. He must have risen from his chair; the sound of its legs scratching the floor was loud against the stillness of the night. "And I don't want to hear about it again."

I padded back to my room and closed the door softly, just in time to hear someone coming up the stairs. At first, I thought it was Ben, but the steps paused briefly outside my room and then continued along the hall. Ben remained downstairs, cleaning up the dishes from the very silent dinner he must've come home to instead of the celebration he'd been expecting.

I really thought I had held it together pretty well, considering everything that had happened. Sure, I was sad for a while, but I had a right to be. Anyone would be. And I felt better now; that had to count for something.

I couldn't trust Mags anymore and it was only a matter of time before she got Ben over onto her side as well. I had to show everyone I was okay. I had to prove to them I could do it, or we weren't going to make it.

CHAPTER 25

As far as I knew, the door to the nursery had been kept tightly closed since the night I retrieved the pieces of the stick baby. No one could bear to go inside the empty room, but now I had to get it ready for the new baby. I needed to breathe a new life into it.

The next morning, I entered the stuffy room, opening both the windows to let some air in. Then, I got to work washing the windows and the windowsills, scrubbing the floor, and organizing the few tiny outfits we'd purchased.

"Jo?" Mags's voice came from the open door. "What are you doing up so early?"

"I couldn't sleep, so I thought I would just start getting things ready." I was on my knees with a bucket of water, scrubbing the floor for the third time. The house was old and no matter how many times I scrubbed, I couldn't get it clean. I tried to resist looking at her; I couldn't forgive her for what she'd said, but my face turned up to hers anyways and I saw pity in her expression. It made me feel so small. "Don't look at me that way!" I snapped.

"I'm not…" She stopped talking, sighed, and came to kneel beside me. "Here, let me help you." She took a brush from the bucket and started scrubbing. "I'm sorry about yesterday," she said. "You're right, I should be supporting you; it's not up to me to decide what's best for you."

This was *not* what I was expecting her to say.

"I'm your sister. I'm here for you," she continued. "I'm here to help, with whatever you need. We can do this together." She put down the brush and took my hand in hers. I couldn't bring myself to speak, so I offered her a small smile in response, squeezed her hand, and continued scrubbing.

We cleaned the room the best we could, and then she helped me carry Ben's grandma's old rocking chair up the stairs. We put it in the corner facing the window, so the baby and I could see the stars at night and the ocean surrounding us during the day. I sat in it, rocking back and forth, letting the motion calm me while Mags sat on the floor beside me.

"I heard you talking to Ben last night," I admitted, finally breaking the long silence. "Do you really think something's wrong with me?"

"No, " she said, leaning the side of her head against my knee. She was silent for a long time before speaking again, and as I waited, I wound my fingers through her long hair. Though she relaxed into me, I could see a tension in her body that usually wasn't there. Finally, she took a deep breath and continued. "I just know something has always haunted you. There's always been a darkness with you, affecting you. You know that game we used to play, where you could see me even with your eyes closed? Well, I always told you I couldn't see you, but I could. It wasn't light and colours like what you described when you saw me. Instead, I saw shadows following behind you, everywhere you went. I never told you; I didn't want to scare you. You were so— not fragile, but—intricate. Complex. Maybe I should have told you, but I didn't know what it meant. I still don't, but I still see it. Them. They haven't diminished over the years. If anything, they've intensified. Gotten stronger. I don't know if it was because of Mother, or because of the baby, but I see them when my eyes are open now. The shadows. The darkness. You've been through so much, and I'm just afraid that, if anything else happens to you, they will overtake you completely."

I took a sharp breath in, sick with what she said. I had always seen them too, the shadows; the darkness in the corner of my eyes, but it was fleeting. I could never quite focus on it. Over the years, I had just gotten used to it. But to know that someone else had always been able to see them too, to know that I wasn't crazy, felt like a huge weight was lifted from me. It was both a punch in the gut and a warm hug.

"It doesn't sound crazy," I finally said. "I see them too. I know they're there."

She looked at me, shock plain across her face. "Really?" she asked, tears in her eyes.

"My whole life, I have felt something pressing on me, moving me in different directions, sometimes in directions I didn't wanna go. When I first met Ben, and then when we first got here and we were happy, it was the first time that I didn't see them anymore. I just want to get back there. That's why I keep seeing Ami. One of the reasons. When I'm with her, they stay away."

She nodded, understanding. "I saw them around Mother, too. I always did. I don't see hers as strongly as I see yours, but whatever they are, you got them from her."

"Hey, how long have you two been awake?" Ben asked, walking into the room and breaking the spell we were both under. "It looks good in here." He smiled and leaned over to kiss me. Apparently, he was just as determined as me to pretend that everything was okay.

CHAPTER 26

Spring turned to summer, and my days remained much the same. Ben and Mags would leave the house in the morning, and I continued spending my days with Ami whenever she was free. Sometimes I would still be at her house when Mags or Ben got home. Most nights, she spent the evenings with us, having dinner, playing games, talking on the porch swing.

Mags couldn't ignore the fact that the shadows did recede when Ami was around, so she stopped interfering with our relationship—whatever it was. If Ben ever suspected anything, he never said. There were times when I looked over and saw him watching us from across the room, but he never looked suspicious or jealous. Only happy.

As the weeks rolled on, I did my best to keep

calm, but as happy as I was to be pregnant again, I was also terrified, and always looking for signs of impending death. I thought that, if I could get ahead of it, know it was coming, it wouldn't surprise me again. I was afraid to sleep, afraid the Banshee would visit me as she had before; and so, I stayed up every night, as late as I could. I stayed up until my eyes closed on their own. If I woke up in the night, it was in a panic, and I immediately had to check the sheets for blood.

I didn't tell Ben how afraid I was. I didn't want to worry him. But Mags could see it, and she did everything she could to make my life as calm and comfortable as possible. On top of school, she cleaned the house and learned to cook so she could prepare meals for us. I felt bad for everything she was doing, and I worried she would sink below and lose herself completely, but I was also grateful for her.

When I asked Ami if she would be the one to deliver the baby, she said no at first. It was too much pressure for her, she said. If anything were to go wrong, she would be too worried about me to think clearly. In the end, though, I begged her, and she relented as long as the pregnancy remained healthy.

She said that, at around eighteen weeks, she would be able to hear the baby's heartbeat with her stethoscope. Even though I still had another ten weeks until then, I asked her to try every week anyway and, of course, every week she was faced with the pulsing silence of only my own heartbeat. She told me not to worry, though; she could feel my uterus starting to expand over my pubic bone and that meant the baby was growing.

Eighteen weeks came and went, and still nothing. If I'd thought my fear was consuming me before, it only got worse as time went on. My mind let me think of nothing but the baby most days, in an uninterrupted loop of surety that something was wrong.

Then, one day, when I was just about nineteen weeks pregnant, Ami put her stethoscope to my bare belly as she had so many times before. But this time, instead of the dull disappointment she faced whenever she had to tell me there was nothing, a huge smile spread across her lips. "Take the earpieces and listen for yourself."

I pulled them from her, my hands shaking, and put them to my own ears. And there it was, the sound of a tiny galloping horse. A heartbeat much faster than my own, though my own could probably have matched it in that moment.

I had expected to feel unimaginable joy the first time I heard it, but the relief that came instead was like a brick wall crumbling around me, and I broke. My hands covered my face and I cried, maybe even harder than I had after my loss.

I was finally able to breathe.

CHAPTER 27

Early one evening, as I was walking home from Ami's, dense clouds moved in above me, causing the midsummer sky to darken. I hurried along the road, trying to make it home before the inevitable rain started, but then I felt something pull at me.

It was so subtle at first that I was almost able to ignore it, like thin wisps of hair tickling at my bare skin. Thunder boomed overhead. Momentarily distracted, I looked in the direction I was being so delicately pulled. There, to my right, was the fairy tree which had gone completely forgotten since the beginning of my pregnancy.

The spring had brought bright green leaves to the dark, barren branches I remembered. I hadn't seen it or thought about it for months and then there it was, calling out to me once again, its power immense and undeniable. It drew me to the fence, and though it pulled at me, I was able to resist going through. My body longed to go, but my head understood it wasn't healthy. I put my hand on my stomach and felt the life there. The air around me beat as though it too had a pulse; as if it were living and breathing around me.

I pushed off from the fence and carried on home to Ben.

Later that night, after fighting it for as long as I could, I fell reluctantly into a fitful sleep. Not long later, a twinkling laugh reached through the bowels of my dreamless state and woke me from the deep sleep I so desperately needed.

My eyes opened and instantly my heart was beating hard in my chest as I began to panic. I pushed the blankets off, grateful and relieved to find the sheets underneath my body still white. I laid back down and listened again for the sound that pulled me from sleep, but the room was as silent as ever and Ben was sound asleep beside me, his breath long and even. The light of the full moon spilled in through the open window, casting everything in a cool glow.

When, after a few minutes, the room remained silent and my anxiety lowered, I matched my breathing to Ben's and tried to calm myself back to sleep. Just as the heaviness began to engulf me, I heard it again, this time clear and so close. A laugh. It jerked me out of the place between awake and asleep so fast I felt sick to my stomach.

Though I tried to convince myself it was just a dream, I held my breath and waited to hear it again. I didn't have to wait long. From bed, I couldn't tell where it was coming from; it came from everywhere, all around me—a tinkling, like a small glass bell, delicate and ringing.

I sat up and gazed around the room, trying to discern the source of the sound, but the room looked as it always did, nothing out of place. I got out of bed to stand before the window overlooking the driveway. Through the glass, I stared, mesmerized, as hundreds of tiny lights swirled around the yard below like fireflies, rhythmically twirling and pulsating through the night, as though set to a melody I could not hear. Charmed, I rushed on tip toes down the stairs and out the front door without another thought.

The moment I stepped out onto the porch and the cool night air touched the bare skin beneath my nightgown, the tiny lights flew up around me, encircling my body.

They weren't fireflies, like I originally thought; they were tiny orbs of pulsing light with no other distinguishable parts. The warmth of them was startling, like small balls of fire. They continued to swirl around my body, lighting the space around me and igniting my skin. Then, all at once, their pulse ebbed, and they flowed away from me, taking their warmth with them.

"Wait," I called, my arms outstretched towards them, but they continued down the driveway.

I rushed after them. They were moving so fast I had to jog to keep up, which was hard and awkward with my belly starting to feel swollen in front of me. I held my hands under it for support and hurried on.

The orbs flowed at a steady pace ahead of me, but managed to never get too far away, like they were always waiting for me to catch up. Then, they made a sharp turn to the left, and it was no longer a mystery where they were going. It also wasn't a surprise. The lights danced just beyond the fence of our neighbour's property, waiting for me.

The tree.

I had ignored its calling before, and now, it had sent for me.

I couldn't fit comfortably through the slats anymore, so I had no choice but to climb over the fence. It wasn't easy and there were a few times I thought I might fall as I tried to maneuver my leg over the top, but somehow, I managed to make it over safely. The moment my bare feet touched the cold, damp grass on the other side, the lights shot off towards the tree, and I hurried after them.

When the orbs reached the tree, they flew directly up the trunk and entangled themselves like string lights within the branches, dancing among the leaves. Then they dropped down out of the canopy as quickly as they had risen and floated around the base of the trunk, waiting. As I approached, they began to circle the trunk. With each rotation, fewer and fewer emerged from behind the tree, until finally the last one disappeared. Confused, I made my way around to the other side, and discovered them swirling together inside a split in the wood just wide enough for a person to fit through. Though utterly dark inside the tree, the floating lights illuminated a set of stone stairs descending into the darkness.

Instinctually, I understood I should be afraid. That, for not only my own safety but for that of my unborn baby, I should turn around and go home. I hesitated, but was unable to ignore the clawing pull that brought me there, and I ducked inside the tree anyways.

Trusting that I would follow, the orbs sped ahead once more. The stairs were steep, slippery and narrow enough that the walls pressed close against my shoulders. This time, the orbs didn't wait for me. They left me behind and without their light it was completely dark. My hands reached out and felt only the hard-packed dirt of the walls surrounding me. The air underground was cold, and the temperature seemed to drop another degree with each step that I took.

Without an end in sight, the stairs went on forever. Down and down, I went, as the weight of the world above pressed down on me. It became so cold I could barely feel my feet anymore. I longed to wrap my arms around my shivering body to keep warm, but I needed them to steady myself against the walls or I was sure to fall. I was keenly aware that if I did, no one would ever find me, and the fear of dying there, alone below the earth, scared me more than anything.

Then, just when I thought I couldn't take it anymore, the darkness around me began to fade. Before I knew it, I could see the vague outline of my hand against the wall. In the distance, a dim light signalled the end of the tunnel. I hurried forward a little faster, stumbling down the stairs.

When I took the last step, it was into a massive cavern carved into the earth and framed by the immense roots of the tree above. The orbs of light nestled overhead , like stars in the night sky.

Slicing through the middle of the cave was a small stream. The sound of the water trickling over the rocks echoed around me. At the side of the stream, a woman kneeled.

I thought of the Bean Sidhe that had appeared to me before my baby was taken, and I stopped dead. Watching it. My chest heaved in fear and dread, and my hands flew protectively to my belly. This couldn't be happening again.

No. No. No no no.

The woman stood, her back to me. She looked achingly familiar, with her long dark hair hanging halfway down her back, and the emerald green dress I knew would be the same colour as her eyes.

When she turned, it wasn't the Bean Sidhe , but my mother. Not the version of her we'd seen strapped to the bed at the hospital, the one wasted away to practically nothing, but the one I remembered best. The one I had spent my whole life afraid of.

Only now, she was smiling. At me.

She was beautiful in the way everyone had always said she was; the way *I* never got to see. Her eyes were warm, and her smile was genuine. This was the version of her everyone *else* knew; the version of herself she withheld so completely from me. She didn't speak, but instead held out her arms as if to embrace me.

I wanted so badly to go to her and to feel her surround me like I had always longed for. I tried to hold myself back; to tell myself it wasn't real; it wasn't possible; but, the child in me, starved for affection, took over and I rushed to her. When her arms enveloped me, something released inside my body like the relief of a long-held breath. I sobbed into the warm green fabric of her dress and breathed in the scent of roses that always followed her around.

"Mama," I cried. "Why?" I wasn't sure if I was asking why she did what she did or if I was asking why she was here now but I just needed to ask the question, no matter the answer.

She was unnaturally still like a statue, her arms stiff around my body. I shivered, my body feeling the cold before my brain could register that she was like ice. I pulled back from her and looked into her face. My heart stopped completely. Gone was the smiling woman I had seen only moments before, and in her place was the woman I last saw strapped to the bed in the hospital—sunken cheeks, long scraggly hair, and dead eyes.

"Josephine Auclair, the little slut!" she growled.

I stumbled back, out of her emaciated arms, but she grasped at me desperately, ripping my nightgown down the front, exposing my breasts and swollen belly.

"Changeling!" she wailed.

I fled for the opening of the tunnel as fast as my frozen bare feet could go, while she staggered after me. I hit the stairs and pounded up them, but I couldn't move fast enough. Her haggard breath and shuffling footsteps stirred the air behind me as her bony fingers pulled at the hem of my ruined nightgown and her nails raked down the backs of my legs.

As they had on the descent, the stairs went on forever. My lungs burned with the effort and my legs were aching and heavy, but I couldn't let myself stop. I couldn't let her get me.

Finally, the moonlight seeped through the opening in the tree above and I pushed myself harder towards it. As soon as I was out into the open air, I collapsed onto the damp grass and the opening in the trunk closed behind me, trapping the thing inside. I crawled up to the tree and ran my hand over the rough bark, looking for some kind of seam in the wood, something to prove that a door had been there, but there was nothing. It was flawless. Like it never happened.

The next time I opened my eyes, alone in my bed, the midmorning light was filtering through my bedroom window. My legs shifted under the familiar weight of my blankets, only to be met with an unfamiliar grittiness between the sheets. Though this dream wasn't about the Bean Sidhe as it had been before, it was just as disturbing, and I pushed the blankets away from me, once more relieved to find the sheets bloodless where I lay.

But, though they weren't stained red, they were no longer white. Instead, they were covered with sand, soil, and dry, crumpled leaves. My hands and feet were filthy, my nails caked in dirt. My nightgown was badly stained, and ripped down the front, exactly as it had been in the dream.

In what I had thought was a dream, but was real.

I flew out of bed. There was no way what happened last night *could* be real; my mother was in a hospital, hours away. But how else could I explain the state of me? I couldn't.

I put on my robe to hide the bare skin behind my ripped nightgown and threw on my shoes, then rushed to Ami's house. If there was a way I could have gotten there without seeing the tree, I would have taken it, but there wasn't. It loomed over the field, seemingly bigger and darker than usual. The pulse of it reached out to me, but my desperation to know that everything was okay was stronger than it was, and I continued on.

When I arrived, her door was locked. I banged my fists against it as hard as I could, but the house stayed dark and silent. I went around to each window on the porch, looked through, and saw no one before making my way to the back door and banging on that one too, but no one came.

Frantic, I ran around to all the windows and the doors, calling Ami's name, but I remained alone. I sat down on the front steps with my head in my hands and started to cry, a certain dread creeping up from the ground, wrapping its hands around my feet, then my ankles, up my legs.

Just when I thought it might overtake me, Ami was there beside me, pulling my hands from my face.

"Jo, what's going on?" she asked, taking in my appearance. "Are you okay? What happened?" Her car was parked in front of the house, door open, the engine still running.

"I think something's wrong with the baby," I cried, covering my face again.

"Let's get you inside and I'll check you out." She hurried to turn off her car, then helped me up.

On the way to her examination room, I told her about the dream and then I told her about how it wasn't a dream. She listened intently, waiting for me to finish before speaking herself.

"Ben told me you sleepwalk sometimes," she said. "You just had a bad dream, and somehow you got out of the house without anyone noticing. It's going to be okay."

I sleepwalked? Ben told her that? That couldn't be right, it had never happened to me before. And, if it had, why wouldn't he have told me?

Ami helped me up onto the bed and laid me back as she undid the tie of my robe, revealing my ripped nightgown and exposed belly. She paused slightly at the sight, but didn't react and didn't say anything else. She put the end of the stethoscope to the roundness of my belly and concentrated for a long time. Then she moved it around to different spots, listening.

With each move of the instrument, my dread grew. I knew exactly what she was going to say. There was only silence inside of me; there was no heartbeat. She was about to tell me that my baby was dead. Again.

My sight dimmed, the darkness moving in.

Finally, she smiled and said, "Your baby's fine, the heartbeat is strong." She handed me the earpieces so I could hear for myself.

I put them to my ears and there it was. The sound of the tiny life both pulled me from and pushed me over the edge, and I broke out into sobs. My heart pounded. I couldn't catch my breath. My sight still threatened me with darkness, and I squeezed my eyes shut against it.

"Jo, you have to breathe," Ami said, slowing down and exaggerating her own breathing, gesturing for me to copy her. I did and when my breath and my heart slowed enough to satisfy her, she hugged me tight. "It was just a bad dream, you're okay. I have you."

"Please don't tell Ben or Mags about this," I begged, pulling back to look into her eyes. "He'll never let me out of his sight again if he knew."

"We have to tell them. It's not safe for you to be leaving the house in the night."

"Okay, but just let me do it my way."

It was clear she wasn't sure if she should believe me, but in the end, she agreed. Ami was right, it wasn't safe, but I couldn't tell them what had happened to me.

I couldn't let them think that I was going crazy.

Because, maybe I was.

CHAPTER 28

When I finally left Ami's, the sun was high in the sky, and I still had hours before anyone would be home. Though I was happy and relieved the baby was okay, I still didn't understand what had happened, and I didn't believe I had only been sleepwalking.

I needed to find out exactly what was going on, and I knew who was going to tell me.

When I came to her property, I climbed the fence just as I had in my dream the night before, but this time, I stalked right past the tree, ignoring its advances, towards the house up on the hill. As the house grew closer, the sight of it stopped me in my tracks. I closed my eyes and opened them again, sure I was seeing it wrong.

The house, so lovingly cared for only months

before, had changed drastically. Not only was it now unliveable, but it was also almost completely unrecognizable. The porch was rotted, sagging, and in some places, completely caved in. Almost all the windows were broken, and the paint had peeled off the siding to reveal the bare, damp wood beneath. Weeds grew up over the railings of the porch, winding themselves around the bannisters so tight they seemed to be pulling the house down into the ground.

"Hello?" I called out, unable to reconcile the memories I had of this place with what I was seeing now.

No answer. Everything was silent except the rustle of the wind blowing through the weeds and some crows cawing in the distance.

I started up the steps to the front porch, but as soon as I stepped onto the first stair, it buckled under my weight. Despite the clawing instinct to turn and go home, I walked instead through the tangle of brush and around the right side of the house.

I pulled my hands into the sleeves of the floral dress I'd borrowed from Ami as I pushed through the tall thorny plants that blocked the overgrown path. Glass crunched beneath my feet, which was odd because I knew it most likely meant windows had been broken from the inside. If someone hadn't been trying to get in, did that mean they were trying to get out? I peered through the empty frames, but despite the brightness of the summer day, the darkness was too thick to see anything but undulating shadows.

"Hello?" I called out again, not really expecting anyone to respond, feeling weighed down by the silence surrounding me.

I had been deeply confused when I saw the state of the house, but now I was starting to feel afraid. Afraid of the house, of myself, what was happening to me.

At the back of the house, crumbling concrete stairs led up to a solid wooden door. Mostly out of habit I knocked lightly, and the sound echoed around me, louder in the silence than it should have been. When no one answered, I tried the door handle and found it unlocked. With a loud creak, the door swung open into a large kitchen.

It appeared as though a family had been about to sit down to dinner, but instead decided to walk out the door and never come back. A large dining table surrounded by six empty chairs dominated the dining area to the right. Before each chair was a place setting, complete with everything needed for a meal—a placemat topped with a dinner plate, framed with cutlery and a water glass. In the middle of the table were various dishes that once held the meal, but only dried remnants of whatever animals hadn't gotten to was left.

The smell of mold mixed with something rotting made my stomach turn and I covered my mouth and nose. Pregnancy had made my stomach even weaker than it usually was, and I found it hard to keep from throwing up even on good days.

The kitchen was filthy and had been taken over by rodents and other small animals, but I could tell it had once been very loved and cared for. Beneath the dirt and debris, the room was tidy, everything was in its place. A mother had lived here. One who had taken care of her family. One who'd cared about what went on here.

Damp leaves covered the floor but still, with each step I took, an unsettling crunching sounded beneath my feet. I got the feeling I was stepping on the bones of tiny dead animals. I tried to push the image out of my mind, determined to see the rest of the house. Light filtered in through the greyed and torn lace curtains covering the windows, barely lighting the space.

A cool wind blew in through the open back door, easing the smell enough that I was able to move forward into a dark, narrow hall that connected the kitchen to the living room. It was as I remembered, though covered in rotten leaves, dirt, and the remnants of animals just as the kitchen was. The couches still faced each other, but one was knocked backwards. The upholstery on both was torn, the wood beneath rotted and chewed through. The wallpaper, once inlaid with thin blue stripes, was badly stained a sinister dark brown in multiple places, and peeling all over.

Over the empty fireplace, the mantel was still filled with family photographs—dusty and yellow with age. I rubbed the sleeve of my dress over the glass to remove the grime and reveal the same family posed over and over again for the same photos. A mother. A father. A young girl with a dark braid. A very young boy with hair so light it was almost white, and eyes so blue that the colour of them was obvious even in the black and white photograph.

In all the photos, the family smiled and looked happy, but as I cleared more of them, I noticed the mother was always looking out of the frame. In every single photo, even though her smile was pointed at the camera or at her family, her eyes were focused on something in the distance. Each picture was taken outside, and the house framed the scene behind them. I opened the front door and saw exactly what she was looking at in the distance.

The tree.

It was clearly visible, just down the hill from the house, and I knew it was what had held her attention all those times in all those photographs. Did she know, as I did, what it was and what it meant?

I looked back into the dark, lifeless house with a complete certainty that something *was* wrong with me, but that something was also just *wrong*. This house proved it. These photos proved it. Most of all, the gaping hole in my chest proved it.

My legs, suddenly weak, shook. I sank to the floor, despair filling me to the top. Holding one of the framed photos, I looked at the mother once more, but instead saw myself staring back from behind the glass. The little boy with the blue eyes haunted me. I threw the photo against the wall, shattering both the glass and the silence.

CHAPTER 29

WHEN I WALKED through the front door of my own house, I was welcomed by Joni Mitchell's voice singing from the record player in the living room and it somewhat quelled the fear and soothed the confusion roaring inside me. The comforting and familiar sounds of cooking came from the other side of the house, and I followed them to the kitchen, where I found Ben and Mags making dinner.

With them unaware of my presence, I watched from the shadows of the hall as they danced comfortably around each other, each acting almost as if the other wasn't even there. They worked together with perfect clarity like a couple who'd been married fifty years. Again, the idea that Mags could step seamlessly into my own life invaded my thoughts. Ben reached around her to grab a knife from the counter as she absentmindedly placed an onion on the cutting board for him, laughing at some small thing he said.

I tried to quell the jealousy that rose up from my gut, but it choked the life out of me, until Ben and Mags together were the only thing I could think of. Their hands touching. Kissing. Her fingers running through his blonde hair. I stepped back, further into the shadows, until my back hit the wall. I used that sensation of pressure against my body to ground me back into reality. Into that moment.

I watched them a while longer, watched Mags as she just stood at the sink washing dishes like it was a completely normal thing to do. I mimicked her movements, trying to commit them to memory, so that maybe one day, I could move as effortlessly as she did through my own life.

I shook my head, left the thoughts behind, and let out a deep breath before letting it go and walking into the kitchen to get the answers I desperately needed.

"Who lives in the house next to ours?" I asked Ben as he cut the onion at the counter.

He jumped slightly at the sound of my voice, and I wondered for a moment if he felt like he had been caught. Did he look guilty? Mags turned from the sink, but she didn't say anything, only looked at me with curiosity as she dried her hands on a towel.

"No one's lived there as long as I've been alive. The house has always been empty," he responded as he transferred the cut onions from the chopping board into a sizzling pan. The scent of them filled the air and stung my eyes.

"Okay then, who *used* to live there?" I persisted.

He hesitated, both hands braced against the edge of the counter, before responding.

"My father told me, when he was a kid, there was a family that lived there. He said the dad died suddenly while working out in the field, and not long later, the mother." He stopped, and looked away, obviously wishing he hadn't said anything. But this was what I needed to know the most.

"The mother?" I prompted.

"She hanged herself from one of the trees on their property. He said the kids were taken in by the ministry. So, I assume, adopted by other families. Such a sad story." He shook his head and moved on to chopping the garlic. "Why do you ask?"

"I met someone over there a while ago, a woman. I thought maybe she lived there, but when I went back today, she was gone," I answered.

"Why would you go there?" Mags asked, coming around to lean against the counter next to me. She waited for my response, but I ignored her question so I could focus on what Ben had to say. "Really? That's odd. I've never seen anyone around that house." By the way he avoided my eyes, I could tell he didn't believe me.

"Yeah, odd," I responded, deciding not to push it any further; not wanting to give them any reason to think something was wrong. I would have to get answers another way.

That night, sleep eluded me once again, and I lay awake while Ben slept soundly beside me, replaying everything that had happened.

The dream. Iris. The house.

My hands stroked the swell of my belly, and I felt my baby moving inside, so alive and so real. I had gotten to the point where I was just starting to feel safe enough in my pregnancy to fall asleep with ease at night. But now, once again, I was too scared; scared of what I'd see when I closed my eyes; scared I would lose control of myself and rise from sleep to walk the night.

So, I lay awake that night and then every night after that, too scared to close my eyes until the exhaustion took over and I had no choice but to sleep, but it was never deep, never enough.

The moment Ben woke up each morning, I awoke too, but remained in bed until he left for work, so he would have no reason to worry about me. I could tell by the way Mags's eyes followed me that she knew something was bothering me, but every time she asked, I told her everything was fine. She obviously didn't believe me, though, and kept close to me as much as she could.

The days grew longer and longer, and I knew that not only did I feel tired, I looked tired. Exhausted. Dark circles rimmed my eyes, and my skin and hair were dull, reminding me once again of the face that had looked back at me that day in the hospital. The day I came here, hoping for freedom and a new life.

Makeup only helped so much. Ben was starting to ask if I was getting enough sleep and suggesting I go to bed a little earlier, but the thought of spending more time in bed, waiting for the dream to get me, was terrifying. I had to do better at hiding my exhaustion.

The fear that something was wrong with the baby returned full force, consuming me. I asked Ami to check the baby every day, sometimes multiple times a day if I couldn't stand it any longer. She tried to reassure me all the worrying was unnecessary and that the baby was doing really well, but I begged her, and in the end she did it for me anyways, anytime I asked. As she said, the baby's heartbeat was always there and always strong, but I just couldn't shake the feeling that something was wrong, and I *would not* be surprised again.

CHAPTER 30

The unrelenting fear and exhaustion went on for months and I grew weaker and weaker. Everyone was worried and I was never alone. While Ben was at work, Ami was always with me unless another laboring mother needed her. On those days, Mags stayed home to watch over me, though I insisted that it was unnecessary.

No longer did I have to beg Ami to check on the baby; now it was she who insisted on it each day. She couldn't understand what was wrong with me. She saw that I ate, and Ben told her I slept each night, but still I lost more weight than was healthy, and, despite my growing belly, my clothes hung from my body once again.

I wanted to tell her what I was so afraid of. I wanted to tell her what had happened to me, because if anyone was going to believe me and maybe understand, it was her, but I couldn't risk her telling Ben or Mags. *They* wouldn't understand. Mags had said I shouldn't have this baby, that I wasn't well enough. If she found out about the sleepwalking and the dream and the house, she would be right. I needed this baby too badly for her to be right.

Then, one night in early December, something woke me suddenly from my reluctant sleep and I gasped. It was happening again. I lay perfectly still, afraid to even breathe, waiting to hear the laugh, watching the window expecting to see the lights floating around outside it, but the house remained silent and the window dark. Despite my heart beating hard inside my chest, the exhaustion once again took over, and my eyes began to close.

Just as they did, it became clear what had woken me so suddenly. It wasn't the dream. It wasn't the fairies. It wasn't my mother. Instead of the laughter and the lights I'd been dreading all this time, a pain rocked through my body, originating deep inside me, clutching my insides, turning my swollen belly rock hard. The surprise of it made me cry out, waking Ben.

He sat up in bed. "Jo? What's wrong?" he asked, fumbling to turn on the lamp.

I couldn't speak. I couldn't move. I couldn't breathe. When the wave finally subsided, I was able to cry, "I think the baby's coming. Call Ami."

Without hesitation, he jumped out of bed and ran down the stairs. The commotion woke Mags, and she appeared at our bedroom door in her pyjamas. When she saw me curled up, clutching the bedsheets in pain, she ran to my side. She didn't have to ask what was happening; she knew. And she understood what it meant to me and for me.

"You can do this," she said with unwavering confidence.

Though I wasn't so sure, I nodded as she helped pull me up into a sitting position. My belly ballooned out in front of me, pulling my nightshirt tight. Just as I was about to put my feet on the floor, another contraction began. I moaned as the wave started out as only a ripple but grew quickly in intensity, until tears flowed from my eyes. Mags grasped my hand, holding me together until it passed.

When the pain receded, Mags got me up out of bed. I turned to look at the space where I had lain, expecting to see blood again, but the sheets were unmarked, and I breathed a little easier. My muscles were tense, so I walked back and forth across the room in a vain attempt to loosen up my body.

Only moments later, Ben returned with Ami. "It's too early!" I cried when I saw her rush into the room. The baby wasn't due for another four weeks.

"It's going to be okay," she reassured me. "Let's get you on the bed so I can check you."

She helped me lay back down. I moaned at the

discomfort as another wave rose and crashed inside my body. Ami put on a pair of gloves, and I felt her fingers reach in to feel my cervix and then a gush of warm fluid soaked the bed beneath me. I tried to sit up, bracing myself on my elbows as panic built inside me.

"It's okay, your water just broke. The baby is definitely coming." She touched me again and said, "Fast. It's coming really fast."

She told Ben and Mags to bring clean towels and sheets, changing the bed and lining it with towels as I paced the floor, back and forth. With each contraction, I stopped, doubling over. Mags massaged my back, while Ben stood to the side, obviously unsure what he should be doing. He looked just as scared as I felt.

Between contractions, I couldn't stay still, or the sensations in my body became too intense and threatened to overwhelm me. I went on that way for what felt like hours, as the contractions became closer and closer together. With each one, shadows darkened my vision, but I pushed them away and focused only on the promise that I would be holding my baby in my arms soon.

Then, the feeling inside me shifted and I felt the distinct sensation of something moving down within my body, dragging itself over my bones. "It's time," I said, panicking. "I can feel it, it's coming. Oh my god, I can't do this." It was getting harder and harder to breathe. The room felt small while the labor felt so big, and I was so scared.

"Come on, let's get you on the bed." Ami led me back to the clean bed and helped me lay down. She put on a clean pair of gloves and went to check me again. "You're right, it's coming now. I'm gonna need you to push."

Mags held my right hand and I put my left hand out for Ben. I squeezed them both as I pushed down as hard as I could.

"Again!" Ami said. "Keep going."

When I couldn't take it anymore, I collapsed back against the pillows, breathless. As soon as one contraction ended, another one started to bloom. I had no time to catch my breath, no time to recover. Ben and Mags stood on either side, holding my hands, urging me, helping me, but no matter how hard I pushed, the baby wouldn't move down any further.

After what felt like an eternity with no further progression, Ami suggested I get into a kneeling position so maybe gravity would help me out. Ben and Mags kneeled on either side of me, holding me up, while Ami positioned herself behind me. The change gave me an immediate sense of relief, and when I pushed again, I felt the same dragging, stretching feeling I had before.

"I can see the head, it's working," Ami cried. "Push again!"

Pain exploded in me like I had never felt before, like I was on fire. It was something I didn't even think I was capable of feeling, of living through. I cried out, screamed.

"The head's out! One more big push!"

I gave it all I had, and then there was this sudden, overwhelming relief. Everything I felt seconds before evaporated, and I collapsed forward onto my hands and knees. A baby's cry filled the room.

Ami said, "It's a girl."

No, that was wrong.

It couldn't be a girl. It was a boy. It was always a boy. I felt it. I knew it like I knew my own name.

But then, Ami brought the crying baby around to me and placed it in my arms. When I looked, I saw that it was, in fact, a girl.

I wanted to puke.

"Do you want to cut the cord?" Ami asked Ben as she clamped it close to the baby's belly.

"Is that okay?" he asked, nervous.

"Of course, it's okay," she said with a lighthearted laugh as she handed him the scissors.

He cut the cord and I felt the half still connected to me fall down between my legs. Ami rubbed at the baby in my arms, who was now letting out a small, mournful cry.

I looked up to find Mags's eyes on me, recognizing that something was wrong. Something the others hadn't noticed yet . Because they were so focused on the baby and had forgotten about me completely.

"This isn't my baby," I whispered, holding it out from my body, willing someone to take it from me.

Where was *my* baby? The one I had grown in my body? I knew it was gone; there was a deep emptiness inside me, and I knew it wasn't in me anymore. The baby I had carried all these months, the one I sang to and dreamed about, was gone.

"What did you say, Jo?" Ben asked, taking it from my hands. He looked down at the thing as Ami helped wrap it in a blanket, with tears in his eyes. He looked so happy. Why didn't he see what I did?

"Jo? What's wrong?" Mags asked. Seeing something in my eyes, she tried to alert the others. "Guys?" she yelled at Ben and Ami, just as I couldn't hold back any longer.

"That's not my baby!" This time I screamed the words and pounded my fists against the bed, making sure they could hear me. "Where's *my* baby?" Tears poured from my eyes and the aching emptiness throbbed inside me.

"Jo, what are you talking about? This is our daughter." He smiled at me, but the crease between his eyebrows betrayed the worry and confusion he was trying to hide.

"We do not have a daughter!" I screamed.

I had to find him. I had to find my baby. Where could he be? I scrambled off the bed and my legs shook with such weakness that I almost couldn't hold myself up, but I reached down into myself and found the strength that I needed. I moved forward though warm blood ran down my legs and dripped onto the floor below me.

"Where is my baby?" I cried, pulling the stained sheets from the bed.

I moved to the dresser and pulled the drawers out, spilling our clothes over the floor. He wasn't in there. Then I saw the chest my father had given me when I was born. I turned it over, spilling the contents, but he wasn't in there either, and everything I had lay broken and crumpled beneath my feet.

Hands grasped at me, and voices spoke, but it meant nothing to me. I couldn't hear them, and they couldn't pull me back. I wouldn't let them.

"They took him," I sobbed, and then I let them take me too.

CHAPTER 31

SOFT VOICES SURROUNDED me, whispering my name, trying to coax me from the darkness. Instead, I sank further and further into it, and I thought maybe I would disappear completely. I thought maybe I would be okay with that. It was as though I had been hollowed out, scraped clean, and all my insides had then been replaced with cold wet sand. I couldn't open my eyes. I wouldn't.

"Why hasn't she woken up yet?" Ben asked. His voice was concerned and sounded far away.

"I don't know, but her vitals are strong. I think she just needs to rest," Ami said.

"Maybe we should call an ambulance," Ben responded. .

"No!" cried Mags. "If she…" Her voice trailed off and she sighed. "They'll take her away. You know they will. I won't lose her again."

Mags took my hand then. I wanted to take hers as well, to let her know I was there, but I was just so tired. Even through the darkness, I could see the colours of her—pink and blue—dancing behind my eyelids.

Why would they take me away? Where would they take me?

My memories felt jumbled and I couldn't quite put together what had happened. I was vaguely aware that I'd had a baby, but as far as I could tell, there was no baby in the room with us. Where was it? Was this the reason everyone was acting so odd?

Did I kill my baby?

The memories darted around and I couldn't make my mind move fast enough to catch them. "Let's give her a little longer to come back on her own before we make any decisions," Ami said from where she sat on my other side holding two fingers over the pulse point in my wrist.

The sound of a baby crying pierced through the darkness and, despite the heaviness inside me, my body responded to the sound. My breasts ached and tingled, my heart jumped, and I had never felt such longing to go to someone, to be with someone. The sand drained from my body, the darkness slipped away, and I opened my eyes.

"She's awake!" Mags yelled. Ben rushed from

across the room to stand behind her and Ami moved her fingers from my wrist to my hand. "What happened? What did I do?" I whispered. My mouth was dry, my voice hoarse as if I'd been doing nothing but screaming. I didn't want to know the answer, but the question was quickly gnawing at me. "You had the baby, but…" Ben hesitated, unsure how to continue. "You lost consciousness shortly after, and you've been out for a while . We've been really worried." He leaned forward, smoothed my hair back and kissed my forehead.

"The baby…" I said. My hands went to my stomach which was now soft beneath the blankets and I noticed the way my body ached in a way it never had before. More than that, it felt completely foreign to me, like it didn't belong to me anymore. My muscles were sore and bruised, my breasts were swollen and I was completely empty. I was right. I had given birth, but there was no baby in the room. Maybe the cry I'd heard earlier was only a dream. A wish. A punishment. Torture. *What have I done?* I put my hand to my mouth in horror.

"It's okay, Jo." Ami put her hand to my forehead and then against my cheek. "How are *you* feeling?"

It was incredulous that she would ask something as mundane as "How are you feeling?" when I was clearly being torn apart from the inside. Why wouldn't they tell me where my baby was? They were keeping something from me. "Where is my baby?" I asked and something about the way I said it and the effect it had on them was familiar. There was something that I needed to remember, something they were avoiding telling me. I searched my mind, going back to the moment I felt the first contraction. I worked my way forward through the labor, but the further I went, the murkier it got.

"She's fine. She's just in the nursery" he answered, his lips moving to my hand, which he then held tight against his body.

Then, I remembered. My son hadn't been returned to me as I'd expected. As I'd hoped. A girl had been born instead and that meant he really was gone forever, and the enormity of that crushed me just as it had the first time. I wanted to wail and to cry, but I remembered what Mags said about being taken away and I knew I had to keep it together. I took a deep breath and my lips trembled under the strain, but I kept the screams in.

Ben left the room, only to return moments later.

"Jo, it's time for you to meet Isla," Ben said, holding a small bundle wrapped in a familiar blue blanket.

Vaguely, I remembered us discussing girl names, something I had done simply to humour him at the time, because I had been so sure the baby was a boy, and that we would name him Jack, for my father. Ben suggested Isla if it was a girl and I agreed without resistance.

Ben's words pulled the grief away from me like a blanket and replaced it with a renewed purpose. My son was gone and maybe it was time for me to finally accept that. Ami helped me get into a sitting position and then moved to make room for Ben to sit down beside me. I pulled myself up even higher so I could see her tiny face peeking out from the blanket. As I took in the sight of her, an image of the stick baby flashed before me, but was quickly replaced with the vision of a tiny, perfect baby girl wearing an impossibly small white hat. It was true that she wasn't what I'd been looking for, but she was something else all her own.

"Hi," I said, my voice breathless and high. At the sound of my voice, she turned towards me, her little face scrunched up like she was about to cry, but instead she just opened her little rosebud mouth, yawned and then was still again. My arms reached out to take her, but Ben was somewhat reluctant to give her to me, pulling back a little at my advance. Pretending not to notice, I gathered her from him anyway.

Her little body fit against mine perfectly, and in that moment, it all fell into place. Suddenly, everything was just as it should be, and it was clear everything that had happened to me over the past year was leading up to this moment. All the pain and the loss became, not only bearable, but worth it, because without it, I wouldn't be here, with her.

I lifted her up closer to my face and breathed in

the warm scent of her and let it fill me, erasing all the fear and the confusion I had carried with me all these months. There wasn't room for it anymore. There was only room for her. I wondered at how silly I'd been all this time. I'd had it wrong all along. It was *always* her.

The others gathered around, smiling at us. They could see it too. They could see that the hard part was over and a new chapter was starting for me, that I would be okay now. I wouldn't have visions or dreams. I wouldn't be called by the tree again. This little girl managed to save me just when I feared that I was almost completely lost.

Ben and Mags went down to the kitchen to get me something to eat and to give me some privacy while Ami examined me. She checked for bleeding and felt around my still tender abdomen, where my uterus would soon shrink down to its normal size. Then she helped me with nursing, teaching both me and Isla what to do. She was a good teacher and in no time, we were doing fine.

Ami stayed completely professional through it all, but once the official midwife business was out of the way, she settled onto the bed beside me and took my hand. Her head rested on my shoulder, and she fell silent. When a shudder ran through her body and into mine, I looked down to see tears flowing over her cheeks. When I asked her what was wrong, she sat up and covered her face with her hands before wiping her tears away.

"I was so scared," she said, her voice shaking. "The baby wouldn't come, and I thought it would be too late to move you to the hospital. I thought I might lose one of you, or both of you. And then, when the baby did come…" she trailed off, staring out of the darkening window.

I knew what she was talking about. I remembered everything now, but it embarrassed me and I just wanted to move on.

"Jo, it was like you were a different person. I thought I had lost you in a completely different way."

I stayed quiet; I didn't want to talk about what happened. I could still remember the pain I felt, the loss as acute as it had been the first time and I refused to apologize for that but I had to say something. I had to explain myself.

"I'm sorry I scared you. I was scared too but I was just confused. I haven't been sleeping very well and I think that, along with the labor, was just too much for me and I snapped. I feel much better now after resting."

Just then, Ben and Mags came in with a tray topped with a steaming bowl of tomato soup, a slice of bread with butter and a glass of milk.

I was grateful for the opportunity to change the subject and I hadn't realised how hungry I was until food was put in front of me. Ben tried to take Isla so I could eat, but I wouldn't let her go, and instead held her in one arm while I ate with the other. I never wanted to let her go again, but as the night went on, it became obvious that no one was going to leave me alone with her.

There was always someone in the room with me, usually Ben. When it was time for bed, Mags stayed with me while Ben got ready in the bathroom down the hall. Then, they switched each other out. When I first realised it, a flash of anger threatened to crack, but when I looked down at my baby, that anger dissipated instantly.

I couldn't be mad at anyone who was trying to protect her, even if they thought they were trying to protect her from me. Besides, if anyone knew the danger she could be in, it was me. I didn't want to remember the things I'd thought or done over the last few months, but I did. As I looked down at my daughter, I took all the guilt, pushed it down and laid my love for her on top of it, covering it completely.

CHAPTER 32

"How's it going?" Ami said, stepping through the front door to find me resting on the couch with Isla, just a few days old, asleep on my chest.

I pulled a blanket from beside me and laid it over her little body to shield her from the cold December air that snuck in through the open door to curl around my ankles and reach up towards my sleeping baby.

"Good." I smiled, holding Isla's tiny body even closer to feel the rise and fall of her little chest against my own. The warm and spicy smell of her filled the air around me and I nuzzled my face against the smooth down of her head and breathed her in deeply. "She's been asleep for a while, but I don't want to move and wake her up."

"She'll be okay. You have to take care of yourself

too, you know."

"Oh, I'm fine," I whispered through the smile. My cheeks were starting to hurt from it. "But, it's Ben's birthday and I haven't done anything for him." He'd left for work this morning before I woke up, and I hadn't even had the chance to wish him a happy birthday.

"Oh!" Ami held up some shopping bags I hadn't noticed. "Don't worry, I got it covered."

In the bags were the ingredients to make his favourite meal—his mom's meatloaf with mashed potatoes, and watergate salad instead of a birthday cake, because, according to Ami, Ben didn't like cake.

I pretended it didn't bother me that I didn't know what his favourite meal was, nor did I have his dead mother's meatloaf recipe. I also pretended to know what watergate salad was, and I tried to hide my surprise when the contents of the bag held green pudding, marshmallows, pineapple, whipped cream, and pecans instead of any vegetables.

Growing up, we always ate very simple food, with the exception of the Christmas party. Day to day, Mother believed food was only for nutrition and not for pleasure or entertainment. It always made her angry to have to pay the caterer at the end of the night, but Father made her understand that people were going to expect certain things at a Christmas party, and she always agreed that, although it was frivolous, it was also necessary.

Since arriving in Halliswell with Ben, I'd made a point of learning how to cook, but now I realised that I was only cooking what I was used to eating my whole life. Plain meat, plain potatoes or rice, and a vegetable. Sometimes they were put together in the form of a soup, but the end result was always flavourless and unenjoyable. As Ami added different seasonings and sauces to the meat, and butter and cream to the potatoes, I felt a surprising amount of shame. Why hadn't Ben said anything to me?

I didn't want to put Isla down, so she slept in my arms while Ami moved comfortably around the kitchen like she had done this exact thing hundreds of times. I supposed that was probably true.

There wasn't much time to feel bad about my lack of kitchen knowledge, because when Isla woke up, her tiny cry engulfed me and pushed all the bad feelings away. I left Ami in the kitchen and went back to my place on the couch to feed and cuddle the baby, and that's where I still sat when Ben came through the door.

He walked right up to where I sat and took Isla from my arms. I stood and kissed him, saying, "Happy Birthday," though my heart was already starting to ache with longing for Isla, and I tried to take her back.

"No, no. I got her. You deserve a break. Plus, I've missed her all day," he said. Kissing me on the top of the head, he walked towards the kitchen with Isla tucked against him. "Smells good!" I heard him exclaim from the other room. "Watergate salad!"

Ami and Ben laughed together, and I felt like an intruder in my own life.

Mags appeared from upstairs and sat beside me. "You okay?" she asked, squeezing my hand.

"Yeah, I'm just a bit tired and…" I hesitated. "Ami is cooking Ben his favourite meal for his birthday, and I didn't even know what it was."

"Don't worry about it, Jo. You're still new around here and you have the rest of your life to find this stuff out. Where would the fun be if you knew everything right from the start?" She was right. She always was. "Come on," she said, pulling me towards the kitchen. "Let's eat."

We all sat around the table eating and laughing as Isla slept in her basket on the floor beside me. I tried to stay a part of the conversation, but my eyes always drifted back to her scrunched up little face. I wanted to remember every little thing about her, and an irrational fear that I would forget her if I looked away always ticked at the edges. Threatening.

I tried to leave her in the basket as long as I could, but it wasn't long before I picked her up. Startled from sleep, she began to cry, and I immediately regretted what I'd done. Three sets of silent eyes looked up making me feel self conscious and on display.

"Oh baby, you woke up," I said with a reassuring smile, so maybe they wouldn't realise it was my fault. "I'll be right back."

I left the room with Isla in my arms and the weight of their eyes upon me.

"Shhh," I shushed, holding her body tight against mine, her head tiny in the palm of my hand. I bounced her up and down on the way back to the living room. By the time I was on the couch, she had settled back to sleep with her cheek pressed against my heart.

After a few moments, Ami followed and sat down beside me. I could tell that she had her midwife hat on by the way she got serious and slightly withdrawn. I suppose she had to close herself off emotionally to a certain extent when working with patients, but it always surprised me when she did it to me too.

"It's been a few days since Isla was born and I just wanted to check in and see how you're doing mentally," she said, tucking her legs up underneath her.

"What do you mean?" I asked, wondering where she was going with this.

"It's really common for new mums to experience something they call the baby blues. It's a really normal bout of sadness that comes on shortly after the baby is born. It has to do with abrupt changes in hormones; but also, having a baby is a huge adjustment. I just want you to know that if you are feeling sad in any way, it's normal and we are here to help you."

"I don't feel sad. I feel so unbelievably happy and at peace," I told her. And it was true. I was happy, but maybe saying I was at peace was a bit of a stretch. I felt so much worry now that I was responsible for such an innocent little baby, but I didn't feel like it was an abnormal amount of worry. "I promise I will ask for help if I need it."

Ami, seeming satisfied with the job she just did, mentally checked a box off in her brain and offered to take Isla while I went for a bath. I didn't want to give my baby up to her, but I had to be agreeable. Ami hadn't given me that talk for no reason. She knew something was up and I knew I had to hide it better.

CHAPTER 33

She wouldn't stop crying.

I was completely alone in the dark with her. Whatever fear the others had about leaving Isla alone with me had been forgotten over the last couple of weeks. At first, they'd all hovered over us, watching my every move with her, and waiting around every corner, ready to jump in and help if she made the slightest noise.

At the time, it was annoying, unnecessary and I was hurt by it. But now, without their supervision and help, I was scared. I bounced her up and down, rocking back and forth just as I had in the weeks after her birth, but nothing worked. Nothing I did could soothe her, when not long ago, I was the only one who could.

I thought back to what Ami taught me after Isla

was born. If she is crying, check her diaper, feed her, burp her, put her to sleep. I could do this. I laid her down on the bed and stared at her, unsure where to start; feeling stuck in an endless loop of feeding, changing, sleeping, crying.

Ben was downstairs fixing the handle on one of the kitchen cabinets, something I'd been asking him to do for weeks and of course he chose this moment to finally do it. He would be back soon, but I couldn't wait any longer. The sound of the crying was giving me a headache and my body was starting to panic despite my mind knowing that everything was okay. I called Ben's name loud enough to carry down the stairs. The sound of my voice scared Isla which made her cry even harder.

I couldn't face the thought of changing yet another diaper, so I picked her up instead and resumed shushing and bouncing.

I'm failing. I'm not a good mother. I can't do this. I can't do this. I can't do this.

Moments later, Ben bounded up the stairs, happy and eager to be there, as always. "Cabinet's fixed!" he called out, entering the room.

"She wont stop crying," I told him, my voice sharper than intended.

He took her from me. She continued to cry in his arms, and for a moment, I was relieved that it wasn't just me who couldn't do it. But then he put her down on the bed to check her diaper. It was wet, so he swiftly changed her into a dry one and she calmed almost instantly. When he picked her back up, she fell quickly asleep nestled against his chest. A moment ago, something as simple as changing a diaper had been a completely impossible task. Now that it was done and had also solved the problem, I felt silly, small. *Stupid.*

"Of course, *you* can get her to stop crying," I spat, again a bit more searing than I'd intended.

I'm a complete failure.

If he noticed the anger behind my words, he didn't react to it. "I think sometimes they just need a change in position or scenery," he said, obviously trying to reassure me.

He chuckled, smiled down at the baby, and walked towards the nursery, singing softly. He always doted on her—going right to her whenever she cried—and was never impatient. Never annoyed like I was.

Though I was sure Ben expected me to follow him, instead I went downstairs to the kitchen to make a cup of tea. I filled the kettle, lit the stove and sat at the table to wait for the water to boil. I found myself doing that a lot lately—sitting, staring, waiting—completely paralyzed with no desire to do anything, not even move. I stared into the distance and simply waited for the day to be over. Hoping that maybe the next day would be better.

Steam poured from the spout of the kettle. I always left it open because the sound of the whistle was as bad as Isla crying. I watched the kettle boil without getting up to take it off the heat. I kept watching it, the edges of my vision blurring with darkness. *What if I just didn't take it off? What if I just let it boil dry?* Maybe it would catch on fire. Maybe the house would burn down and I would just sit here, staring, and do nothing to stop it.

I got up, took the kettle off the burner, turned off the gas and poured the boiling water into my mug before returning to my chair. That's where Ben found me later with a mug of cold water on the table in front of me. I wasn't sure how long I'd been sitting there, I wasn't even sure if it was night or day anymore.

"Hey, what are you doing?" Ben asked, pulling out a chair and sitting next to me.

"Oh, I'm just trying to think about what to make for breakfast," I told him.

"Breakfast? It's almost dinner time." He laughed, standing back up to look in the fridge at what food we had.

"Yeah, I guess I haven't had anything to eat today so it's breakfast for me."

"Speaking of breakfast, Isla's awake and I think she's hungry. Why don't you go up to feed her and I will take care of dinner down here." He kissed me on the cheek and started pulling things out of the fridge.

Of course she was hungry. She was always hungry. I thought back to how long I had sat in the kitchen not doing anything. I could have spent that time trying to get ahead. I was always behind now. The house was a disaster. There were clothes, diapers and dishes everywhere. They all tried to help me, but everyone had a job to go to but me. Mags had done the majority of the household chores since she arrived, but she recently started working at the grocery store in town and was gone most days until around dinner time when the store closed.

Now I had to go upstairs and start the whole cycle again. Feed, change, sleep. And tomorrow wouldn't be better. It would be exactly the same. I left Ben In the kitchen and made my way upstairs. Each step I took felt like I was walking in quicksand. I was sinking into the ground and fighting to pull myself back out again. But with each step, I fell further in and found it harder to make my way back.

What if she's dead?

Well if she is, there's nothing I can do about it now.

But what if she is dying right this second?

Isla could be dead right now. Her blanket could be strangling her and I am just doing nothing. The panic hit me and the quicksand poured away. I ran up the stairs now, straight to the nursery. I threw open the door and flicked on the light. Immediately I heard stirring from the crib.

What if it's the stick baby?

Thinking that I was too late, that the fairies had come and taken my child again, I ran to the crib and sobbed with relief to find Isla starting to stir, but not quite awake yet. Her tiny mouth rooted around, the instinct to eat strong.

"Oh, thank god," I cried, scooping her up into my arms. "I will never let them take you. I promise."

CHAPTER 34

THE NEXT MORNING, I was set to have a visit from Ami before she left to make her rounds around the town and some of the neighbouring communities. She stopped in just after Ben left for work and it didn't feel like an accident that she was catching me alone.

She asked the mandatory questions she had to ask all the new moms. How was my bleeding? Was I able to use the bathroom normally? How was I sleeping? Did I have any concerns about myself or Isla?

"Everything is going great," I told her, hoping my smile wasn't too big.

"What about your mood? Have you noticed any signs of those baby blues that we talked about?" She was making notes in a notebook.

"My mood is good. I haven't noticed anything out of the ordinary." Maybe that was true. How was I supposed to know what was ordinary after having a baby?

Ami wrote something in the notebook again and then took a blood pressure cuff out of her bag. What was she writing about me? She was suspicious. She didn't believe me.

"What are you writing in there?" I demanded.

"Just keeping notes. It's hard to keep everyone straight by the end of the day." She took my blood pressure and then wrote it down as well.

"Okay, everything looks good with you. Now it's Isla's turn." She stood up and bent down to pick her up from where she was sleeping beside me on the bed.

"What?" I put my hand over her to guard her. "Why do you need to check her?" People were always trying to take her from me and I was starting to think that they were planning something. Planning to keep her from me.

"I just want to make sure that she is growing okay and gaining enough weight. It won't hurt her." Despite me obviously not wanting her to pick her up, Ami reached down and scooped Isla into her hands. Startled, her little arms and legs flew out and she started to cry. The sound hurt my ears and made me wince.

"Her reflexes are good," Ami cooed as she undressed Isla before wrapping her in a sling. She attached a scale to the top of it and lifted Isla up. I compulsively watched her every move. Never letting my eyes stray from my baby. "Six pounds thirteen ounces. She's gaining well. So, is feeding still good?" She removed Isla from the sling and passed her back to me to redress.

No. It was really hard. I couldn't get her to latch half the time and then when I finally did get her on, she fed for hours. More than once I had fallen asleep with her attached and had woken to her cries feeling completely bled dry.

"Yeah. It's been fine." I told her. I didn't want her to think that I couldn't do it. I was doing it and I had to believe that it would get easier. Having a baby was hard. Everyone knew that. I just had to get through this bit.

"Jo, I have to ask? Are you really feeling okay?" She moved closer to me. "You can tell me if anything is wrong."

"Why would you ask that?" *How did she know?* Someone must be watching me and reporting to her.

"Ben told me a few things that I find worrying and as your midwife and as your friend, it's my job to check in on you."

"What did Ben say?" I focused on doing up each of the little buttons on Isla's sleeper and not the pounding of my heart in my chest.

"Just that you sometimes seem a little out of it. That you've been pacing back and forth with Isla in your arms. You've mentioned that you can't trust anyone else to watch her." She placed one of her hands over mine and I realized that I had been worrying at the final button, unable to get it through the hole. She pulled my hand away, did up the button herself and then held my hands in hers, waiting for my explanation. I had to give her something.

"I'm just really tired. I haven't been sleeping very much and I think it's messing with me a little. I really am okay. Ben is just worried. I'm definitely not pacing or paranoid." I chuckled.

Ami gave a little smile that meant that she didn't quite believe me but at this point she had no choice but to listen to what I was saying.

"Okay. You let me know if anything changes." She started packing up her bag. "I'm going to go and see a few women in town. Then I have an appointment at my clinic. After that I am going to come back and cook you all dinner." She kissed me on the cheek, cupped Isla's head with her hand and left as fast as she came.

I couldn't believe that Ben had told Ami those things and it was clear that she was only coming back later so that she could spy on me. I really couldn't trust anyone. With Ami gone, the room suddenly felt hot and stuffy and small. I went to the window to open it, but then remembered that Isla was asleep on the bed. I didn't want her to get cold. Plus, I didn't want anything to come in and take her.

I went downstairs where Mags stood at the barre Ben attached to one side of the living room wall so she could do her exercises inside during the long winter months.

The whole house suddenly felt hot and small, and I was stifled inside it. Seeing me reflected in the mirror behind the barre, Mags stopped what she was doing and followed me. Without a word, we put our feet into the boots lined up by the door, grabbed our jackets and went outside. The air was icy, the snow crunched under our boots, and I could breathe again. She took my hand and followed me to the edge of the yard overlooking the water below, where we stood together for a long time. She was patient and it was comforting to know that, with her, I didn't have to say anything until I was ready.

I concentrated on the shapes forming in the misty puffs of our breath. Trying to focus on anything other than what I was feeling. After a while, when the cold started to make its way through the layers of fabric and into my body, I finally said, "You were right. I don't think I can do this." Mags watched me closely, letting me finish. "I'm not a mother. I don't know how to be one and how would I? All I know of mothers is *our* mother, and look at what she was. What if I'm like her?"

She stopped me there. "Look at me." She turned me towards her. "You are not her. You could never be her."

I tried to turn away. I didn't want to hear it and I

definitely didn't want her to make me feel better, but she refused to let me go.

"Listen to me!" she said. "You are everything that she isn't. She taught you how *not* to be as a mother. She taught you how not to be in *life*, and every moment you pretend you are anything like her brings you closer and closer to that being true. Do not let her win this one."

Her words struck something deep within me. By believing the lies I told myself, I was letting our mother win. I was letting her hold herself over my life like a dark cloud always on the verge of bursting.

I tried to keep it in. I tried not to show the weakness that I felt, but a sob burst from my aching throat. Mags released me from her grip, letting me wrap my arms around myself as the tears came. They dripped down my face freely, ice cold against my hot skin. She gathered me up, my chest against hers, and let me cry. I thought I might never stop. I had kept it all inside for the last few weeks, all my frustrations and my failures.

After my miscarriage, I had thought having another baby would make everything better. I thought being a mother would come easily, that it would heal me. Now I could see how wrong I'd been. Being a mother was impossible, and it was the very thing that made me feel as out of control as ever.

"You can do this. I will help you and we will get through it together," she said into my hair. "It's

Christmas time," she whispered then, and I could hear the smile in her voice. It was our favourite time of the year and my memory transported me back to the Christmas party almost one whole year ago. The lights, the gifts, the food. The magic. "Let's have a party."

I pulled away from her, my cheeks wet with tears, and nodded. The idea of planning a party filled me with excitement, distraction, and purpose. It was something I could control, something I knew I could be good at.

CHAPTER 35

THE AISLES OF the grocery store glistened with the bright colours of the different products lining the shelves, intermingled with sparkling Christmas decorations. Slowly and with purpose, I walked down every single one, gingerly selecting items and placing them in my cart, which was already overflowing with different meats, cheese, crackers, cakes, and chocolates, along with all the fixings for a traditional turkey dinner.

It was December twenty second, the day before our annual Christmas party, and I was at the small grocery at the edge of town, the only one we had. The selection wasn't what I was used to. In the city, we had everything you could possibly imagine, and my parents hired people to put it all together for us. Obviously, I'd never been in charge of a party like this —or anything at all—but I wanted everything to be just as it always had been. I needed it to be perfect, because I knew that if I could do this one thing, everything would be okay.

In the produce section, I reached for one of the last bags of fresh cranberries. Just as I was about to drop them in the cart, like a cherry on top of everything, the sharp, shrill sound of a baby crying pierced through my calm.

My baby.

I would recognise the sound of his voice anywhere. Startled, I dropped the bag. It broke open when it hit the ground at my feet, sending red berries in every direction. They weren't solid like they normally were; they were soft and wet. When they struck the floor, the displays, and my own body, they ruptured, spraying everything.

I looked down and saw the red juice flowing down my legs, only it wasn't juice. It was blood. The berries were gone, the bag was gone, and all that remained was a puddle of blood on the floor beneath me. Confused and terrified, I screamed. And then I screamed again, as I dropped to the floor, unable to hold myself up any longer.

Everyone in the store was staring at me, but no one was helping. I screamed at them to help me, but instead they all backed away quietly, until a man in a shirt and tie with a name tag that said "John— Supervisor" moved towards me with his hands up as if I had a gun pointed at him.

"Ma'am, are you okay?" he asked.

Of course, I wasn't okay. Something was wrong with me, why couldn't he see that? Why hadn't he called an ambulance?

I started to tell him this, but when I looked down to show him the blood, I only saw a bag of cranberries unbroken at my feet. There was no blood to show him. I didn't understand how it was possible. I'd seen it, smelt the metallic tang of it, tasted it in my mouth. And now, it was all gone.

"I… I'm sorry," was all I could manage to say as I brushed past him and ran out the door into the cold relief of the outside air. My face burned with embarrassment and confusion.

Ben and Mags were at the car waiting for me. They'd gone to buy decorations and a few gifts while I shopped for the food. When they saw me without any bags, they jumped out and ran towards me, looking as confused as I felt.

I composed myself quickly and told them that I had forgotten the money. Ben bought the story and gave me some cash out of his wallet. Mags, though, could tell something was wrong, and her eyes burned into me as I turned to head back into the store. I didn't want to go, but I knew if they went instead, they would find out what had happened, and I couldn't allow it.

My cart was just where I had left it; no one had gotten around to returning my items to the shelves. I pushed it towards the cashiers as if everything was fine, but I could feel the eyes on me once more. When "John—Supervisor" started towards me, I gave him a pleading look and he backed off, letting me pay for the groceries and leave in peace. The store breathed a palpable sigh of relief when I walked out the doors with my full cart and, apparently, my sanity in check.

Back at the house, Ami was laid back on the sofa reading a book as Isla slept peacefully against her chest. As we bustled through the door, she put her finger to her lips, indicating that the baby was sleeping, and we all quieted down. Of course, Ami could get her to sleep; even she was better than I was.

One of my bags slipped from my hand and hit the ground with a loud thud. The sudden noise startled Isla and she started to cry but Ami immediately patted her bottom gently, a quiet "shhh" sound coming from her mouth. Isla calmed instantly, but I knew she needed me, so I rushed over to the sofa and picked her up.

"Hey, Jo, she was okay," Ami said in a voice as calm as the "shh" sound she used on the baby, as if speaking that way had become a habit. A habit that should be mine.

"She was crying. Obviously, she needs to be fed and I'm the only one who can do that, so don't tell me what to do," I snapped before walking from the room with the baby in my arms.

The silence I left behind was thick, but I didn't

care. I was sick of being patronized and they needed to be reminded sometimes that I was Isla's mother, not them. I could tell they wanted to follow me, but a whisper of voices told me someone had suggested they leave me be. I retreated upstairs, leaving them to prepare the house for the party tomorrow.

In the bedroom, I settled onto the bed with my back against the headboard. Once comfortable, I positioned Isla at my breast, but no matter what I did or what position I tried, she wouldn't feed.

What had come so easily in the beginning seemed almost impossible now. Shortly after she was born, Ami told me not to feel ashamed that we were having difficulties nursing, and that feeding her formula was okay, but I knew the truth. The only thing she needed was my milk, and I didn't want help from anyone who didn't believe that too. So, I stopped telling Ami that anything was wrong at all.

But sometimes, no matter what I did, she wouldn't eat from me, and that meant I was already failing as her mother—failing to do one of the few things I was made to do.

Giving up, I laid her down on the bed beside me as I cried along with her. I wanted to wail with the disappointment inside of me, but I couldn't let the others hear, so I pushed my face into the pillow to stifle my cries.

Moments later, Mags came in to see how I was. To check up on me. "Jo?" she called out in her singsong voice, as though she were calling out to a child.

I sat up as soon as I heard her enter, wiping the tears from my face and smoothing my hair down. When she saw my red eyes and wet cheeks, she rushed to the bed to see if something was wrong with the baby. As if *I* would let anything happen to her.

"Are you okay? Is Isla okay?" she worried.

I jumped up right away and insisted, "Everything is fine. I'm just really tired." Suddenly, I felt silly for being so upset about nothing. I smiled at my sister to reassure her that everything was okay, but she wasn't convinced. "Really! I promise. Everything is great. I am going to go and start hanging the lights. Oh, and I have to start getting the food prepped. Maybe you can help me with that? I wonder if Ben picked up the Christmas trees. I better check. We need three of them at least! I hope we have enough decorations."

Mags called out after me as I left the room, but I skipped down the stairs to get away from her accusing look and the cries of my baby. I was so excited for the big party, and I had a lot that needed to be done by tomorrow. Now I understood why our mother hired so many people when she was the one throwing it all those years. It was a lot of work.

Later that day, I was helping Ben lower one of the Christmas trees into its stand when Ami came downstairs carrying something that stopped me dead where I stood. All the hair on my arms and the nape of my neck stood up and my skin crawled under the presence of it. She held a bundle of sticks, tied together with twine, and wrapped lovingly in a blue blanket.

The stick baby—the one I burned months before—was back, and there was Ami carrying it around as if it were a real child. Bile filled my mouth as Ben and Mags gathered around her, laughing, cooing, and touching the disgusting bundle of sticks, pinching the area where its cheeks would be. They crowded around her so tight that I couldn't see it anymore.

Unable to just stand by any longer, I pushed through them, but when I did, in her arms was my Isla, hypnotized by the fairy lights we hung around the house for the party. Though I was glad I had been mistaken, I was also confused, because I had been so sure of what I saw. It was there. It was right there.

Ben and Ami disappeared with the baby to make a quick dinner for everyone, and as soon as they were out of the room, Mags approached me.

"What is wrong with you?" she hissed under her breath. "I know something is going on. What happened just now?" she demanded.

Though a part of me knew she was only worried about me, there was another part, stronger than the first, that was sick of being watched and criticized all the time. No matter what I did, she was always looking for something wrong with me. I thought back to when I'd overheard her say I would surely be taken away if they called an ambulance after Isla was born.

She really did think that I was crazy. She really thought that I was just like our mother, and if she thought that, there was nothing I could do to change it now. Nothing I could do at all. If she wanted a show, I could give her one. If she wanted our mother, I could give her that, too.

"There is nothing wrong with me, you bitch!" I growled; my voice low but my words loud enough that she flinched away from me violently as though I'd slapped her. "Why are you always trying to prove that I'm crazy?"

I stepped towards her, and she stepped back, stumbling a little, the fear warping her beautiful features. I stopped. I knew I sounded angry, but mostly I was hurt because she was supposed to be on my side, no matter what. The look on her face proved that I was more alone than ever.

"Wh... what?" she stammered. "I'd never do that." She moved towards me, but this time I was the one to back away from her. "I know you aren't crazy. I'm just so worried about you. You've been through so much after Mother and then the baby. Now, with Isla, I'm just scared that it's all too much. After what you said the other day, I just want to help you."

She reached out to take my hands in hers, but I ripped them from her grasp. I couldn't stand the thought of her touching me now, when all I could see was the pity in her eyes. She winced at my rejection and the hurt on her face pierced through my resentment leaving me filled with shame.

"Just leave me alone," I said, unable to meet her eyes again.

Her green eyes, just like my own, looking after me through the shadows. She didn't follow me into the kitchen, and we didn't see her again for the rest of the evening. Feeling guilty for how I treated her, I went to her room to leave a tray of food outside her door. I knocked gently and called out, but she said nothing in return.

The space under the door was dark, her light off, but I knelt anyway and pushed my fingertips through the gap as far as they could go. I held my breath, waiting for the warmth of her to comfort me, but it never came. The space on the other side of the door remained empty and silent.

I knocked three times.

Nothing.

CHAPTER 36

AFTER GIVING BIRTH, I thought I would be able to sleep again, that the fear would subside and I would finally get some rest. Now, it wasn't the fear that kept me up, but a nervous energy that made me feel electric, like I could do anything. Like I didn't even need to sleep anymore.

Once again, I spent all night awake. Ben woke up every couple hours and each time found me gone from bed. When he asked later where I'd been, I told him that I'd been up with Isla and we slept in the living room to let him sleep, but really she slept in a basket most of the night and I didn't at all. The truth was, I was too excited to sleep and I spent a lot of the night puttering around the house, making sure that everything was perfect for the party. I was wired and I knew this was my chance to prove that everything was okay. That I was okay. So, I re-swept the floors, rearranged the decorations on the tree, repositioned the furniture, re-plated the food, washed every dish, wiped every counter, washed the windows. I couldn't stop until everything was finished, but as soon as one chore was done, another presented itself until the sun started to rise and Ben came down to find breakfast on the table and me smiling in an apron.

"Wow, what's all this?" He looked around the spotless room. I expected him to be happy, but instead he looked worried. "It's barely seven in the morning, when did you have time to do all this."

"Oh, Isla had a hard time last night. The only thing that would get her to stop crying was carrying her around so I wrapped her in the sling and got to work. Don't worry, we were only up for a couple of hours and then we both slept like babies." I laughed, but Ben didn't seem entirely convinced so I walked up to him and threw my arms around his neck. "What are you so bothered about? I'm fine! Great even. I've never felt better and I'm so excited about the party."

He pulled me into a hug and said, "Jo, I'm worried about you."

I pulled back and looked him in the eyes. Behind his glasses, they were darker than usual and a deep line had formed between them. "Why are you worried?"

"It's not healthy to get so little sleep. It can mess

with your head."

Ah. I could see what he was getting at. Just like Mags, he thought I was crazy. I reminded myself that he didn't know the things that I knew. He was in the dark and that wasn't his fault. "If I promise to sleep tonight, will that make you feel better? Maybe I can stay in Mags's room and you can take Isla."

Given a plan of action, Ben's demeanour visibly lightened. "That's a great idea. I will bring her to you if she gets hungry, but otherwise, I will pace the house with her in the sling if I need to."

"Deal," I said, although I had no intention of letting that happen. I needed Isla with me. I couldn't trust him to take care of her properly. I couldn't trust anyone. They were all against me and I had to protect us from them.

But first, the party. Ben requested that it just be the four of us, plus Isla, but that wouldn't do. If it was going to be just like before, the house needed to be full of people, like it always was.

So, I asked both Ben and Ami to invite everyone they knew, and I asked Mags to invite any friends she had made since moving to Halliswell. They were reluctant, arguing for a quiet Christmas, but in the end, they conceded, and that evening our brightly decorated house was full of brightly decorated people from town. It was absolutely perfect.

Surprisingly, not one person declined the invitation, as they all wanted to come see the new baby. I found myself standing in one place for a lot of the evening, Isla becoming heavier and heavier in my arms, as guests formed a line to greet us one at a time and to present Isla with a Christmas gift.

My eyes searched the crowded room for my sister, but I couldn't find her anywhere. The fight from the night before was still fresh in my mind, and we hadn't made up the way that I hoped we would when I went to her room. Somehow, she'd managed to avoid me for most of the day and I hadn't found time to be alone with her—to apologize for how I treated her.

Then, a glimpse of her, in a light pink dress made for a ballerina, peeked through the crowd. My gaze followed her as she danced around people, flitting from one group to the next as though with wings.

I motioned for Ben to take over for me and he took Isla, glad for the opportunity to show her off. I rushed away towards the corner of the room where I had seen Mags last. Just then the crowd parted a little and there she was, waiting for me. I smiled at her, and she back at me, and I knew then that we were okay, as we always were, as we always would be. Side by side, we hovered around the edges of the party, watching everything, and devouring the large plates of food she got for us like she always did.

Obviously, the party couldn't be as grand as we were used to, but it was perfect, nonetheless. The Christmas music came from a record player instead of a grand piano, and there were only three brightly decorated Christmas trees instead of ten, but by the laughter and the singing, I could tell everyone was having a great time. Despite the number of bodies that were crammed into our small house, people swayed and danced to the music, and they laughed and kissed under the mistletoe hung in various places throughout the first floor.

Best of all, under each tree, the gifts from the guests were starting to pile up. "For the baby," most of them said as they handed the brightly wrapped packages to me.

This was the first time we would be allowed to open them. Even better, when I woke up in the morning, everything would still be as it was now. There wasn't a team of people waiting in the wings to erase this night from our memories as soon as the clock struck midnight.

The hours ticked by and the party was in full swing. The food on the table was starting to run out, and we couldn't replace the rum and eggnog fast enough before it was gone again. Everyone was enjoying themselves, but I was unable to join them. This was supposed to be the party I fully experienced, but I still found myself on the sidelines, only observing. As I watched, the room began to spin along with the undulating guests. The music got louder, the singing got louder and the laughing was so loud it made my heart quicken. I looked down at my empty glass of eggnog and tried to recall how many I'd had. Was I drunk?

Then, over the sounds of "Have Yourself a Merry Little Christmas," I heard Isla's cry. She had been passed around all night and I was grateful for the break, but the realization that I didn't know exactly where she was caused a panic to grow so fast that it took my breath away in an instant.

How could I be so stupid?

Now she needed me, and I couldn't find her anywhere. I stood up on my toes and looked frantically around the room. Her cry was loud, and I knew she couldn't be far. I scanned the room again, listening closely, and then through the crowd I saw a man, one I recognised from town, carrying something in his arms.

Relief washed over me when, at first, I thought it was my baby, but when he moved again and I got a better look, I recognised the same bundle of sticks from yesterday. He wove between the other guests, rocking it in one arm, smiling and waving to someone across the room. He passed the thing to someone else, and they lifted it up to their face and kissed it.

Hot and feeling faint, I could still hear Isla crying, but the only baby I could see was the stick one, and then all at once I knew. I knew exactly what was happening to me. It was happening again. The fairies were coming for me. They were already here.

I had to find Isla before the switch could be made. Worried that I was already too late, I pushed my way into the crowd and started calling out for her, but there seemed to be so many more people than I remembered inviting.

I looked into their faces, but couldn't recognise a single one. I had never seen these people before in my life. What were they doing in my home? I pushed through them, shoving them aside. I called out Isla's name, but I couldn't hear my own voice over the sound of the music and the unrelenting laughing that beat down into my head, making it pound to the beat of the music.

"Isla!" I called again, but no one seemed to hear me.

Then, I saw a woman holding her across the room. I saw only a glimpse of my daughter before the woman turned away, obscuring my view. I rushed through the crowd and grabbed the woman's arm, pulling her to face me.

It was the woman from the house –Iris Bower – but she wasn't holding my baby anymore, she was holding the other, the changeling, looking down on it with love.

"What are you doing with that? Give it to me!" I tried to take it from her, but she screeched and pulled it away from me.

Hands pulled me back from behind and Ben's voice said, "Jo, what the hell are you doing?"

I whipped around to look at him, ready to tell

him something was incredibly wrong, that I didn't know where our baby was, that this woman was hiding her from me, but when I looked at his face I saw fear. Not the same fear I was feeling; instead, he was afraid of me. His eyes were on mine, wild, but he kept glancing over my shoulder. I turned to see what he was looking at and saw Mrs. Watson from further down the road, holding Isla in her arms protectively.

Protecting her from me.

I spun around, looking for Iris and the changeling , but they were gone and, in their place, only shadows remained.

"I don't understand. No. Where is she? She was right here! This isn't right." I looked around the room frantically. I had to show them or they would think I was crazy.

Ami emerged from another room and took Isla from Mrs. Watson, as Ben's arms wrapped around me. "Come on," he said, leading me away from the party.

As we left the room, the music and the talking resumed, but there was an underlying whisper running through the house now. Everyone was talking about me. Ben brought me into the kitchen where Mags was waiting. She took me from him with a meaningful look that I couldn't decipher. "I'm going to go check on Isla and Ami. I'll be right back," he said before leaving the room. When the door to the kitchen closed behind him, it muted the sounds of the music and the whispering coming from the rest of the house.

Out of the crowd, I realised my body was in overdrive, shaking, my breath ragged. "Mags you have to believe me. The fairies are coming for her. They're coming for Isla," I clawed at her, desperate for her to believe me.

Mags grabbed my arms and held them away from her. "Jo, you need to stop this!" She yelled at me and I stopped short.

Why was she yelling at me? I wasn't the one doing this. I was just trying to protect my baby. To protect all of us. "What are you talking about? It's not me. It's them. They are here and they are going to take her. How are we going to live with that?" I was crying now, but she led me to the table and helped me into a chair. She pulled her own chair close to face me, sat down, and took my hands in hers. She held them for a long time, her head down and she looked like she was praying, but that was impossible. Despite being brought up Catholic, Mags never believed in God. Neither of us did. But maybe he *was* real. If Mags believed now, maybe I was wrong. What if God was the one doing all this. Punishing me for getting pregnant in the first place. No. It was impossible. I couldn't get distracted from what was really happening.

Mags's shoulders shook slightly. She was crying and the sight of her upset sobered me instantly. As always, only one of us could break down at a time.

It was her turn.

"Hey, what's the matter? Isla was found, you don't have to cry," I said, squeezing her hand to comfort her, but she pulled her hands away to wipe the tears from her eyes with the palms of her hands.

She shook her head, exasperated. "Jo, we need to talk. I know you don't want to, but you have to listen to me." She looked at me, waiting for me to argue, but I didn't. I could see she was serious, and that this was important. "You are not okay. Something is wrong, and it's scaring me. It's scaring all of us. We thought you were better after Isla was born, and you *were* okay for a while, but you aren't now —"

"What do you mean?" I interrupted her. I hadn't been perfect, I knew that, but I was doing my best.

"Look, my manager at the store told me what happened yesterday. He told me you dropped a bag of cranberries and then you lost it. You started screaming and crying out that you needed to find your baby. He said you screamed at the customers and pulled whole displays down."

Wait, that wasn't what happened. He was lying. "No. No, that's not right." I shook my head and tried to stand but Mags pulled me back down.

"Listen to me!" she shouted, and it was so unexpected and so unlike her that I flinched. "It's not your fault this is happening, but we cannot leave the baby alone with you when you are this confused about what's going on. You need to let us get you some help. I should have listened to Ben and Ami before, but I didn't want to lose you. Now I know that if I don't get you help, I *will* lose you, and I'm afraid that it might be permanent."

"What are you saying?" I asked, though I knew. She wanted them to take me away. She wanted to put me in the hospital, like Mother.

"I talked to the doctor at Riverview, and he thinks he can help you. It's normal to experience this kind of thing after the trauma you have gone through, and then with having Isla–"

"Riverview?" I screamed, cutting her off. "You think that I need to be hospitalized? You think that it's going to be good for me to be in the same place as our mother after what she did to me?" I couldn't believe what she was saying. She was trying to get rid of me. It was all coming together. She was trying to take Ben and Isla from me.

"I know Mother's there, and that is scary, but Dr. Hayes promised me that you won't see her. You'll be on completely different ends of the hospital. You'll be safe there, and we can come and visit you every week until you're better. We can bring Isla with us too."

I couldn't believe what I was hearing.

"I can't leave her. I can't leave my baby," I cried. "She needs me!"

"If you stay, Jo, you could end up hurting her."

At this, I looked at her, shocked. There was no way that I would hurt my baby. Everything I did was to protect her. "No. No, I would never!"

"Jo, I know it's not intentional and you probably aren't even aware of it, but there have been so many times where you've left her alone," she whispered, so quiet that I almost thought I heard her wrong, but then she continued. "You've forgotten her on the bed or on the couch. In the car. And just now, the way you tried to rip her away from Mrs. Watson, you could have really hurt her."

I wanted to say it wasn't true, but I couldn't force the words from my mouth. She was right. I knew she was. Something had been wrong with me for a long time, and this was it. Apparently, everyone could see what my mother had sowed in me that night. She planted it like a seed, and it had grown this past year to consume me completely.

Mags was hoping I would agree to go to the hospital willingly, because the other option would be to force me, and we both knew I wouldn't come back from that. But I didn't agree. I couldn't go there. Even if the doctor kept his promise that I wouldn't have to see our mother, I would feel her in every inch of that place; in every inch of me. I wouldn't go.

I knew exactly how much I could stand, and this was it. This was as far as I could go. I knew what I had to do.

"Okay. You're right. I'll go," I told Mags, and the relief she felt was palpable.

It floated in the air between us, and it hurt me to know that I lied to her. It hurt me to know the relief she was feeling would be brief. Her pain would only be temporary, though. I would be okay. Mags could stay here with Ben and Isla. She could take care of them in the way that I couldn't. Just like she wanted.

She hugged me tight, and as I breathed in the scent of her, it transported me back through my whole life. She had been there for all of it, from the very beginning until the very end, just as I had been for her.

CHAPTER 37

T HE NIGHT WAS in the complete darkness of a new moon as time rolled over from the twenty third to the twenty fourth. Christmas Eve.

It was my first real one, and I was supposed to be free to celebrate my daughter's first Christmas along with my own. It was supposed to be a magical day– special– but by the time the sun came up, I would be gone.

I knew that, for all of them but especially for Isla, this day would be tainted forever, and I felt guilty. I did. I wished I was stronger. I wished I could have been the mother Isla deserved. The partner Ben deserved. But, I'd run out of time.

The chest at the end of our bed, the one my father had given to me, was filled with everything important to me, but when I opened it, there was only one thing I was looking for. Wrapped in a square of black velvet cloth was the fairy figurine that Nan had given me all those years ago. I rewrapped it in the cloth and placed it in the drawer of my bedside table for later.

As I was closing the drawer, Ben appeared in the doorway. He leaned against the frame, arms crossed, eyes glittering with tears. "Mags told me that you've agreed to get help. Thank you," he said.

His head was down, and he was having a hard time looking at me. Sometimes his weakness annoyed me, but now I only felt sorry for him, and I knew it was only going to get worse for a while. I went to him and gathered him to me, as he had done for me so many times.

"It's going to be okay. I'm gonna make it better," I whispered into his chest, and he nodded in response.

"I know," he said as he wiped the tears from his cheeks.

Mags showed up behind him, holding my daughter. The image of the three of them together stabbed through my heart in a way that was both hurtful and validating. This image was right. This was how it was always supposed to be. Mags replacing me in the photograph of my life, replacing the shadow of myself that I had been all this time. Maybe this was the solution. A way we could all get what we wanted which was for me to get better.

"Ami is going to come by in the morning to pick

us all up and we will drive there together," Mags said. Ben turned his head and nodded to her.

"Can I see her?" I asked, reaching my arms out towards my daughter. If I was strong enough to go through with my plan, this would be the last moment she'd have with her mother and I wanted it to be a good one. Ben and Mags exchanged glances, hesitating, but then Ben nodded and Mags stepped into the room to hand her to me. I looked down into her sleepy face and the site of her blurred behind the tears in my eyes. "Hi, baby. I'm so sorry. I love you and I'm going to make everything better."

My left hand went to the buttons of my dress, but as I started to undo them to prepare to nurse her, Mags interrupted, "Actually, Ami brought bottles and formula. I was thinking that we should try them out while you're still here, just in case she won't take them."

My breath caught in my throat. They were preparing for me to be gone. They were already adapting to life without me. It cemented my plan. I was doing the right thing. I wanted to cry out. I wanted to scream, but instead, I handed Isla over to her, laid down and pretended to go to sleep, but really I was paralyzed as the final parts of myself broke away. In the deepest part of the night, when I knew for sure everyone was asleep, the walls of the house rising and falling with each of their breaths, I got out of bed as slowly and quietly as I could. I couldn't risk waking Ben now, or all this would be for nothing.

He didn't stir when I stood up and he still didn't when I closed the door behind me. I crept across the hall and into Isla's room, knowing she wouldn't be there, certain she was in Mags's room with her, safe from me. In the empty crib, I placed the fairy figurine, so she would always have something from her mother, along with a letter explaining that I was sorry.

Out in the hall again, I shoved a letter under Mags's door before slipping down the stairs. There, I waited, my ears straining for any sign that someone was following. When I heard the floor above creak, I opened the hall closet and pulled out a coil of rope before taking off into the night.

I knew exactly where I needed to go because I was always going to end up there. I'd tried to fight it before, but now I succumbed, and when I stood before the tree, I knew it was right. It rose above me, black against the night sky. Its bare branches looked much the way they did the first time I saw it. Empty, barren, longing for something. Longing for me.

"This is what you want. Isn't it? A life. It doesn't have to be Isla's. You can have mine, I don't want it."

A small part of me still wanted to run. To continue on to Ami's house, beg her to make it better. But Ami was in on the plan to take me to the hospital and I was no longer safe there.

When the other part of myself found me there, she screamed at me, begging me to stop. She cried and reasoned and failed. No one could change my mind now, not even myself, and to silence the part of me that fought so hard, I wrapped my hands around her throat and watched until the light in her eyes dimmed, but didn't go out.

The lowest branch was out of my reach, but it lowered itself to me, allowing me to tie the rope around it.

I didn't know how to tie a knot, but something guided my hands and I did it. Still, that other part of me fought it. She kicked and screamed and begged, but in the end, she lost when the lowered branch of the tree returned to its place above, taking her with it.

I expected to feel fear or shame or regret, but all I felt was relief. And, as the air was squeezed from her lungs, I could finally breathe.

First position. Second position. Third. Fourth. Fifth.
Fall.

EPILOGUE: MAGS

T_EARS SLIPPED FROM_ my eyes as my sister's coffin lowered slowly into the ground. I dabbed at them gently with a tissue, praying the tears wouldn't give away the amount of makeup I was wearing.

Ben cried silently beside me, clinging to Ami the way I *knew* he would if given the chance. I bristled on the inside but pushed it down as I disappeared into the oversized sweater under my heavy coat.

I tried to ignore their incessant weeping. They hardly knew her. What did they know about losing half of your very being? They didn't understand what it was like to be faced with an entire lifetime without something that essential. And, worse, with the knowledge it was all my fault.

I did this to her. I could have stopped it. I could have sacrificed myself instead, but I couldn't let Isla grow up without me and I couldn't let Ben do this alone. This was *my* chance to be the person I'd always wanted to be, and I had no choice but to reach out and take it.

When she was settled into the earth, I shakily stepped forward to throw my handful of cold dirt into the grave. My vision blurred as the darkness, stronger than ever, flashed forward.

I reached up and grabbed it, wound it around the part of myself I was sure I could control, and then pulled it back where no one could see it.

When everyone had said their final goodbyes, I took my baby into my arms, smiled—not too big—and said, my voice a little too high, "Let's go home."

ABOUT THE AUTHOR

JENNIFER WEST lives in British Columbia, Canada with her husband and three daughters. When she's not painting glitter onto little girls' eyelids or reading, she is cohosting the In Her Good Books podcast and hiking the mountains of the Okanagan. In 2018, she opened her own coffee shop so that she would have a place to write and that's where you can usually find her—writing horror and pouring latte art.